PEGASUS DOWN

Also by Philip Donlay

The Donovan Nash Series

Speed the Dawn

Seconds to Midnight

Aftershock

Deadly Echoes

Zero Separation

Code Black

Category Five

PEGASUS DOWN

A NOVEL

Philip Donlay

OCEANVIEW PUBLISHING
SARASOTA, FLORIDA

ISBN 978-1-60809-309-0
Published in the United States of America by Oceanview Publishing
Sarasota, Florida
www.oceanviewpub.com

10 9 8 7 6 5 4 3 2

PRINTED IN THE UNITED STATES OF AMERICA

For my son, Patrick

ACKNOWLEDGMENTS

THIS BOOK WOULD not have been possible without the wonderful support of the people of Eastern Europe. In my travels through Poland, Hungary, Slovakia, Austria, and beyond, your warmth and kindness is second to none. Thank you all so very much.

For their patience, friendship, and insight, I offer my deepest thanks to my long-time friends who never fail to keep me pointed in the right direction. Scott Erickson, Bo Lewis, Gary Kaelson, Pamela Sue Martin, Richard Drury, Kerry Leep, Nancy Gilson, and Brian Bellmont. You've played a bigger part in all of this than you'll ever know. To my brother Chris, the smartest guy in the room—any room. Thanks for being there when I needed you. Thanks also go to my agent, Kimberley Cameron, and her team of talented professionals. You all do phenomenal work.

A very special thanks goes out to Dr. Philip Sidell, as well as Dr. D. P. Lyle, for their remarkable medical expertise. As always, I'm most appreciative on many levels. To all of my brothers and sisters who battle ankylosing spondylitis, and the associated nightmares that go along with the disease—you inspire me each and every day to keep moving forward.

I'd also like to thank the experts, the people who shed light on a myriad of subjects. To Captain Dave King, for educating me on the Boeing 727, I can't thank you enough for your patience and support. Thanks also go out to the amazing flight staff of Airbus

Helicopters for taking the time to try to educate an old fixed-wing pilot about the world of helicopters. Samantha Fischer, Vicki Harlander, Liz Lange, Victoria Dilliott, and Maddee James, you're all amazing, and I'm the first to admit that I couldn't do what I do without your efforts.

Finally, to Oceanview Publishing, the people who turn my words into books. Utmost praise goes to Patricia and Bob Gussin, Emily Baar, and Lee Randall. I know there isn't a better team anywhere.

PEGASUS DOWN

CHAPTER ONE

THE FLASH OF the explosion lit up the night sky and the shock wave resonated deep into Lauren's bones. Thrown hard against her seat belt, her ears rang, and bright spots swam in her vision as the cabin of the Learjet plunged into darkness. The crippled jet banked hard to the left. What few lights were visible out of the small windows confirmed they were headed down. The familiar whine from the jet's twin engines faded to nothing, replaced by the shrill sound of bells from the cockpit and urgent voices of the pilots.

The pitch-black night was replaced by the glow of the emergency lights, and Lauren saw the frightened faces of the two other passengers, both men clutching their armrests as the airplane shuddered. One man she knew well; he was an old friend, Dr. Daniel Pope, an MIT colleague from years ago. The other was a man she'd only met a few days earlier. His name was Jakob Kovacs, a freelance operative brought in by the CIA. Their fear was justified. Lauren knew each second without the engines put them closer to the ground.

One of the pilots turned and yelled into the cabin. "Everyone strap in tight! We're going down!"

Lauren cinched her seat belt until it hurt. She'd chosen a seat that faced aft, she knew enough about airplanes to know that facing the tail was safer in the event of an emergency landing. She also knew that a dead-stick landing at night, in a powerless plane, had a survival rate of nearly zero. The smattering of lights she'd seen earlier were gone. They were too low.

She thought of those she'd left back home and how much she wished she could be there for one more minute, to tell them goodbye and not to grieve. She looked across the aisle at Daniel; his face had gone shock white. He'd closed his eyes. At least she wouldn't die alone. The last thing she saw before she, too, closed her eyes and leaned down to cover her head with her hands, was her wedding ring. She whispered goodbye to her husband and her daughter.

Her fear was at a level she'd never known. Every muscle in her body wanted to flee—fight was an option long vanished. Lauren was slammed hard into her seat as the Learjet decelerated violently. The roar of the impact coursed through her body and reverberated in the small cabin. The airplane lurched sideways, and she was thrown savagely to the side as a final tremor ripped through the shattered airframe.

Lauren heard the unmistakable roar of water as it exploded upward and then cascaded down. The crippled Learjet spun in the current and quickly began to sink. Jolted into reality, she felt the first touch of cold water pouring into the cabin, as it swirled around her ankles. Lauren sensed the airplane was sinking nose first. She turned and saw that the cockpit was already flooded, telling her that the forward fuselage had ruptured in the crash. There was no way to reach the pilots.

She threw off her seat belt and on unsteady legs went to Daniel. His eyes were closed. A single groan told her he was still alive. In the glow from the emergency lights she could see Kovacs. His eyes were unfocused, his neck bent at an impossible angle. He was beyond help.

As the water rushed in, the torrent almost toppled her. She reached beneath the surface, and by feel, unfastened Daniel's seat belt and heaved hard to raise him up out of his seat. Lauren rolled him on his back, slid her right arm underneath him, and part swimming, part wading, hurried toward the over-wing exit. She planted her feet and furiously pulled on the handle. The hatch gave way, the open exit only inches above the water level.

She shed her shoes, and gripping Daniel's collar, she climbed out into the darkness and crouched on top of the wing. The rising water level inside the plane let her float him face up. Standing on the wing, she leaned back, and then with all of her strength, pulled Daniel's unconscious body through the emergency exit.

Moments later they were free of the Learjet and floating alone in the pitch-dark water. Lauren kicked away from the airplane and watched the sleek tail pitch upwards and then slip below the surface. The jet was gone. Lauren and Daniel were all that floated away in the swirling current. She cradled Daniel's head in the crook of her arm and used her free arm to tread water. She kicked to inch them closer to the bank, while allowing the current to do the bulk of the work carrying them downstream, away from the crashed jet.

Distant lights had told her there was civilization somewhere up ahead, but she had no idea how far. Lauren was swimming at a slow methodical pace, fighting the urge to panic as she continued to propel them toward the tree-lined shore. When her feet finally touched bottom, she pulled Daniel as far up the bank as she could, so they could hide under leafy branches she'd snap from the low-hanging limbs.

Once she felt as if they were somewhat hidden, Lauren knelt and checked Daniel again; he was still breathing. A warm wind rattled the leaves above them and the constant buzzing of insects was the only other sound. The night was cloudless, and the stars of August filled the sky. Lauren waved at the insects that buzzed unseen in her face. She'd been deep in thought about who would come looking for them when the sun rose. A new sound began to fill the air, and it took her several seconds to understand she was hearing the roar from an approaching boat. She pulled Daniel closer and adjusted the leaves as well as she could to camouflage them both.

When she saw the high-powered spotlight searching the water ahead of the vessel, she reacted immediately, taking a handful of mud from the riverbank and smearing it on her face, then repeating the process on Daniel. Then she drew her legs up and made herself as small as possible.

The light pierced the darkness and in the harsh beam she would have been blinded if she hadn't looked away. In that instant she saw that Daniel's eyes were blinking open and she was terrified he'd try to move. She inched closer and whispered into his ear. "Daniel, it's Lauren. Don't move, don't make a sound. Do you understand?"

In the sweeping light from the approaching boat she saw him slowly nod his head.

Lauren thought they'd have until daylight before anyone searched for them. It was a miscalculation she'd not make again. Earlier, she'd been trying to calculate exactly where in Eastern Europe they'd crashed, but all she could say with certainty was they were somewhere between Bratislava and Budapest, which put them in either Slovakia or Hungary. There was a current, so they'd crashed into a river, but it seemed small for the Danube. Her biggest concern was being found by the people who'd shot them down, though being arrested by the police could be just as bad. At times, the Slovak and Hungarian governments were indistinguishable from its criminals. She remembered the detailed briefing she'd received at Langley. The mission was covert. The CIA would maintain complete deniability, which meant no help was coming. She and Daniel were alone in a very hostile environment.

Lauren was almost afraid to breathe as the boat cruised closer, its throaty engine pushing against the current. The searchlight reached out from the bow and swept both banks and the water in between. She could see the brown, muddy water, as well as the tall trees that lined the shore. In the residual light she spotted armed men along the deck. As the boat cruised past, questions flooded her mind. How deep was the water, was there floating jet fuel from ruptured tanks, or other debris that would reveal the location of their crash? If the authorities found the wreckage, would they have any idea how many people were onboard? Would they be looking for survivors? She pictured the open emergency exit and instantly answered her own question. Of course they would—and then the hunt would be on.

A gurgle sounded from deep in Daniel's chest, and blood trickled from the side of his mouth. His body stiffened. "I'm sorry I dragged you into this."

Lauren cradled him protectively in her arms, her eyes fixed on the stern of the passing boat, looking for any sign it was slowing or turning. When she deemed it safe she replied. "Why did you ask for me?"

"I didn't think anyone else would come."

"That's not true," Lauren replied, absently stroking his face.

"I had to try to protect my daughter, Samantha, as well as be heard, and maybe get out of this place," Daniel said as he found Lauren's hand with his. He pressed a rubber-covered jump drive into her palm. "It's all in here. It wasn't for me, it was for the others."

"Samantha is safe," Lauren said, relieved to see that the drive that Daniel had given her was a high-quality military grade. Whatever data Daniel saved would have easily survived the crash and the prolonged immersion in the river. "What do you mean? What others?"

"I built . . ." He choked and spit up more blood. "A small, stealth-capable jet. Remember the *Phoenix*? I reengineered it to be invisible to radar. It has the radar cross section of a sparrow."

Lauren remembered the *Phoenix*, a design from their days at MIT, when they were together.

"My design was meant for a surveillance platform." Daniel was now gasping for breath. "They modified it, turned it into a weapon."

"Who are these people, and who do they want to spy on?" Lauren held him more tightly now.

"I don't know." Daniel's voice was barely audible, the gurgling in his chest worse. "They might be Ukrainian, or Chechens. I don't know, but when they do decide to act—I believe they will be able to use the *Phoenix* to deliver a nuclear weapon."

"They have a nuclear weapon and you built them a stealth aircraft?" Lauren felt a cold stab of fear rush through her body as the implications fully registered.

"I didn't know. When I made the discovery, I sabotaged the plane," Daniel said. "I don't know how much time I bought. Not long."

"Where is it? Tell me where you were?" Lauren pleaded, but she knew he was fading.

"I'm sorry," Daniel said his voice weaker. "I changed—different than before. Only you—"

Lauren heard the last wisp of breath slowly leave Daniel's chest and then he was still. A wave of anguish welled up within her, and she wanted to scream at the heavens and demand to know why. Daniel Pope was a good man, he'd reached out to her in his moment of need, and she'd come, only to have him die in her arms. She closed her eyes as a kaleidoscope of images of their time together assaulted her from every direction. She reeled at each crystal-clear memory, tears forming as she remembered the day they met, his impish uncertain smile, the flash of interest in his eyes. His laugh, his clumsiness, his intellect, their walks, the late nights, the seasons in Boston, but now he was gone. She was battered by the thoughts and images of the life they had once shared, and finally she had no choice but to give in to grief. She cried silently, for him, for his daughter, and for herself. The memories kept coming, an avalanche of their time together that gathered momentum, and threatened to completely unhinge her. Lauren's tears rolled down her face, fell on Daniel's skin, and then, drop by drop, met with the river and were swept away toward an unknown destiny.

CHAPTER TWO

DONOVAN NASH AWOKE as the sensation of soft breath tickled his cheek. He opened his eyes with a smile. His five-year-old daughter, Abigail, still in her pajamas, was perched wide-eyed, hovering over him.

"Daddy, my tummy is empty. Make me pancakes like you promised!"

Donovan reached up and grabbed her under her arms, lifting her free of the bed to hold her at arm's length. She squealed with delight and put her hands out like wings, and Donovan spun her around like an airplane until he finally allowed her to drop next to him into the soft bedding.

Amidst Abigail's giggles, Donovan threw back the covers, sat on the edge of the bed, and pulled on a t-shirt. He picked up his cell phone. No message from his wife, Lauren. That perplexed him. As a consultant for the Defense Intelligence Agency, she'd been called away to a meeting in Geneva, Switzerland. That had been five days ago, and she was scheduled to arrive back home at Dulles Airport this afternoon. Her flight out of Geneva departed at what would have been five in the morning Washington D.C. time, so she promised she'd send a message that she'd made her flight so as not to wake him. The lack of a message was odd, but not cause for immediate alarm.

He turned and motioned for Abigail to jump up for a piggyback ride, which she did without hesitation. With a firm grip on both his phone and his little girl, he headed downstairs for the kitchen.

"Special pancakes!" Abigail cried out as she slid off Donovan's back to sit on the kitchen counter.

Donovan opened the refrigerator, pulled out the orange juice, and poured Abigail a glass. "There you go, sweetie. Let Daddy start the coffee, and then we'll make special pancakes, okay?"

Abigail nodded as she drank her juice.

With the coffee started, Donovan found the bowl with the spout he liked, pancake mix, milk, and eggs. He set the pan on the stove and began to prepare the batter to the perfect consistency.

"What time does Mommy get home today?" Abigail asked as she finished her juice.

"You know the answer to that question." Donovan said as he whipped the batter with a wooden spoon. "We've talked about it every day since Mommy left for Europe. You tell me what time Mommy gets home."

"Two fifty-five!" Abigail held up both hands as if she'd scored a victory, clearly overjoyed at her mommy's return.

"What are we going to do before Mommy gets home?" Donovan asked, knowing the answer was going to further super-charge his daughter.

Abigail's eyes grew even larger as her excitement accelerated. "Horseback riding! Daddy, make me a pancake of Halley."

Donovan dropped some batter in the pan to test the tempera-ture and found it perfect. Halley's Comet was the full name of the Welsh pony that Abigail rode and loved dearly. Halley had been her pancake request for the last two months. Using a spoon, he carefully poured batter to make the horse's torso, and then run-ning legs, a neck and oval head, then he used tiny drops of batter for the ears, followed by a flowing tail. He grabbed two plates,

butter and syrup, and returned to the stove just in time to carefully flip his creation. With Lauren out of town, he and Abigail
often ate in the kitchen with her sitting on the counter, one of the
many father-daughter rituals they enjoyed.

"Ready?" Donovan asked as he slid the spatula under the horse
and placed it on Abigail's plate. Her face lit up and a peal of delighted laughter filled the kitchen. Donovan helped her with the
butter and syrup, and she smiled with each bite.

"Your turn, Daddy. What are you going to make?"

"I'm going to create a Gulfstream pancake," Donovan said as he
poured her a glass of milk.

"You always make an airplane," Abigail challenged.

"I like airplanes." Donovan grinned as he measured out the fuselage, wings, and tail of a sleek jet. From long practice he expertly
added the batter that became the engines and then waited, spatula in hand, for the batter to bubble. He'd been making pancake
shapes for Abigail since she was little, right after she'd fallen in
love with the Little Mermaid. His first efforts were more symbolic
than accurate, but he quickly improved. It was their special treat,
one that Lauren left to him. A deft flip of the pancake and a perfect, golden-brown Gulfstream was cooking in the skillet.

"Is it an Eco-Watch Gulfstream?" Abigail asked with her mouth
full.

Donovan smiled. Eco-Watch was the company he'd founded
and now ran. It was the premier private scientific research foundation in the world. With two highly modified Gulfstream jets as
well as two ocean-capable ships, Eco-Watch's services were sought
out by some of the most advanced universities, laboratories, and
scientists in the world. A third ship was being built, and there were
plans to add to the aviation section as well. At fifty-one years of
age, Donovan had lived two lifetimes' worth of success, and it was

Eco-Watch that made him the most proud. Very few people knew he'd founded Eco-Watch with his own money. Only seven people in the world knew the truth about Donovan, and his past, and he went to great lengths to keep it that way. The more he could distance himself from the man he'd once been, the more freedom he enjoyed. He was able to do work he was passionate about, and still do what he loved most, which was to fly. Eco-Watch was home.

"Daddy, make me another," Abigail said as she took the last bite of pancake number one.

Donovan stirred the batter and went to work. Two more horse shapes and one little surprise turtle pancake, and Abigail was finished and happy. As Donovan lifted her down from the counter, he got an impromptu kiss on the cheek before she bolted for her room to change clothes. He cleaned up the kitchen and managed to down some coffee before he, too, headed upstairs to get ready to go to the equestrian center. A quick glance at his phone produced a frown, still nothing from Lauren. He tried to call her mobile, but it went straight to voice mail.

"Daddy, come help me," Abigail called out from her room.

Donovan rounded the corner and found his daughter half-dressed. She was wearing her tan jodhpurs, a white blouse that needed to be tucked in, and she was combing her long reddish-blond hair in preparation for a ponytail. He helped her smooth her hair, gathered it in, and then secured the ponytail low on her neck so it wouldn't interfere with her riding helmet.

"I need my ribbon, Daddy," Abigail declared the instant her hair was set.

Donovan found two ribbons on Abigail's dresser, and held them both up for her to choose. Without hesitation she pointed at the white one dangling from his right hand. Abigail was the perfect mix of her mother's high IQ, matter-of-fact approach, coupled with his sometimes-impetuous adventuresome streak. She was already a handful, but he wouldn't have it any other way.

Donovan carefully tied the ribbon the way Lauren had taught him, and got a nod of approval as Abigail checked his work in the mirror. Then he helped her fix her shirt. Once that was finished, Abigail launched herself on the bed and held up her right leg. He slid the first black paddock boot into place, then the second. She jumped up, made sure her boots were pulled up just below her knee, and then she slid on her jacket.

"You look perfect," Donovan said.

"Let's go!" she called as she strode past him for the hallway.

"Not so fast," Donovan said. "I need to take a shower and get dressed. You make sure you go to the bathroom, wash your hands, and then brush your teeth. Oh, and don't get any toothpaste on your jacket. No television. If you're bored, sit down and read something. I promise I'll be quick."

The exasperated sigh of an impatient five-year-old was all he heard as she tromped off to the bathroom.

Donovan glanced at the time, it was eight-thirty, late enough to make a call to Lauren's section at the DIA. If there had been a delay of some kind, hopefully they'd be able to tell him what was going on. He dialed the direct number, but didn't recognize the voice, or name, of the woman who answered.

"This is Donovan Nash. I'm Dr. Lauren McKenna's husband, and I was wondering if you could give me an update on her ETA to Washington."

"I'm sorry, Mr. Nash. I don't have that information."

"I'm just looking for what flight she may have taken. We're expecting her to arrive this afternoon."

"I'm sorry, you'll have to get that information from Deputy Director Reynolds."

"Fine," Donovan said. He'd known Calvin Reynolds for years, but why would Lauren's itinerary have to come from her boss. "Let me talk to him."

"I'm afraid he's off-site today."

"If you talk to him, have him give me a call," Donovan said. "He's got my number."

"I'll pass your message along, Mr. Nash."

"Thanks." Donovan hung up, checked his phone once again for any message from his wife, still nothing. He hurried toward the bathroom for his shower. As the hot, needle-sharp spray peppered his skin, Donovan found he couldn't shake the cloud of questions swirling in his head. Where was Lauren? Why hadn't she contacted him?

CHAPTER THREE

LAUREN OPENED HER eyes and found that the sun had risen far above the horizon. Something had woken her from a restless sleep. The mud on her face had cracked and dried, and the smell of putrid fish hung heavy in the air. Daniel was still in the shallow water beside her. During the night she'd managed to take his belt and used it to secure him to a log so he wouldn't float away. In the sunlight, she studied his slack features. They'd been in their mid-twenties when they were together. He was in his mid-forties now, but the man she'd known was still clearly visible. He was thin, a runner, with dark hair and brown, fiercely attentive eyes. He never possessed leading-man looks, but she'd been attracted to him for his clumsy sense of humor and considerable intellect.

From his dossier she knew that life hadn't been easy or kind to him since school. He'd married years ago, not long after graduating from MIT. His wife had left him and their daughter, Samantha, and run off with another man. Daniel had raised his daughter as a single parent since she was ten. From what Lauren had read, Samantha had never been in trouble, and Lauren had no doubt that Daniel would have given her the love, attention, and energy his daughter needed. Over the years, Daniel had gone from project to project without any real focus or drive only to end up here, dying in a muddy river in Eastern Europe. Lauren had no real idea how all of this could have happened.

When Lauren heard the sound of men talking, her attention immediately snapped from Daniel to the voices. She could make out at least three different men. Farmers, soldiers, she had no idea, but they were getting close. She caught sight of them through the brush. There were three of them and they were on foot. They were only thirty feet away on what looked like a crude path. As they walked past, she remained motionless until they moved beyond her hiding place. Then Lauren quietly slithered out from beneath the pile of brush, and climbed the bank until she spotted the men in the distance. She crouched behind a thick bush and evaluated her situation. Two of the men were in uniform, carrying rifles. The third looked to be a civilian. He wore gray pants and a shirt that may have once been white, a blue bandana around his neck, and a straw hat perched on his head. A farmer perhaps, a man used to being out in the sun.

Lauren took in her surroundings. Where the trees ended, there looked to be a wider path or a primitive road; on the other side of that were more trees. As much as she wanted to get away from this place, in broad daylight, the best move was to stay where she was. Careful to mask her footprints, Lauren slid down the bank and crawled back under her makeshift canopy.

She thought back to the night before. The pilot briefed her that he intended to stay low until they reached the outskirts of Budapest, where there was a small airfield. He was going to climb into Hungarian airspace from there, appearing as if they'd just taken off. From there, the plan was to fly to Vienna. They hadn't been airborne very long, which meant someone either knew where they were going or that Daniel had been followed. High in the morning sky, Lauren spotted the contrail from an overflying jet, it was headed west, the direction she wanted to go. Home was due west, but help would not be coming. The entire mission to extract Daniel was off-book, which gave the United States government complete deniability.

Lauren began to grasp the enormity of her situation. She swatted a large bug that was crawling on her wrist and grimaced as it fell away. She fought the overwhelming desolation of being alone in a hostile land. Her first order of business was Daniel. Her eyes filled with tears at what she needed to do, how horrible it was for him to end like this. She couldn't help herself as her thoughts drifted back to a different time, to when she'd met him, how different they'd been, yet they'd gravitated to each other.

It had been a fall afternoon, she was leaving class, and up ahead of her, Daniel had just pushed through the doors to leave the building. He'd glanced behind him and spotted her just as he'd let go of the door. He'd tried to recover, to get the door, but his momentum was all wrong. He twisted his ankle, swore, and managed a partial recovery as Lauren, amused, watched through the glass. He was embarrassed, hopping on his uninjured foot until he could finally pull open the door for her.

Lauren smiled at the memory—classic Daniel. He was so wounded and harmless, she agreed to have coffee with him, and that's how she discovered the intellect behind the boyish charm. She remembered being struck by how dissimilar they were. Looking back, maybe that was part of the attraction.

His work at MIT in aerodynamics had garnered attention from aircraft manufacturers around the world. He was a fierce lab rat, not a field guy. Growing up in Chicago, he'd been a gifted student but avoided athletics, or any team sports, preferring to be inside. She, on the other hand, jumped at any opportunity to go out in the field when she was in school. She loved chasing tornados in Kansas, flying with hurricane hunters in the Atlantic and Pacific Oceans, and observing volcanoes in Alaska. After graduation, their differences had outweighed their connection, and they'd finally broken up. She'd gone to work for the Defense Intelligence Agency and Daniel began to drift.

Lauren replayed the sequence of events that brought Daniel back into her life. Ten days earlier, Daniel had managed to send an email message to the Defense Intelligence Agency. The short paragraph explained that he was being blackmailed, held somewhere, perhaps in Slovakia, and that he was going to make his escape, but his action would put his daughter, Samantha, in danger. The only person he trusted, or would surrender to, was Dr. Lauren McKenna.

The email launched an immediate investigation by both the Central Intelligence Agency and the National Security Agency and Lauren was summoned by the CIA to Langley. Technically, Lauren was a contractor to the Defense Intelligence Agency, her PhD in Earth Sciences from MIT having led to her recruitment years ago. She was an analyst, but over the years, her close proximity to Donovan Nash and Eco-Watch had molded her into a field agent of sorts. Her most formidable weapon would always be her brain, but she also knew rudimentary field craft, and how to use a weapon.

Accompanied to Langley by her boss and friend, Deputy Director Calvin Reynolds, she'd sat down across from a man named Quentin Kirkpatrick, who had been placed in charge of Daniel's extraction from Eastern Europe. Lauren found him overdressed, overmanicured, a little too polished, as if he were trying hard to project something he wasn't. Once she and Calvin had taken their seats, Kirkpatrick dawdled in a clear attempt to emphasize his superiority.

"Can we get this meeting underway?" Lauren didn't bother to mask the fact that she'd had dealings with the CIA before and she didn't much care for their tactics.

"Yes, of course," Kirkpatrick took one last look at the papers in front of him before addressing them both. "The CIA has the hardware and manpower in position, but we need you, Dr. McKenna, to anchor the mission to extract Dr. Daniel Pope. The situation requires you to fly to Geneva, where you will meet with a field unit. They will brief you based on local conditions and the fluidity of the operation."

"Does Daniel know we're coming?" Lauren asked.

"We have no idea. Using the email address he used to send the original message, we sent Daniel Pope a single phone number, with instructions for him to use when he was in position at one of three airfields in Slovakia. Once he surfaces, we'll fly in and get to him before anyone else does. That a world-class aeronautical designer has been blackmailed to work on a project of unknown origin is, how shall I put it, worrisome."

"What about his daughter?" Lauren said. "Have you found her?"

"Samantha? She's in an Orange County, California, hospital. She was injured in a car accident, but she's expected to survive. We're looking into the accident itself, but on the surface it looks like another driver ran a red light. He was tested at twice the legal blood alcohol limit. It's not his first DUI; he's still in jail."

"Is Samantha conscious?" Lauren asked. "Does she know her father's whereabouts?"

"She's in and out. She had surgery to remove her spleen, and she has two broken legs, a fractured collarbone, as well as a concussion. All she's given us is that her father is working on a contract in Europe, for a company in Germany."

Lauren nodded. Several years ago she'd read that Daniel's latest project for a company called Dynamic Composites, had failed to produce a viable prototype for DARPA, the Defense Advanced

Research Projects Agency. The failure had resulted in the company being dissolved. It struck Lauren as odd that Daniel would accept a contract abroad. From what she remembered about his conservative nature, he just wasn't that adventuresome.

"We're checking to see if any aerospace companies have contracts or joint contracts in Slovakia," Kirkpatrick continued. "We're also trying to retrace Pope's movements prior to getting on a plane for Europe."

"How long has Samantha been in the hospital?" Lauren asked.

"Five days."

"That's not Daniel's style. I doubt that he ever went to work for any company in Europe. It's a cover story for his daughter," Lauren said. "I wonder if she was being used as leverage. If so, she's still a target. My guess is that Daniel, is, or was, being forced to work in exchange for his daughter's life."

"If he failed to deliver, they probably threatened to kill her," Calvin added. "Daniel would get to talk to her at certain intervals, and if she wasn't available, as in being in the hospital, Daniel would no doubt presume the worst and try to bolt."

"We're of like minds, Dr. McKenna. Samantha is under twenty-four hour guard," Kirkpatrick said and then tapped the face of his watch with a forefinger. "Dr. McKenna, if there are no more questions, your flight to Geneva leaves in a few hours. Your cover is that you're going to a meeting with your European intelligence counterparts. You can study the dossier we've prepared on the flight over."

"Slow down for a minute," Calvin pointed a finger at the CIA agent.

"Problem, Calvin?" Kirkpatrick replied.

"We're a long way from anyone climbing aboard a plane. We're here as a courtesy, and just so we're clear, we're not under any directive to cooperate. If Dr. McKenna wishes to proceed, she'll do so as a volunteer, not because you said 'jump'. I'm also going to want to hear your assurances as to how you will safeguard Lauren's well-being. And while we're at it, let's have a little reciprocity here, Quentin. What does Dr. McKenna get in return for helping you?"

Kirkpatrick extracted a thick file from the top drawer, and never taking his eyes from Calvin, let it drop to the table. "There's your reciprocity. Dr. McKenna still owes us. She can volunteer for this mission, or I can have her locked up for treason. Instead of Geneva, she'll be on a flight to a classified federal holding facility. Dr. McKenna, it's your call."

Lauren didn't need to open the file. She already knew the contents. It was the official investigation into her actions in withholding information from the CIA, and aiding a known fugitive and suspected spy. A CIA agent in Paris had died two years ago. She'd avoided major issues when it happened, but only by the slimmest of margins after Donovan had intervened. She'd always suspected that her actions would resurface. Now they had.

"Lauren, we can fight this," Calvin said.

"It's okay, Calvin. I was going to volunteer anyway, even before the slimy tactics. All I ask is that this makes us even. I go get Daniel, the file goes away."

"That decision is above my pay grade." Kirkpatrick said, a not-so-subtle smirk lingering.

Lauren's focus on Kirkpatrick was broken by a large insect crawling on her neck. She flicked it away and forced herself not to look at its size. She thought about home. Donovan would be worried that he hadn't gotten a text from her when he'd woken up this morning. Abigail would be going a million miles an hour because it was horse-riding day. Donovan would have his hands full.

Lauren felt her throat tighten as a barrage of images raced through her mind. She and Donovan, after surviving a difficult time in their marriage, were healing. They were back together, talking, planning. It was as if a severe storm had enveloped them and their relationship, and they'd survived, stepped out into the aftermath, and found the air sweeter, the grass greener, as if their problems had been scrubbed clean by the maelstrom. Donovan, despite his many demons, had managed to shed most of them. He'd become a better husband and father and as a result—a happier man. They were as content as they'd ever been. Sooner or later, he'd understand that she'd lied to him about why she was going to Europe, that the mission involved Daniel Pope, a former lover.

When she didn't check in, Lauren knew that Donovan's first move would be to reach out to Calvin. Even if Calvin would confide in Donovan, she wondered how much intelligence her office at the DIA would be able to uncover. All anyone really knew was the plane was missing, as were the five people onboard. Satellite surveillance would show nothing, no wreckage; the crew wouldn't have transmitted a Mayday call, so there'd be no intercept by the NATO AWACS planes typically watching Russian airspace. By crashing into the water, the Learjet had simply vanished. Lauren had no idea what protocols or time frames were in place to notify the next of kin, but Donovan would be told fairly soon that she was missing, and presumed dead, along with Daniel Pope. She could only imagine the pain and betrayal that he would feel, and there was no immediate way for her to prevent it.

Lauren took a deep breath, it was time to get to work. She ventured away from the river and began to look for what she needed. It took her the better part of an hour, and several trips, but she finally gathered enough rocks to do the job. She slid down into the water next to Daniel and waved away the insects that had

CHAPTER FOUR

DONOVAN LEANED AGAINST the fence encircling the paddock. Abigail was atop Halley, using both the reins and her knees to guide the pony in figure eights around the corral. Ms. Taylor, her coach, was never far away, giving both horse and rider gentle encouragement. Donovan marveled at Abigail's focus as his daughter controlled the horse while maintaining her poise, heels down, head up, hands in the correct position. Each detail, combined with her riding clothes, served to remind Donovan how quickly his daughter was growing up.

As he glanced across the paddock, Donovan spotted the black Crown Victoria as it pulled up and stopped. The front door opened, and a man in a suit, dark glasses obscuring his eyes, surveyed the area. Satisfied, he then reached for the rear door and stepped to the side as it opened.

In the Virginia summer heat, Donovan wore cargo shorts and a loose-fitting polo pullover, his concealed Sig Sauer within easy reach. A quick glance around the perimeter confirmed that the immediate threat was from the Crown Vic. Donovan watched a figure emerge from the back of the car and relaxed as he recognized Lauren's boss. Deputy Director Calvin Reynolds spotted Donovan and held up his hand in greeting. Dressed in khakis and a knit shirt, Calvin's visit wasn't official, but there was no way Calvin's presence at his daughter's riding lesson was accidental.

Donovan let Calvin come to him. The driver held his position at the car, while Calvin walked toward Donovan. The two men shook hands warmly, but without smiles. They'd known each other for years, their common point of interest being Lauren. His wife thought of Calvin as a father figure. Donovan had mixed feelings about any high-ranking official in the intelligence community, though over the years Calvin had proved loyal.

"She's learning fast," Calvin said as he turned to watch Abigail ride. "You must be proud of her."

"Where's my wife?" Donovan was in no mood for small talk.

"Did you know that Lauren has a code name in the CIA?"

"Yes, it's Pegasus, given to her by an operative in Paris. Calvin, answer my question. Where's my wife?"

"This morning I received a message from the CIA via secure text. All it said was 'Pegasus Down.'"

"What does that mean?" Donovan felt real fear, his fight or flight response coming at him hard.

"I have serious reservations about telling you any of this. I know you're concerned. I know you called my office this morning. What I have to tell you I couldn't say on the phone, but you're a friend, and so is she. I know very little at this point, but I also know how you're going to react, which is poorly, and probably impulsively."

"Calvin, is she alive?" Donovan said the words almost as a warning, his anger and frustration starting to spiral out of control. Abigail circled close on Halley, and all Donovan could think about was how devastating it would be for her if her mother never came home.

"We don't know," Calvin replied. "I'm being stonewalled by the CIA. They're distancing themselves from this and refuse to confirm or deny anything. I'm running into interference from the top, and it's quickly becoming something beyond my scope."

"She's not in Geneva, is she?" Donovan felt his world tilting out of balance as Calvin shook his head. "Where is she, and what is she involved with?"

"Ten days ago, the DIA was contacted by a scientist. The message was tagged for Lauren and marked urgent. We, as well as the NSA, took a look into the matter. There was enough evidence to believe that the scientist had been kidnapped and forced to work for an unknown group. The scientist called for an extraction, but the only person he'd turn himself over to was Lauren. She agreed, and last night the mission went active. As of this morning, the plane she was on is missing. Langley has no idea if it's crashed or been captured. It's vanished, along with all five people aboard."

The effect of Calvin's words was quick and devastating. Donovan felt the sudden heat as his face flushed, there was a ringing in his ears, and his knees started to buckle as if he was being squeezed from all directions. He couldn't draw a full breath. Donovan closed his eyes, as if he could ward off the implications of the news. "What kind of plane are we talking about?"

"A Learjet 31."

"Nothing draws a crowd faster than a plane crash. If it crashed, don't you think you'd know?"

"Normally I'd say yes, but in this case I have to say—maybe. There are mountains, rivers, and wetlands in the area, so it's possible for a crash not to be detected. We don't know anything for sure. She may have escaped. She could simply be out of contact. Just because we don't know where she is, doesn't automatically mean the worst case."

Donovan raised his head, his eyes found Calvin's. "What's being done?"

"I can tell from the look on your face I was right in being hesitant to tell you about this," Calvin said quietly. "I understand how you're feeling, I'm feeling the same things, but you can't barge into Langley demanding answers. They'll shut you down."

"I'm not going to Langley," Donovan said. "You're the spy, you go deal with those people. I'm going to find my wife. Where was the extraction being made, and who is this scientist she went to rescue?"

"As to where, I don't know for sure. It's classified."

"You don't know where she went?" Donovan's hands drew up into tightly balled fists that he wisely kept at his sides. "Didn't you have to sign off on this? Aren't you her supervisor? The CIA can't just waltz in and start picking out members of the DIA to use as they see fit, can they?"

"She and I both signed off on the operation," Calvin lowered his head. "Under some duress."

"Explain," Donovan snapped.

"They played the Paris card. They said if she didn't volunteer, they'd reopen the investigation and transfer her to a federal interrogation center."

"Who said that to her?" Donovan whispered the request. His rage had grown white hot. "Give me a name."

"Quentin Kirkpatrick. One word of warning. If the CIA catches wind that you're involved, they'll take measures to shut you down," Calvin explained. "With their airplane and people missing, they're hoping it's completely destroyed, or in such a remote area it'll never be found. They're gambling this will go away. They're also doing whatever it takes to maintain complete deniability."

"I'll ask you again," Donovan said. "Where was all of this happening?"

"Last I heard it could be Slovakia," Calvin replied. "Or maybe Hungary."

"What's the scientist's name?"

"Daniel Pope."

Donovan wasn't entirely surprised that Daniel was somehow involved. Long ago he'd been Lauren's boyfriend. Donovan had met him several times and liked him, even consulted with him on several of Eco-Watch's aeronautical modifications. He was a nice guy, a little introverted, but highly intelligent.

"What are you going to do?" Calvin asked.

"What you hoped I'd do, the single reason you came here to tell me all of this. First, I'm going to make some phone calls while I watch my daughter finish her lesson. Then, I'm going to do what no one else will do, which is go find my wife, and God help anyone who tries to stand in my way."

"I'll help as much as I can."

"Thank you. I'm counting on it," Donovan turned to watch his daughter as his mind filled with everything he'd just heard and what he was going to do about it. Without another word Calvin turned and walked away. Donovan thought the DIA deputy director's shoulders were a little more stooped, as if what he'd just set into motion weighed heavily on the man. He waited until Calvin was out of earshot before he selected a number and dialed.

"Donovan, good to hear from you," William VanGelder said as a way of greeting. "I was going to call you later today."

Donovan was relieved that William had picked up. His best, as well as oldest friend, William had raised Donovan from the age of fourteen, and now, thirty-seven years later, Donovan's first call for help was still the elder statesman. Heavily involved in the oil business for years, William was now nearly a living legend inside the State Department. There weren't many within the beltway that hadn't heard of, or felt the impact of William VanGelder.

"William, I can't talk on an open line, but it's about Lauren. We have a problem. How soon can you be at my place?"

"I'll be there inside of an hour," William said without hesitation.

"See you shortly." Donovan disconnected from William, thumbed through his contacts until he found the one he wanted, and pushed the call button. Moments later a pleasant young woman answered.

"Good morning, Omni Jet Charters. How can I help you today?"

"Is Mark around?" Donovan asked. Mark Foster was a friend who owned and operated one of the top jet charter and leasing operations on the East Coast. Donovan had known Mark for years. The businessman had a passion for airplanes and had helped Donovan set up aircraft purchases for Eco-Watch. No one, least of all Mark, knew that Omni was financed in part by Donovan's vast fortune.

"He is. May I tell him whose calling?"

"Tell him it's Donovan Nash."

"Of course, Mr. Nash, please hold."

"Donovan," Mark said as he picked up. "Good to hear from you. What's going on?"

"Hey, Mark, it's a zoo over here. Scheduling-wise, I'm in a bind and I need an airplane. I'm hoping you can help me out."

"I have the Gulfstream V available. Are you looking for a charter or a lease?"

"I need it to be a charter from Dulles to Vienna, Austria." Donovan had quickly calculated the geography. He didn't want to risk barging into Bratislava in a United States-registered Gulfstream, and Vienna was only forty miles away. "I'd like your crew to stay around for at least a week. It's hard to tell, but we may need to fly to some other cities."

"No problem, when do you want to leave?"

Donovan looked at his watch. "Can we be airborne in four hours?"

"Sure, let's call it a three o'clock departure. How many passengers?"

"Three, besides Michael and I, there will be a Ms. Veronica Montero, I believe you have her information on file."

"Yeah, I've got her here. I'll make everything happen at this end," Mark promised. "Is this billed to the Eco-Watch account?"

"No," Donovan answered. "Use the other account, and if you could, can you eliminate any paper trail that mentions Eco-Watch?"

"Sure, I'll bill this to sales. We'll call it a demonstration flight. Anything else I can do?"

"We're probably going to need to charter a helicopter while we're there as well. Can you find out what might be available?"

"Okay, what size are you thinking?"

"Let's find one that will hold at least six passengers."

"I'll check it out. It's already late afternoon, but I have a guy over there I can call. I'll do my best. Is that all?"

"That's it for now. Thanks for doing all this on a weekend."

"It's never a problem for a friend. Glad I could help. I'll see you later."

Donovan disconnected the call and slid his phone into his pocket. He applauded as Abigail brought Halley to a clean halt, and then, reins in hand, she slid off the horse without any help from her coach. Donovan took a long moment to collect his thoughts, to compartmentalize everything he was feeling. Then he prioritized what needed to be done next, making a mental list of the tasks he needed to accomplish. The thoughts that his wife might be dead, he buried the deepest, losing her was something he couldn't begin to process—or possibly accept. His mind raced between why Daniel might be involved and the fact that Calvin had breached security protocols to bring him what little information existed. Then there was Quentin Kirkpatrick. Donovan set the thoughts of the CIA agent aside for the moment—Quentin would not go unpunished for his actions; he'd be the dessert Donovan would relish when everything else was finished.

Donovan returned Abigail's wave and glanced at his watch. He had time for one more phone call before his daughter finished getting Halley back into the stable. Donovan stared at his phone, at the icon simply labeled Montero. He was hesitant about bringing Montero into the professional fold due to their complicated history. His relationship with Montero had begun badly, recovered, and now she was truly one of his closest and most trusted friends. He'd been hesitant to offer her a position within Eco-Watch, though, not long ago, Lauren had made a compelling case to bring her aboard to fill the position that had once been filled by another friend—one who'd died. If Buck were alive, that's who he'd be calling next—but Buck was gone, and as much as that still hurt, right now he needed Montero's skill set. He pushed the icon and she picked up on the second ring.

"Montero, it's me." Donovan addressed her by last name only. Only in an emergency would he dare use her given name of Veronica, which she hated.

"Donovan, it's the twenty-first century, I have a smartphone. I know who's calling. What's up?"

"We have a situation. Can you be at my house in an hour?"

"Of course. Wait, is this administrative, or tactical?"

Donovan debated with himself one last time. Former FBI Special Agent Veronica Montero could be impatient, and at times, infuriatingly annoying. She could be direct or manipulative and deceptive. In short, she was a pain in the ass. A highly decorated former FBI agent, who, on any given day, if provoked, could become a force to be dealt with. A weapons expert, a former martial arts instructor, she'd worked undercover and brought down dozens of high-profile criminals. Most of all, and the reason he finally relented, was that Donovan trusted her. Montero was one of seven people in the world who knew the truth about his past, and she was an asset Donovan needed right now.

"Hello? Are you still there?"

"Tactical. Pack a bag, we're going to Europe," Donovan said. "We'll be going via chartered jet, no TSA."

"I understand. I'll see you in an hour."

Donovan needed to make one last call and he steeled himself for what was to come. Michael Ross was his best friend, they'd started Eco-Watch together, and while technically Donovan was the boss, those lines had blurred long ago. Michael was a world-class pilot, maybe the best Donovan had ever seen. Theirs was a unique friendship based on the trust forged over the years in the cockpits of sophisticated jets. Michael's wife, Susan, and their two kids, Patrick and Billy, were like family. The relationship was so important to Donovan that he dared not tell Michael the secrets of his past. To jeopardize what they'd built would be unimaginable. Therefore, as always, the moment Donovan made the call, he put himself in the mindset of omission, a reflexive mode not to divulge anything that Michael might think suspicious or out of place.

"Donovan, what's up?" Michael said as he answered.

"Hey, Michael." At the sound of his friend's voice, Donovan considered the words he was about to say, and he felt his rising emotions trying to constrict his throat. He paused for a second, fighting down thoughts of Lauren, and the worst-case scenario.

"Are you all right?" Michael asked.

"Not really," Donovan said the words, though he didn't expect his voice to break. "It's Lauren. She's missing."

"What do you need me to do? I can be at your house in ten minutes."

"I have something else in mind."

"Name it."

"Meet me at Omni's hangar at three o'clock. I had Mark Foster set up a charter. I'm going to Europe to find Lauren—and I need your help."

"I'll be there." Michael hesitated a moment as if thinking. "Is it just going to be the two of us?"

"No, there'll be one other. I don't know if you've ever actually met her, former FBI agent Veronica Montero?"

"I've met her," Michael said. "About a month ago, when you were in New York, Lauren brought her by the hangar. The three of us went to lunch. Lauren explained that she wanted us all to get to know each other. We ended up having a barbeque at my place later that evening with Susan and the kids. We all think she's amazing. I mean the whole world knows about her. Hell, she was on the cover of every magazine in existence after she took down that terrorist. It was good to hear firsthand what she managed to accomplish on our behalf, first in Florida, then in Guatemala. You do know not to call her Veronica, right? She hates that name."

Donovan was mildly surprised, more by the continued deception surrounding exactly how she and Donovan met, though it came as no shock that his wife had taken Montero to meet Michael. Lauren hadn't made it a secret that she thought Montero would be a perfect fit within Eco-Watch. "Yes, I'm well aware of her sensitivity to her name. I'm glad you've met her, it makes all this easier. We need to be a team the minute we hit the ground."

"I have to ask. Is she coming with us as an independent contractor, or did you make her a job offer?"

"Contract, I can't think about the other right now. Let's go get Lauren, and if we both think Montero is a good fit afterwards, we'll offer her the job."

"I like your attitude," Michael said. "Hang in there and I'll see you in a few hours."

CHAPTER FIVE

LAUREN HEARD A BOAT on the river long before it came into view. She'd heard several in the last few hours and wasn't overly concerned. From her hiding spot she was invisible from the water, as well as from the path. Earlier, while contemplating what Daniel had told her, she'd grown restless. Barefoot, she'd paced the same pattern over and over in a small open section of green grass, while she wondered about the jump drive and its contents. She wasn't sure what he'd given her, and without a computer, she had no way to know for sure, but Daniel would have crammed as much data as was available into the drive's memory.

The boat steadily cruised past, then the motor slowed, and shouts erupted. Lauren checked to make sure the path was clear and quickly crawled to a spot where she could survey the river.

The boat was maybe twenty feet long and looked to be a civilian vessel. The helm was set forward, with a flat wooden afterdeck where several pallets of cargo sat. Two men were starboard, pointing into the river as a third man positioned the boat. One of the deck hands used a long-handled gaff to hook something below the surface. He set his feet and pulled. His deck mate joined in, and an object finally broke the surface. Lauren put a hand over her mouth when she realized it was a body. She glanced down and found Daniel still secured out of sight next to the log. The sailors slowly walked to the stern, careful not to lose what they'd found.

Together, they heaved and strained to get the water-soaked corpse up over the low gunwale.

The instant the body broke the surface, Lauren saw the aviator's epaulets; the four gold bars meant it was the captain. Once the body was on the deck, the boat sped upstream, turned, and began running up and down the river, searching. In the distance, Lauren heard the faint thumping of rotor blades. She listened until she was positive it was getting closer. Startled birds called out sharp warnings as they took flight. A large animal, either a deer or something else, fled through the underbrush.

Lauren listened to the helicopter as it approached. She couldn't see it, but it sounded less than half a mile away, which would put it overheard in twenty seconds or less. She was about to move when she heard another threat. Lauren crouched behind a tree trunk and made herself as small as possible. A small truck was trundling down the crude trail toward her. A quick glance told her there were two men in the cab, plus two riding in the bed, the men in the bed were holding weapons. The discovery of the body, especially one wearing a pilot's uniform, would draw hordes of people, police, military, and finally recovery crews. She needed to go. Now.

Coming up behind her, the helicopter roared overhead at treetop level and then banked upstream. It was French built, an Alouette. From her years of studying satellite imagery for the DIA, she recognized it as an older model, the tail boom an open assemblage of tubes and wires. The Plexiglas bubble surrounding the cabin gave it the look of an overgrown wasp. As the truck rounded a small curve and rolled out of view, Lauren was up and moving. She dashed to the river. A quick look up and down the waterway and she didn't spot any more boats, though from the sound of it, the helicopter was circling back around.

Lauren slid down the bank, and knelt until only her head was above the brownish water. As the helicopter closed on her position, she undid the belt holding Daniel at the surface, took a deep breath and submerged. Eyes closed, Lauren put her hands around Daniel to keep from drifting away. The beating of the rotor blades permeated the water and it sounded as if the helicopter was directly overhead.

Lauren's lungs began to burn. She willed herself to remain calm and not to move, to save every molecule of energy. She risked opening her eyes in the murky water and turned to look upward. Silhouetted against the sky was the slender shape of the helicopter. It was flying away from them. Lauren held on to Daniel and eased her head above the surface and gulped huge quantities of fresh air. She took one last big breath and slipped back underwater.

Lauren still clutched Daniel as the helicopter flew overhead once more and then slowly moved away. When she popped to the surface, she could feel the current pulling at her. It felt strong enough that she thought she'd be able to move faster in the river than on foot. She listened for the helicopter, the beating blades filled the air, but it seemed to still be moving away from her, flying in a large arc.

Lauren kicked hard and pulled Daniel's rock-laden body as far out into the channel as she dared. She lifted his face out of the water, kissed the fingers on her left hand and pressed them to his lips.

"Goodbye, Daniel," Lauren whispered, her vision blurred by tears as she released her grip on him, and he slipped below the surface for the last time. Lauren took a breath, submerged, and swam toward the shore while letting the current propel her downstream.

Moving downstream, the road was above her and out of sight to her left. The helicopter was still in the area, but now seemed to be hovering in the sky upstream. Lauren could only assume they were looking for, or perhaps had already found, the crashed Learjet. She needed to keep moving as fast as she could, because by sunrise there would be divers in the water, and once they found the emergency exit door open, the search for survivors would intensify.

Lauren swam into a small cove before she saw the wooden dingy where a single man sat quietly monitoring several fishing poles. Her bare feet dug into the mud and she used her arms to counteract the current. She furiously kicked toward the shore. When the river was shallow enough for her to touch bottom, she clawed her way up the bank. Through the trees to her right, a truck engine cranked to life.

She sprinted across the road, down a faint trail that took her deep into the woods. Behind her, she heard shouts that became more urgent, and then they abruptly ceased. Lauren could only guess that she'd been spotted and now she imagined men spreading out, weapons at the ready, as they followed. In the distance, the sound of the Alouette drew closer.

Lauren came to a sudden stop as the trees gave way to an open field. She took one look at the hundred yards where she'd be exposed and made the decision that she couldn't risk being spotted out in the open. She ducked off the path just as the helicopter, flying only feet above the treetops, roared overhead.

Lauren hid as the helicopter wheeled in a tight bank and circled back around and began to slow. Lauren realized the helicopter was landing, and her immediate impulse was to bolt in the direction she'd come, but then she'd risk running straight into the men from the road. She held her position, calculating her odds of escape as the helicopter touched down in the field. The instant the first man dropped to the ground, Lauren started moving deeper into the brush. She glanced back and took a long look at the man who appeared to be shouting orders. Even at this distance she could see that he had dark hair, cut short, accentuating his sharp facial features. He stood just shy of six foot and looked solid without being fat. Despite the heat, he was dressed in black clothing, and in his left hand, he held a pistol. Two men with shouldered Kalashnikov automatic weapons jumped to the ground behind him and began moving toward her.

Lauren ran as fast as she could, roughly paralleling the path she'd used before. She weaved in and out of the trees, trying to make use of the thinner undergrowth where the trees blocked the sunlight. Behind her the helicopter throttled down, and the beating rotor faded in the forest. She scanned ahead, hoping to see her pursuers before they spotted her.

After running as far as she dared, she stopped and leaned against the trunk of a tree, waiting, listening. The sensation of being hunted from two separate directions was unnerving. Lauren was about to continue when the snap of a branch echoed through the trees just ahead of her. She instinctively dropped into a crouch. Undetected, she slowly peeked around the trunk.

A man was moving cautiously in her direction, leading the way with a rifle. His clothes were civilian, he was stocky, bearded, and he walked with his eyes cast downward, as if he were looking for tracks. There were dried leaves all around Lauren's feet, if she moved, she'd certainly be heard. On an impulse, she grabbed a limb above her head and used her bare feet to gain traction on the rough bark. With surprising quickness, she silently climbed until she was crouched on a sturdy limb nearly ten feet above the forest floor. She steadied herself with both hands, trying to keep her breathing under control, while beneath her, the armed man moved closer. The only sound that reached her ears were the drops of water falling from her saturated clothing and pooling in the rough bark beneath her feet.

as possible until someone tells us what we want to know. Where was the jet headed? Who's involved, who the bad guys are, and finally, where do we find them? The second issue is geographical. We need to be in Eastern Europe—now. Third, we need answers from Dr. Pope's daughter. If she's in protective custody, maybe I can call in some favors from the FBI and we can lean on her. She may know more than she thinks."

At other times in their relationship, Donovan had felt the need to tone down Montero's take-charge attitude—but not today. His decision to include her had been a wise one. They'd come a long way in three years. The first time they'd met, she'd been a special agent with the FBI. She'd been in her late thirties then, blond, pretty, and athletic. She was attractive and knew it, using her looks as one of the many weapons she had at her disposal. Armed with confidence and intelligence, as well as an innate dislike for rules and structure, she'd breezed into an interrogation room in Boca Raton, Florida, and put Donovan in the middle of her investigative crosshairs. In the course of her investigation, she discovered the truth about his past, and instead of revealing this truth, she'd blackmailed him into helping her find a killer. They'd succeeded in a spectacular fashion. Montero was publicly hailed as the federal agent who had brought down one of the most dangerous terrorists in America and averted a catastrophic attack that would have killed hundreds of thousands of civilians. In reality, Donovan and Lauren had killed the terrorist, but Lauren brokered a deal to give Montero the full credit and deflect attention from Donovan and Eco-Watch. Montero became a household name, as well as a media centerpiece for all of law enforcement. She'd kept an earlier vow and promised Donovan that his secret would remain safe.

Eventually, she grew to hate every minute of the attention and adulation and resigned from the FBI. A year ago, Lauren contacted

Montero to bring her in on a problem that required her unique blend of superb investigating skills as well as her ability and willingness to apply force when required. After that, his wife and his former blackmailer had become great friends, and now, if he made her the job offer, Montero was going to be a permanent fixture.

The blond, outgoing, impetuous FBI agent he'd first met was now a dark-haired, quiet, confident, more mature woman, who did as much as possible, short of surgery, to downplay her appearance. Montero and Donovan had much in common these days, and the irony wasn't lost on either of them.

William nodded his agreement and produced his phone. "I'll start with the Secretary of State, and perhaps he'll bring in the Attorney General."

"Wait," Donovan said. "Let's think about this. If we start strong arming people on the Hill, the CIA will most certainly take notice and try to stop whatever we're doing. I think we need to keep everyone in the dark except Calvin at the Defense Intelligence Agency. He said he'd help us, and I believe him. That said, it doesn't mean you can't reach out to people outside of our government, as long as there's no chance of blowback to the CIA."

"I have contacts in Poland, but really no one in Slovakia." William stroked his chin as he thought. "Considering what's at stake, have you considered Kristof?"

"Who's that?" Montero asked.

"Kristof Szanto?" Donovan's eyes narrowed at the thought, the implications far too complex to process all at once. "Do we know if he's even still alive?"

William shrugged. "From what I understand, no one has seen him for years. I could make a call."

"No, leave it to me," Donovan said and then turned to Montero. "You're right, though, we need to be in Eastern Europe."

"Okay," Montero nodded her agreement. "What have you already put into motion?"

"We're wheels up on a chartered Gulfstream V for Vienna at three o'clock."

"You're not taking an Eco-Watch jet?" William asked.

"No, I don't want anyone to know I'm involved. Plus, with a charter, the three of us can get some sleep and be ready to go once we arrive."

"Vienna?" Montero said and then cocked her head. "Wait, three of us? Who else is going?"

"I set up the charter to Vienna, which puts us close to Slovakia without making it obvious. Once we land, the plane will remain with us," Donovan explained. "We're taking Michael. If needed, Michael and I can, at a moment's notice, fly the Gulfstream anywhere. We might ruffle a few feathers, but a Gulfstream allows a level of flexibility we can't get any other way."

"What will you tell Michael?" William asked. "Especially if you end up contacting Kristof?"

Donovan knew what William was driving toward, the three of them sitting in this room all shared the secret that Donovan would go to any length to protect—the one thing that Michael Ross could never know. Donovan Nash was born Robert Huntington, the heir to the Huntington Oil fortune, a family-held company, founded by his grandfather and turned into an industry giant by his father. Robert's trajectory from birth was that one day he'd take his place at the head of the family business. It was something young Robert never questioned.

When he was fourteen years old, he and his father, mother, and a crew were yachting in the South Pacific when they were caught in a savage storm. Battered by the storm, the ship capsized and broke apart, and everyone but Robert perished. It was the day Robert became an orphan and also the day he learned how quickly loved ones could be taken and how profound that loss could be.

Once rescued, Robert fell under the guardianship of William VanGelder, his father's right-hand man. William, childless, assumed his position as acting chairman of Huntington Oil and raised Robert like his own son, grooming the young man for the course set for him at birth. Robert went to Dartmouth, then Oxford. He graduated with honors, but spent more time indulging his passions than studying.

Flying topped the list of Robert's loves. A licensed pilot since he was seventeen, he collected advanced ratings as well as exotic airplanes. With Robert in the cockpit of his prized P-51 Mustang, the residents living in the English countryside heard sounds they hadn't experienced since the war. Hearing the Mustang was often all the people on the ground could do, for Robert loved to fly low, weaving through hedgerows for miles until he pulled back on the stick and climbed the spectacular machine straight up into the sky. If he wasn't attending and flying in local air shows, his other passions included snow skiing, fly fishing, European sports cars, and redheads. In typical Robert Huntington style, he excelled at each particular pursuit.

Upon graduating from Oxford, Robert returned to California and took his seat as the chief executive officer of Huntington Oil. William was elevated to chairman emeritus, and together, they proceeded to build the company into a first-rate global energy conglomerate.

A newly minted billionaire, Robert believed in the philosophy of work hard, play hard. His business savvy became front page news in the financial community; his social life became front page news on the Hollywood gossip circuit. Robert was often photographed with the latest A-list starlet on his arm as they

boarded one of his private jets, bound for some glamorous destination. He mostly ignored what was said about him and lived as
he chose, focusing on building Huntington Oil, his growing collection of planes, and dating whomever he wanted. His carefully
orchestrated life began to unravel at a Malibu fundraiser to save
the whales.

Meredith Barnes was an environmental activist, bestselling au-
thor, star of her own nature documentary, and a staunch opponent
of anyone harming the environment. It didn't matter if the offender
was a farmer using pesticides, a car maker unconcerned about emis-
sions, or the CEO of a major oil company, she'd put a bull's-eye
on their back and use her considerable influence to effect change.
Part scientist, part celebrity, Meredith Barnes was a media darling,
and had grown her platform to include a global collection of presi-
dents, kings, and captains of industry. At home on the world stage,
she was loved by millions, and her message of uniting each inhab-
itant of our fragile planet to do everything possible to make sure
we don't destroy our only home, resonated throughout humanity.

Known wherever she went, Meredith Barnes, a beautiful, fiery
redhead, was singularly brilliant at using her intelligence and
charm to influence nearly anyone she chose. If the situation called
for more forceful means, she was just as adept at unleashing a legendary temper. Robert was moved by her speech, and afterwards,
wrote a personal check for three million dollars. In what became
legendary footage, Meredith chased him down and famously tore
up his check. She stood on her tiptoes and poked him in the chest
with her finger and accused Huntington Oil of a dozen practices
that were harming the planet.

That night, Robert decided she was right, and he made the
commitment to make Huntington Oil a model for environmental change. With Meredith's help, he implemented directives that

changed the energy business forever. Their romance was as swift as it was unexpected, and Robert had never been happier. Weeks before an epic environmental summit in Costa Rica, Robert had proposed. The deliriously happy couple decided to defer the news of their engagement until after the summit. With leaders from all over the world in attendance, there were powerful resolutions on the table to limit overfishing of the oceans, end rain forest depletion, and move towards alternative energy solutions. Enthusiasm was high, and the world press focused on the event as the summit that could save our planet.

In a fraction of a second everything changed. Gunfire, screeching tires, Robert brutally assaulted as Meredith was dragged screaming from their limo. Despite all of his wealth and influence, Meredith Barnes was found dead in a muddy field outside San José. A single gunshot to the forehead had ended her life.

Robert was beyond devastated, as the rumors began to circulate that he'd had a hand in killing Meredith, that the oil billionaire had used the beloved environmentalist to get close to her and then finally silence her forever. His enemies fanned the flames of Robert Huntington's destruction by releasing photos of Robert on an unknown beach with a young woman at his side. The pictures were bogus, but the public cries became shrieks. The public outcry was so fierce he was unable to attend Meredith's funeral. He was never able to say goodbye as the backlash intensified. Boycotts of Huntington Oil were implemented, and threats against all senior executives were received daily. Bombs were exploded at Huntington Oil facilities, and employees injured.

Robert was even further vilified by his silence. He'd made no public appearances or statements since Costa Rica. He was in the home he and Meredith had bought together, crippled by the pain of her death. He was drinking, taking pills, anything to try to escape his anguish. It was William who asked him if he'd thought of taking his own life. Robert admitted that he had. It was that evening the two of them set plans into motion for the death of Robert Huntington.

Several weeks later it was reported that billionaire Robert Huntington had died when his plane crashed into the Pacific Ocean. As Robert floated to earth that night in a parachute, the world began to celebrate the demise of one of the most reviled men on earth. As media speculation ran rampant as to the exact cause of Robert Huntington's death, he began the secretive journey to Europe, where his appearance would be changed forever, and Robert Huntington would start fresh as Donovan Nash. It remained a secret, which if discovered, would instantly destroy everything he'd built, including Eco-Watch, Donovan's memorial to Meredith. Unofficially, he was one of the ten richest people in the world, but only seven people knew the truth and that's how Donovan wanted it to stay.

"Lauren's situation is real enough. I'll tell Michael a version of the truth, that Kristof used to be a friend," Donovan replied. "Though, if we end up involving Kristof, we'll have to do it very carefully."

"Okay, so who is Kristof Szanto?" Montero asked. "What's the connection?"

"A long time ago he was one of my closest friends," Donovan said with a wince. "Our fathers were both in the oil business as well as good friends. Kristof is a few years older than I am, but I've known him almost all of my life. His family is Hungarian, but Kristof grew up like I did, jumping from home to home. We spent a lot of time together as kids, and again when I went to school in Europe. We had a falling out of sorts, and he ended up being one of the people I left behind, one of my bigger regrets."

"What makes him a potential ally in finding out what happened to Lauren?" Montero probed.

"After his father died, he was positioned to take over the family empire but discovered he had no taste for the corporate world or the oil business. He sold the company, and promptly lost his fortune with unfortunate and ill-advised investments. Kristof went broke, and then discovered a business he did have an affinity for—organized crime. In Eastern Europe he's known as Archangel."

"Oh, for God's sake!" Montero's eyes grew large. "Archangel, for real? Everyone in law enforcement knows about him. He's a ghost. Untouchable, he's part legend, part myth, and rumored to be one of the most powerful and ruthless men in Europe, and one of the wealthiest. That would certainly make him an asset."

"There've been whispers over the years that he's dead," William said. "But never any proof."

"Let's say for the sake of argument he is alive," Montero said. "What makes you think he'll be receptive?"

"I don't," Donovan replied. "I have all kinds of reservations about trying to find him. Even looking for him is enough to get us into serious trouble. He's not going to have a clue who I am, and if I do tell him, he might still be angry enough to kill me."

"Let's see if he's alive first," Montero said. "If he's dead, it's a moot point, and we need to move on. I'll start a discreet search for him."

Donovan snapped his head around as the phone on his desk rang—the phone that rarely rang, because it was a secure line installed and maintained by the DIA. Lauren needed such a connection when she was working from home. Donovan picked it up on the second ring.

"I was hoping you'd be there," Calvin said.

"Not for long," Donovan said.

"I might have something. Earlier today, satellite reconnaissance spotted an unusual group of boats on the Danube River, south of Bratislava. In one image, there appeared to be a male body on the deck of a small boat. The body appeared to be wearing a pilot's uniform."

"One of the Learjet pilots?" As Donovan said the words, his stomach tightened, his emotions threatening to rush to the surface unchecked.

"We think so," Calvin continued. "We also spotted something else a short distance away. The area is mostly wetlands, but there are a few small clearings. In one of those clearings, is what looks like a crude crop circle, we can make out a faint pattern trampled in the grass. It's a letter, and depending on your perspective, it's either a small b, or a capital P."

"Pegasus," Donovan felt the air rush from his chest. "If anyone would know how to get the attention of a satellite analyst, it's Lauren."

"My thinking exactly."

"Give me the coordinates," Donovan said as he put pen to paper.

"47.53.03 N, 17.27.27 E. The place is twenty nautical miles southeast of the Bratislava airport. That section of the Danube serves as the border between Slovakia and Hungary. I'm tasking more surveillance assets to get better coverage of the area. How soon are you leaving?"

"We're wheels up at three o'clock in a chartered G-V, flying nonstop from Dulles to Vienna."

"I'll be able to track your progress. Let me give you a new number. Call me when you land."

Donovan wrote down the number. It had a 703 area code, he assumed it went to an untraceable disposable phone. "Got it.

Thanks, Calvin," Donovan ripped the paper from the notepad, folded it in half, and slid it into his pocket.

"I'll protect you as much as I can from here. Go find her."

Donovan hung up and repeated to William and Montero what Calvin had told him.

"It makes sense," Montero said. "Lauren wouldn't want it to be obvious to anyone on the ground looking for her, but something that might be noticed at the DIA."

"It's thin," Donovan said, "but it's all we have at the moment. I do want to say something while it's just the three of us. This is my wife we're talking about. I'm not going to sugarcoat this: there are no rules, no boundaries, and no limits on what I'm willing to do, or spend, to get her back alive. Montero, we're not cops with regulations, we're essentially vigilantes. William, you have access to my money, spend it all if you need to, but for this one, we're not leaving anything on the table."

CHAPTER SEVEN

LAUREN BALANCED HERSELF on the branch poised on the balls of her feet, ready to push off into space. She'd remained motionless in the tree, waiting, holding her breath until the man below moved past. Water from her soaked clothes began pooling at her feet, threatening to overflow at any second. A rivulet broke loose and raced down the channels of the bark before dropping off into space. She followed the freefall until the drop collided with the man's shoulder.

He snapped his head sideways, then immediately looked upward while raising his gun. Leading with her heels, Lauren jumped, her feet crashed into the man's right shoulder, ruining his aim. Lauren felt a distinct pop as his collarbone snapped under her weight. He let out a strained cry as he was driven down into the dirt. His head snapped backward as he hit, and then he was still.

Lauren rolled on impact, adrenaline coursing through her body. She picked up the rifle, then fished in the man's pockets and found five rounds of ammunition, plus a wad of bills. There was nothing else, no wallet, no radio. She stuffed what there was into her pocket. The man wasn't all that big, a good four inches shorter than she was, and she eyed his boots. She placed her foot next to his, close enough she thought, and quickly relieved him of his footwear. She slid them on and laced them as tightly as she could. They were a little large; still, they were better than nothing.

Lauren stood, and flexed her legs to make sure she was okay, and then gripped the gun so it rested unobtrusively along the side of her leg. Her friend Veronica Montero had told her that the best way to get shot was to wave a gun around. Montero also told her the best way to win a gunfight was not to get into one. Now that she was armed, she felt less vulnerable and began to retrace her path to the clearing. She went straight to where the Alouette had landed, it was still running, but at idle speed, the main rotor and tail rotor blades spinning in the sunshine, the cockpit door open, the pilot sitting inside, waiting.

Lauren briefly entertained hijacking the helicopter but ruled out the play. The noise would most certainly bring the others running. Then another thought came to her. Lauren worked her way into position behind the helicopter where the pilot couldn't see her coming. With both hands, she gripped the rifle near the trigger, like choking up on a bat. She tested its weight, and then her grip. Satisfied, she began moving quickly toward her target.

Lauren stopped just behind the open door and used her booted foot to kick the thin aluminum skin of the helicopter. The pilot spun his head to find the source of the noise. Lauren was already swinging. She delivered an uppercut and the wooden forearm of the rifle connected with the man's jaw line. His eyes rolled up into his head, and he sagged against his seat belt.

She stepped over him and took a quick glance into the cockpit. She found what she'd hoped to find—a pistol, a chart, binoculars, and a bottle of water. She snatched all of them and hurried to the rear of the helicopter.

Lauren stopped at the tail rotor housing, the blades a blur as they turned. She planted her feet, and with her hand on the butt of the rifle, she shoved it toward the blades, the most vulnerable part of the helicopter. She turned away and ducked as the wooden stock of the gun exploded. Something metal snapped, and she dropped to the ground and covered her head. The noise of metal tearing itself apart echoed throughout the clearing. Lauren risked a peek and saw the blades were bent, slamming into the metal housing as they still tried to spin. The entire frame of the helicopter shuddered under the onslaught. She couldn't imagine the helicopter would fly anytime soon.

She spotted the rifle; it was twisted and bent beyond repair. She collected her stolen items and ran, trying to be as quiet as she could while not compromising speed. For a solid twenty minutes, she moved as quickly as she could in the rough direction of the lights she'd seen the night before.

Lauren finally stopped, out of breath, as well as hot and thirsty. Her clothes were soaked with sweat. The strap from the binoculars she'd stolen had rubbed her neck raw, and she eagerly pulled them off. She sank to the ground and then produced the bottle of water and held it up, finding it two-thirds full. She took a small sip of the warm water and then another until only two inches of the precious fluid remained in the bottle. She ignored the rumbling in her stomach and opened the chart. As she did, two folded sheets of printer paper tumbled to the ground. She picked them up and as she unfolded them, she recognized the first image was Daniel, it matched the photo in the replacement passport the CIA had given her to get him out of Europe. The second sheet was her passport photo. The only way they could have possession of these was if they'd found the plane and the documents. Lauren slumped, she'd expected more time before the Learjet was found.

She began to study the chart, searching each grid along the water without luck, searching for something she could tie to her current position. The wetlands along the Danube were a labyrinth of channels and waterways. She'd seen no landmarks, nothing she could tie into the chart.

Lauren listened as she caught a faint sound that seemed to blow in with the wind. It was indistinct, but she thought she could make out a constant drone. She guessed it was coming from a large engine, perhaps a piece of farm equipment, definitely bigger than a car or truck. She folded the chart and photos, got to her feet, and carefully worked her way parallel to a worn pathway, stopping every now and then to listen, but all she heard was the distant sound of the large engine, which seemed to be fading. She stopped and spotted a hint of a trail that led toward a cluster of trees situated away from the path. She decided to follow it.

She eased into the thick grove of trees and found a fallen log well hidden by the canopy of leaves above. She gingerly sat on the ground and used the log as a backrest. She closed her eyes, and while catching her breath, she took an inventory of her battered but still intact body parts. As she sat, her thoughts drifted to Daniel. The sight of his face slipping beneath the water as he sank would stay with her always. She thought of what he'd said—that the *Phoenix* was a stealth aircraft with possibly a nuclear payload.

Lauren allowed herself to be transported back nearly twenty years, to when she and Daniel were together at MIT. He'd shown her some preliminary designs he'd made for a super quiet, efficient, light jet. She remembered it clearly, he'd been so excited, and all she could think was that it was so unusual looking. The craft was no more than thirty feet long with a wingspan of about thirty feet. It had an unconventional V tail, instead of the more common vertical and horizontal stabilizers. Overall, the jet was nothing but smooth rounded edges, so much so, it looked like a spaceship. Instead of sweptback wings, Daniel had used a forward-swept wing design. He'd explained the jet engine was buried in the fuselage to reduce drag. It was a combination of parts that seemed to come from other planes. She'd laughingly named it the platypus.

Unamused with Lauren's suggestion, Daniel immediately tried to find a suitable name for his creation. Over dinner, he settled on the *Phoenix*, from one his favorite movies, the original 1965 black-and-white version of *Flight of the Phoenix* starring Jimmy Stewart. Hollywood actually built a flyable prototype from the wreckage of a crashed Fairchild Flying Boxcar. A mishmash of components were eventually made into a smaller flyable plane the stranded crew used to fly to safety. Daniel's odd design became the *Phoenix*.

She remembered all the drawings and scale models. How all the components were blended, there were hardly any sharp edges. Then there were the engines buried deep in the fuselage to reduce drag, plus the V-tail design, all which would be beneficial for a stealth platform. Despite the fact that it all happened so long ago, she remembered those days clearly. The *Phoenix* marked the beginning of the end for her and Daniel's relationship.

Daniel had been distraught when she'd broken things off. She'd never intended to be with Daniel for so long, but the rigors of the MIT doctoral program made him a habit she hadn't had time to break. They'd never really fought, were sexually compatible, if not incendiary, and overall made a comfortable relationship—it was just lacking some undefinable element. Finally, before she was leaving Boston for a summer internship in Florida to join the Air Force Hurricane Hunter squadron, she broke up with him.

Lauren pondered her and Daniel's time in Boston. As with most relationships of any significance, there was always a certain amount of second guessing, and Daniel was no exception. She'd gone to Florida, and after some tears and late-night phone calls with Daniel, he'd grown desperate and when he issued an

ultimatum, their relationship collapsed completely. Not long afterwards she'd taken up with an Air Force pilot. Ultimately he
was all flash, no substance, but Lauren liked hanging out and especially flying with the pilots. She was exposed to enough of the
pilot swagger and charm to develop an attraction to the type, and
the memories of reserved, awkward Daniel had quickly faded.

Years later she met Donovan Nash, a pilot who had just the
right amounts of flash and substance, and he was definitely char-
ismatic. Donovan was tall, his tousled brown hair a contrast to
his deep blue eyes. He carried himself with the easy confidence of
a man who was in charge but didn't flaunt the fact. She remembered how he zeroed in on her from the moment they met and
she'd been swept off her feet by a man who was smart, capable,
had a strong silent side *and* was one of the handsomest men she'd
ever dated. Their chemistry clicked, and they'd begun a torrid
romance in between missions flying his Eco-Watch Gulfstream
jets high above the fury of Atlantic hurricanes. They were heady
times, right up until she'd left him.

Her attraction to him had blinded her. Donovan had a private
side, which at first seemed romantic and mysterious, but which
she could never break through, let alone get invited in, and eventually the secrets, the half-truths, the evasiveness, became too
much. His inability to communicate past a certain point made
her decision for her, and suspecting another woman, she walked
out on him. She'd been heartsick, the first month beyond misera-
ble, but she pushed past her breakup with Donovan and put him
firmly in her past, knowing it was for the best. Two weeks after
that decision, she discovered she was pregnant.

Something moved in the brush to her left, and Lauren quietly
raised the pistol and waited. The grass rustled again and a fawn
stepped cautiously into the clearing. Round doe eyes finally

spotted Lauren, and the startled deer flinched twice and then stopped and studied Lauren briefly before slinking out of sight in the overgrowth.

Abigail would have been so thrilled to see the fawn, and Lauren felt her state of mind crumble at the thought of her daughter. Abigail was so perfect, a little mixture of her intelligence and her father's fearlessness. It was a potent combination for a five-year-old, but Abigail was also poised, articulate, and self-assured. For months, after she found out she was expecting, Lauren went back and forth as to whether to tell Donovan he was going to be a father. In the end she decided that her reasons for letting him go were valid. There was no way she was going to live with a man who was emotionally closed off and distant. Both she and Abigail deserved better. It would be in everyone's best interest if that door remained closed.

She didn't see him again for almost eighteen months. It was in Bermuda. There was a car wreck and she was dying, trapped upside down in an overturned car, while Hurricane Helena rolled in from the open ocean and pummeled the tiny island. Torrential rain began to fill the car with water. She remembered every detail. Trapped upside down, she called for help, as inch by inch, the water reached her head then slowly covered both her eyes and nose. She remembered thrashing frantically, trying to stretch for just one more breath, to live a few more seconds. The next thing she remembered was choking up water, looking into Donovan's blue eyes.

Three days later, he told her he loved her and confessed his secret: that Donovan Nash was a name he'd taken from a very distant relative, that his real name was Robert Huntington. In that instant, with those two words, Lauren understood. Long-dead parents, Meredith Barnes, the murdered fiancée the world blamed him for killing. The onetime playboy with unlimited resources had staged his death and then changed, evolved into the bravest, most capable man she'd ever met. Fiercely loyal, impatient, intelligent, and one of the most loving, yet fragile and damaged, souls she'd ever met. She loved him, and no matter what happened, she would always love him, and she took great comfort in the knowledge that he felt the same way about her.

Lauren took in her immediate surroundings. The sun was low on the horizon. By now Donovan had most likely been given the news, probably by Calvin. She had no idea what the DIA knew, or what Donovan's state of mind was, or how he was reacting. In his life he'd experienced the deaths of those closest to him, and survived, but barely. Those events had scarred him deeply. Lauren's hope was that if she didn't survive, Abigail would be the difference. Maybe their daughter would create a foundation that would keep Donovan grounded, stop him from retreating and spiraling into himself and the darkness that waited there.

She felt the jump drive in her pocket. Its contents needed to be seen—but how to do that quickly? She didn't have a ready answer. The one thing she knew for sure was that the CIA wasn't coming. She was on her own. Her thoughts returned to Donovan. Whatever he was doing, more than anything, she needed him to be on his way to her.

CHAPTER EIGHT

DONOVAN SAT RIGID in the leather seat of the Gulfstream V, impatient for the pilots to start the takeoff roll. The twin turbofan engines finally spooled up and sent the airplane hurtling down the runway for the six hour and fifty-one minute flight to Vienna.

"How's Abigail?" Montero asked.

"She's good," Donovan said. "You know her, everything is an adventure."

"Wonder who she inherited that from?" Montero said.

"I explained that Mommy had been delayed in Europe, and that I was going to go help her and would she mind if Grandpa William took her to her grandmother's for a few days. Her only concern was that she'd be able to go to her next riding lesson. I promised her she'd not miss a single day with Halley. I packed her a bag, and she blew me a kiss from the back of William's car. She's fine." Donovan didn't want to consider how much of what he'd just described would change if something happened to Lauren.

As if reading his thoughts, Montero turned her attention out the window.

The airplane broke ground, and Donovan listened for the familiar sounds of the landing gear being pulled up into the wheel wells, the flaps being retracted, small power changes as they turned northeast. Donovan knew their route would eventually intercept one of the designated North Atlantic Tracks, invisible airways calculated to separate the traffic as well as take the best advantage of the prevailing westerly winds across the ocean. He'd done it himself hundreds of times, though for once he was happy to be in the back of the plane instead of flying.

Donovan heard a phone ring somewhere in the cabin and then someone calling his name. He turned and found Karen, their flight attendant, standing in the aisle.

"Mr. Nash, Mr. Foster is on the phone," Karen said, as she politely gestured toward the compartment that held the satellite phone.

"Thanks," Donovan pulled out the phone, more than a little curious why Mark would be calling so soon after takeoff. "Mark, what's up?"

"I wanted to reach you before you tried to catch a nap. It's about your helicopter."

"That was quick." Donovan reached for the pen in his pocket.

"It was quick because there are no helicopters to be had. There's some sort of big auto race beginning this week in Vienna and everything is booked solid. The closest helicopters for charter are out of Berlin, or Geneva, and even then they only had a few days of availability. Sorry. I told them to contact me if there were any changes."

"Thanks, Mark." Donovan replaced the phone, threw off his seat belt, and nodded to Montero to join him in the back of the plane. Michael had a chart spread out on an open table. As Donovan approached, he knew exactly what Michael was studying, the Danube River between Bratislava and Budapest.

"What was the phone call?" Michael asked.

"I'd asked Mark to charter us a helicopter," Donovan said. "Turns out there aren't any available in the area. The closest one is in Geneva, and even then there was a pretty small window where we could have guaranteed access."

Montero pulled her laptop closer and began typing. Seconds later she'd pulled up a page and spun the screen around so Donovan could see.

Donovan leaned down and saw that she'd found an aircraft broker in Europe and there were listings for thirty-seven individual helicopters. Montero may have opened the door to a solution, but now there were several other problems. "Let's say we can talk William into fronting us the money to buy one, who do we get to fly the thing?"

"I say we call Reggie Cornell." Michael reached for his briefcase. "Remember him? He's the former SAS operative in London who put together the team that extracted Lauren, Abigail, and Stephanie from Paris. I assembled all the after-action reports. He's a solid guy."

"Do it," Donovan returned to his seat as Michael scrolled through his tablet and then picked up the phone and dialed.

"Is this Reggie? This is Michael Ross with Eco-Watch. I appreciate you taking my call. I'm sorry for the late hour, but we need your help. I'm going to hand you off to my boss, Donovan Nash."

Donovan took the phone from Michael. "Mr. Cornell, Donovan Nash here, it's nice to finally be able to thank you in person for saving my family."

"Mr. Nash, it was my pleasure, that was one of the easy ones. How can I help you tonight?"

"I can't say much on this line, but I need a helicopter pilot in Vienna by tomorrow."

"Same bit of business as Paris?" Reggie asked.

"Something like that, can you help me?"

"What kind of machine are we dealing with? Is this an urban job, open terrain, over water?"

"No open water, probably urban. Let's call it an Eastern European theatre of operation," Donovan glanced at the screen of Montero's computer. "As to what machine, find me the best pilot you can, and then ask him what he prefers, and it'll be made available."

"Same pay schedule as before?" Reggie asked.

Donovan had no idea what the rate had been, and he didn't care. "If you can put this together, and the pilot can be in Vienna by noon tomorrow, I'll double the rate."

"You sound like a man going to war. Are you sure you don't need the services of more than just a single pilot? I have a team I can assemble on short notice."

"I'll keep you in mind, but for now, one pilot is all I need."

"I have someone I trust. Call me back in ten minutes," Reggie said and promptly hung up.

"What did he say?" Michael asked. "Can he help us?"

"He said he's got a guy in mind. We're to call him back in ten minutes."

Montero spun her computer around. "I'm going to separate these helicopters geographically, and then by type. Once we know what the pilot prefers, we can make an offer on the best available helicopter within a workable distance in relation to Vienna."

Michael's eyes shot back to the screen of his tablet. "If the deal with Reggie falls through, then our next option might be to contact Airbus Helicopters, they'd love to sell a helicopter to Eco-Watch."

"That's the problem, we're not Eco-Watch," Donovan said. "Officially, we're friends of Lauren McKenna, who is currently presumed missing while traveling in Slovakia. Technically, we're mercenaries on a rescue mission."

"Are you carrying a gun?" Michael asked Donovan.

"I'm in charge of the guns, among other things, and we're all going to carry them," Montero said without looking up. "We all know how to defend ourselves, so it makes sense we should have the tools. Once we're on the ground, I'll issue firearms, and there will be a briefing."

"Wow," Michael said. "No hesitation there."

Montero stopped writing and looked up. "What's the one thing you'd like to have if you find yourself in a gunfight? Exactly—a gun. As someone who'll likely be in the same gunfight, I want you to have one as well. Okay, I think I've narrowed this down. These are all of the helicopters that are available in Europe within a three-hour ferry flight to Vienna. There are eleven. I've listed them by type and location."

"Nice work." Donovan scanned the list. "What are these numbers?"

"Prices," Montero said, "I converted them all to U.S. dollar amounts."

"I see," Donovan nodded his understanding. She'd included that information purely for Michael's benefit. She knew as well as he did that money wasn't an object.

"It's about time to call Reggie back," Michael said.

Donovan studied the satellite phone momentarily and then pressed redial.

"Right on time," Reggie said as a way of greeting. "His name is Trevor Emerson, former SAS, none better. I have a phone number. Are you ready to copy?"

Donovan wrote down the number, read it back, and then thanked Reggie and severed the connection. Using his thumb, Donovan punched in Trevor's number and then waited for the call to go through.

"Hello," a man's voice answered.

"Trevor, my name is Donovan. Reggie said to call."

"How's the missus and the little one? Doing well, I hope?"

"You were there?" Donovan asked.

"I'm always Reggie's first choice, so, yeah, I was flying that one."

"Thank you so much, you saved lives that day."

"Very good, then, how can I help you?"

"We have a missing persons case. Their last known whereabouts are not certain, but we believe it could be Slovakia. Right now I'm on a jet flying to Vienna, and I want to add a helicopter to the operation to be used for possible extraction. You pick the machine, I'll make it available."

"How many missing persons are there?"

"I'm not certain, no more than two."

"How large is your team?"

"Three."

"Lean and mean, eh?" Trevor replied. "My preference would be a Eurocopter EC-130. There are plenty around, so it won't draw all that much attention. It's the right size and can take some punishment, if you know what I mean."

Donovan scanned the list Montero had prepared. "There's a three-year-old EC-130 T2 listed for sale in Salzburg, Austria. Would that work?"

Montero clicked on the link that pulled up the entire listing, complete with photographs, and turned the screen toward Donovan.

"Salzburg? Is it red with gold stripes?" Trevor asked.

"Yeah. Are you familiar with this machine?"

"I delivered it to the owner and did a bit of training for his crew. Rich bloke, another one of his odd toys, I suppose. I'm not surprised he's selling. I heard he'd buggered up his fortune in the market. Yeah, it's a nice machine, it'll do nicely."

"I'm going to put this in motion. Can my people reach you at this number?"

"Yeah, text me the information when you have it, as well as how I can reach you," Trevor said. "How soon were you thinking?"

"I'm hoping we'll close on this helicopter in the morning," Donovan said. "Where are you now?"

"London, West side."

"We're going to charter a jet to get you to Salzburg. Would Farnborough Airport work?"

"Um yeah, sure, Farnborough's fine."

"Perfect, we'll make the arrangements through TAG Aviation."

"Mr. Nash, you're in an awfully big hurry and spending a great deal of money," Trevor said. "May I inquire exactly who it is that's missing, and how messy this could end up being?"

"It's my wife, and it could end up being very messy."

"I'm sorry to hear that, but I appreciate the candor," Trevor said. "I'll see you soon."

Donovan was pleased with Trevor. The former SAS pilot hadn't hesitated for a second about flying into a fight. Donovan exhaled slowly to clear his mind and then dialed William.

"William, it's me. Are you somewhere you can talk?"

"Yes, I just delivered Abigail to Lauren's mother, and I'm home now. Is there any news?"

"Nothing, though I do need to ask a few favors, and maybe borrow some money."

"I'm listening," William said, his voice letting Donovan know that he understood that Michael must be close.

"I need to buy a helicopter. Montero is sending you all the information as we speak. I need it as fast as humanly possible."

"Let me walk to my computer," William replied. "Okay, I'm

opening her email. Got it. Salzburg, Austria? A Eurocopter E-130 for two point three million dollars?"

"That's the one."

"Shall I buy it through one of the Swiss companies?"

"Yes." Donovan had layers upon layers of corporations, trusts, and financial entities that were used to keep his Huntington Oil fortune separate from Donovan Nash, who, as far as the world knew, was a salaried employee for a nonprofit organization.

"Okay, what else?" William asked.

"Can you set up a charter through TAG Aviation out of their Farnborough, England, facility? There's a man by the name of Trevor Emerson, we'll designate him as our agent in the purchase. He needs to get to Salzburg in time to coincide with the closing of the helicopter. All of his contact information should be in your inbox by now."

"I'm assuming this is our helicopter pilot?"

"Yes, we got lucky. Have you heard any news from your Eastern European connections?"

"I made a few calls, nothing yet. Is there anything else I can do for you?"

"Not that I can think of. I'll keep you posted."

Donovan hung up, then turned toward the galley and caught Karen's eye.

"How can I help you?" she said as she joined them in the rear of the plane.

"Do you have any Canadian whiskey aboard?" Donovan asked.

"Of course," Karen smiled. "I believe you prefer McLoughlin & Steele?"

"Nice. Can you bring us three of those on the rocks?"

"Right away. When would you like me to serve dinner?"

Donovan had very little appetite, so he looked at Michael and Montero, who both shrugged indifference. He turned back to Karen. "Let's eat early, and then maybe we'll try and get some sleep."

Moments later, Karen appeared at Donovan's elbow with three whiskeys on a tray.

"Let's take a short break," Donovan said, passing out the drinks. "I want to thank you both for being here. I can't imagine going at this alone." They clinked glasses and then drank. Donovan savored the smooth whiskey and relished its satisfying heat in his chest.

"Here's to none of us ever being alone," Montero tipped her glass and finished her whiskey in a single swallow. "I think we should go over the high-resolution satellite images of where we believe the Learjet went down. Then I want to examine every possible escape route Lauren may have taken and every possible means we have of finding her."

CHAPTER NINE

LAUREN FLINCHED, FRIGHTENED, as out of nowhere a high-intensity searchlight ripped through the darkness and lit up the tops of the trees. Afterimages danced on her retinas as she shook her head and blinked them away. Moments later the harsh beam of light returned. Squinting in the brightness, Lauren started to paddle toward the shore. She'd been swimming in a channel to travel quietly in the night, but now she was exposed. As her feet found purchase on the muddy bottom, she pushed forward and climbed out of the water.

The searchlight continued its bizarre sweep above her, illuminating the forest, this time further away, and when it swung away from her, the ink-black night came crushing down once again.

Lauren stood with her hands on her knees, her eyes adjusting from the high-intensity assault to what little light was being produced by the star-filled sky. She had no idea what time it was but most likely nearing first light. She felt like she'd been slogging through the wetlands for hours. Moving downstream, her progress was easier, though the unseen splashes around her were at first unnerving, though by now, Lauren only paid attention to the largest disruptions. She could feel the first signs of fatigue tapping her energy, and hunger gnawed at her insides. She pushed all of that away and studied her immediate surroundings. She was in an area of trees and brush, but across what looked like a dirt road, was a field. The trees were sparse, and she spotted something faint—a green light moving from right to left.

Lauren kept her eyes on the light and put the binoculars to her eyes and realized at once that the right tube was dark, most likely filled with water, but the left side still worked, and she turned the thumbwheel until the green light in the distance jumped into focus. She panned each direction from the light, and when she contemplated the mystery of the searchlight and the rising and falling sounds of a large engine, she understood that she was looking at the wheelhouse of a tugboat.

Hearing a vehicle off to her left, Lauren hurried down the embankment and hid out of sight. She drew the pistol from the waistband of her slacks and pressed against the riverbank. The headlights danced above her head, and she suppressed her alarm at being so close to danger. The vehicle powered past only feet from her head, and as it receded in the distance, a cloud of dust settled over her. She studied the sky to the east. It might be her imagination, but she thought she could detect the first hint of the coming day nibbling away at the darkness.

Lauren debated going back into the dark water or staying on land. She chose land for the simple reason she'd have to hide as soon as daybreak drew closer. She pulled herself up the embankment and hurried across the road into the field. She made good time. The land was flat and dry, and the plants only came up to her knee. Lauren stopped and looked behind her. In the dim light of the stars she could see the trail her passing had left in the dry grass. She backtracked and then angled towards a row of trees to try to find some bare ground so her trail wouldn't be so easy to follow.

Lauren walked on in silence, acutely aware of any new sounds in the night air. She topped a small rise, and straight ahead, the glow she'd been chasing became distinct lights. Through the trees she spotted a cluster of buildings grouped together on the other side of the river. A town beckoned, the sight of civilization was a relief, but Lauren knew it also represented another level of danger. It seemed like an eternity, but she finally reached the edge of the trees for an unobstructed view.

"Shit," Lauren whispered in the silence as she knelt behind the last of the foliage.

Lauren took in the sight downstream. Bathed in lights and spanning the half-mile wide river was a dam. Lauren still had the binoculars. She raised them and slowly panned the entire structure. On the far shore was a breakwater; on the other side was a set of locks for the barge traffic. There was a towering control center that would give the men up there a commanding view up and down the river. Lauren viewed the end of the dam and stopped. Two military trucks were parked grill to grill, acting as an effective gate to any traffic wanting to cross.

She was blocked from crossing the main channel, unless she swam, and she wasn't anxious to swim against the current above a large dam. She lowered the binoculars, and using the light from the dam, she began to carefully separate the now soaked sheets of the chart. She peeled the last section apart and found the sector of the map she needed and set aside the two grainy passport photographs. She quickly located the dam on the chart; it was near the town of Gabčíkova, in Slovakia. She scanned downstream until she found a small town on her side of the river. It was miles away. If she tried to go west, once she emerged from the forested wetlands, all she could discern on the chart was open farmland. She thought about the pictures, as well as the time that had elapsed since the plane crash. As far as she knew, she and Daniel's faces

CHAPTER TEN

"WAKE UP!" MONTERO whispered. "Donovan, wake up, you're having a bad dream."

Donovan's eyes flew open to find Montero hovering over him. In that last instant, before he was fully awake, he was slogging through a Slovakian swamp searching for Lauren. He kept finding body after body, each face he recognized—though none of them were his wife.

"There's coffee in the carafe, help yourself," Montero said as she returned to her seat and slipped on her reading glasses.

Donovan sat for a moment, letting his nightmare subside. He ran his hands through his hair and took in his surroundings. All the window shades were closed, making the cabin dark. In what little light there was, he found Michael still asleep in one of the forward chairs, a blanket pulled up under his chin. Montero was where he'd left her before he dropped off to sleep, sitting in a chair, her computer on the table in front of her. The coffee sat tantalizingly close on the credenza. He poured himself a cup.

"Do you want to talk about it?" Montero said.

"Not really." Donovan blew into his cup to cool the coffee and then took a tentative sip.

"How are you holding up?" Montero asked. "Should I be worried?"

"I'm okay," he answered, knowing full well he wasn't even close to being okay. The bad dream was predictable. Earlier in the evening, as they had gone over the satellite imagery of where they thought the Learjet crashed, all Donovan could think about was how improbable it was that anyone had survived. Even if the pilot could see the water and tried to ditch, the odds were nearly impossible that anyone could walk away. If someone did survive, they'd have to escape the sinking airplane before they drowned, a task made even more difficult in moving water and further compounded if that person were injured. All he had to grasp onto was Calvin's report about a single letter P trampled into the grass, which could be anything, something completely random, a trick of light, or just wishful thinking.

Earlier, as he'd laid there trying to drift off to sleep, he'd been caught up in a loop of imagining a flight home without her. The thought of living without Lauren was crippling. They'd had to fight so hard to be together, and the reward for their perseverance was a stronger relationship, a more intense love than he'd ever thought possible. Then he pictured himself having to face Abigail, telling her that Mommy—at that point, Donovan felt his throat begin to tighten. The big surprise was that he'd slept at all.

"The expression on your face is telling me something else," Montero said softly. "It's okay to be a little messed up. If you *were* fine, I'd be worried. I've seen you operate under enough stress to buckle and crush most men, yet you get through. No, let me rephrase that, you somehow do more than get through, you prevail. One of these days you'll have to teach me how you pull that off with such regularity."

"I think the scars on my body would seem to discount that theory. Did you get any sleep?" Donovan asked, anxious to change the subject. "When did you start wearing glasses?"

"I slept a little, and I just got these, and I don't want to hear anything about my advanced age," Montero said as she finished typing. "I got to thinking about a few things. The guy Lauren went to rescue, Daniel Pope. It's a fair assumption his daughter was threatened so he'd cooperate. With that in mind, I went ahead and instituted round-the-clock surveillance on Abigail and Lauren's mother, as well as Michael's family. It'll be undetectable, but I'd always rather err on the side of caution."

"When you say undetectable, what exactly do you mean?"

"The subjects won't be aware they're being protected. With no visible deterrent, it also allows any threat to reveal itself. Then, of course, be eliminated."

"Thank you." Donovan was both relieved and mortified at the thought that once again, his five-year-old daughter needed armed protection. "What else have you been doing?"

"Looking into things," Montero replied. "Daniel Pope. Have you ever met him?"

"Yeah, several times, brilliant guy. I like him. He's a part of Lauren's history. They dated when they were at MIT which isn't a big deal. I can't change Lauren's past any more than I can change my past. Why does any of this matter?"

"It probably doesn't. I'm just being nosey, but I do want to know what to expect from you if he somehow survived."

"I don't dislike the guy, unless he's got some kind of hidden agenda. If the reason he asked for her was based strictly on a trust issue, I understand. However, if he has something else in mind, then he and I might have a little problem."

Montero handed her laptop across the aisle to Donovan. "This is a file from a contact who works at Interpol. It's not Archangel's actual file; he's not part of any active investigation, and hasn't been seen for almost eighteen months. This is more of a summary, you probably know most, if not all, of the contents. It was more for me than you, but I need to know what you can add. I think you should read it before Michael wakes up."

Donovan took a long swallow from his cup. He needed more caffeine to keep up with Montero. He glanced forward at Michael, who was still asleep, and began to scan what Montero's contact had sent. She was right; he knew most of what was said.

Kristof Szanto, aka Archangel, is a fifty-four-year-old of Hungarian descent. He was born in London into a wealthy family, and twenty-seven years ago, upon the death of his father, inherited Szanto Petroleum. Within a year, he sold his business to a European subsidiary of Huntington Oil and began to spend his fortune. Two years later, his money nearly gone, he was arrested on charges of weapons smuggling, but walked, as all of the witnesses recanted earlier testimony. He was never arrested again, but in a criminal career that spanned nearly twenty-five years, he's been a suspect in weapons smuggling, political corruption, election tampering, and in that time has eliminated or merged with several other criminal syndicates in Eastern Europe. It is suspected that virtually every level of weapons dealing in four continents passes through Archangel.

His current whereabouts are unknown, but his criminal enterprises are thriving, leading some to believe he's deceased, or been quietly pushed aside, and someone new is in charge. Interpol has no new leads in locating him. He is reported to have several homes in Europe, an apartment in downtown Budapest, plus an estate in rural Hungary, as well as a flat in London. A chalet thought to be owned by Archangel in Innsbruck, as well as the country home outside of Budapest, were recently renovated and modernized. There is speculation that these properties may go on the market, further substantiating the rumors of Archangel's passing.

"The part about his homes strikes me as strange," Donovan said as he handed Montero her computer. "I remember the chalet outside of Innsbruck. We'd stay there sometimes when we came to visit in the winter. He bought a flat in Chelsea, but he also loved Treviso, Italy, and Nice in the South of France. Hell, he could have a dozen homes that aren't even on this list."

Donovan heard the engines change pitch and felt the Gulfstream begin its initial descent. Michael opened his eyes and threw off his blanket.

"What time is it here?" Donovan needed to set his watch.

"It's a little after five o'clock in the morning," Montero replied.

Donovan said good morning to Michael as his friend trundled past them, mumbling something about zombies and jet lag, as he headed for the lavatory.

"Is he going to be okay?" Montero asked.

"He's not a morning person," Donovan said. "He'll improve with coffee."

"I have rooms for all three of us at a hotel near the airport. I thought we could all shower and perhaps have breakfast. My thought is to let Michael stay at the airport and meet Trevor when he arrives. Maybe by then we'll have a clue to where we're headed next."

"Do you have a theory about Kristof?"

"I always have a theory," Montero said. "But at this point it's too disjointed to even talk about. Ask me later today."

"What are you and I doing once we land?"

"We're going to meet with Klaus Mikos, the interior designer who did the design work on Kristof's country house in Hungary."

"How do you know this interior designer?"

"I don't. He was featured in a magazine and he mentioned the property. He's famous and he lives in Vienna. We'll start with him. Someone was giving the orders for all of those renovations."

Karen came back to the cabin with fresh coffee and an assortment of pastries. She folded the blankets and opened the window
shades in preparation for landing. As she was finishing, Michael
emerged from the lavatory. He'd shaved, changed his shirt, and
his hair was combed. He took a cup of coffee and a Danish from
the tray and plopped down in the seat across from Montero.

"You look like you slept," Montero remarked. "How do you
feel?"

"Not bad," Michael yawned. "Has there been any news about
Lauren? Anything that gives us a better idea of what we're going
to do first?"

"We were just talking about that," Donovan said. "Nothing
new, but we've decided we're going to split up. Montero has some
friends at Interpol we're going to go meet. I want you to stay at the
airport. Montero made us room reservations at one of the local
hotels. I need you to wait for Trevor to arrive with the helicopter.
Check it out, brief him on everything we know so far."

"Sounds good," Michael said, turning to make sure Karen was
out of earshot. "I was thinking about guns, what are we doing
about Customs?"

"There won't be any," Montero said. "We're being pre-cleared
through customs and immigration, courtesy of William and the
State Department. Speaking of customs, I have a nine-millimeter
Glock and two extra clips of ammo for you. I'll transfer it to you
once we're off the airport grounds. Is that satisfactory?"

"Yeah, I'm familiar with the Glock." Michael said.

"Good," Montero continued. "Now, here's the drill. If you draw
your weapon, it's because you're going to use it on someone who
is about to harm you. A weapon is not a conversation starter. Do
not use your weapon to warn your adversary. If you pull it out,
use it to kill. Fire your weapon until the threat is neutralized, and

then leave the scene immediately. Either William VanGelder or I will handle things from there. Understand?"

"Yes," Michael said.

Montero turned to face Donovan. "I have a forty-caliber Sig for you. Same briefing as Michael, except I know you'll do what you want regardless of what I say. Just be careful, both of you."

"There is one more bit of news I need to share with the two of you. My contact at Interpol passed along an unverified report channeled through an informant in Poland. It's possible that a clean-up team has arrived in the vicinity of where we believe the Learjet went down."

"Are you telling me the CIA sent in someone to get rid of the evidence?" Donovan asked. "They can't be troubled to send a rescue team, they send in cleaners?"

"It's more than likely not the CIA directly. If anything, it's a subcontractor. It's also an unsubstantiated rumor. I needed to bring it up because it's how things work in the real world. We could run into these guys," Montero continued. "What I'm telling you, is we have no friends once we land. View everyone as an adversary until proven otherwise. I'm sure Lauren was briefed, and is well aware of the situation, and we need to be equally prepared. Word of our arrival is going to spread fast, so we need to be ready."

"How far will the powers that be go to stop us?" Donovan asked Montero. "When I was on the phone with Reggie, he offered his services. Should I have taken him up on his suggestion?"

"To answer your first question, I'm going to assume they'll do whatever they deem necessary to cover their asses. The closer we get to causing problems in their world, the more pressure they'll apply. As for Reggie, the more people there are, the more complicated everything gets. I say let's leave Reggie and his former

Special Forces chaps out of the equation right now. It's my hope the three of us will be able to do this quick and dirty, and be gone before anyone knows exactly what we've done."

"Is your Interpol connection reliable?" Michael asked.

"Very. She owes me her life," Montero said. "When I was with the Bureau, I found out she was passing classified Interpol information to her boyfriend, who was connected to a real jerk of a drug dealer. I could have turned her in, and the drug dealer probably would have had her killed to keep her from testifying. Let's say she was most cooperative in helping me bring down her boyfriend and the entire drug ring. She's been very helpful ever since."

Donovan had once been on the receiving end of Montero's tactics, and the story was classic Montero. She was all about finding maximum leverage, then using it to her advantage.

"Realistically," Michael asked, "how much time do you think we have to be effective?"

"No more than forty-eight hours," Montero said. "Obviously, we'll keep looking for her as long as it takes, but I think inside of two days, we'll be all jammed up by either the CIA or the local authorities—which is why we need to work fast."

CHAPTER ELEVEN

THE SUN QUICKLY burned away the mist, giving way to another hot muggy day. Lauren sat cross-legged with the binoculars, studying the dam and its surroundings. She could see the high-voltage lines that stretched off to the east. The fact that this was a hydroelectric dam meant that the water coursing through the turbines was consistent, which explained the current in the watershed. She was thirsty, and she'd long since finished the water she'd taken from the helicopter. Beyond hungry, she could feel her energy level waning. She had found a stand of trees surrounded by some camouflaging grass and weeds. She had a good field of view across an open area and the road and the river beyond. Though now in the daylight, Lauren could clearly see that the canal feeding into the dam was man-made. Through at least a hundred and eighty degrees, she could see a threat coming from a long way off. If someone were coming up from behind, she hoped they'd be making enough noise for her to hear.

She lowered the binoculars. The trucks and soldiers were still in position. Maybe six or eight men per truck, which meant a minimum of twenty-four armed men guarding the road. There were security cameras on top of each light pole and an operations platform, which looked like a control tower, giving whoever was up there a commanding view of this entire section of the canal.

Lauren had the map opened in her lap. She'd pinpointed her

exact position between the original channel of the Danube and the canal. She was still in Slovakia, though the border to Hungary was less than half a mile away. Right behind her was one of the larger forks of the Danube. On the map she traced the path of the river as it snaked back and forth for miles. The closest civilization on this side of the canal was several miles upstream, a village named Bodíky. Downstream, the map ended before it showed her anything resembling a town or a major road.

No matter how many times she studied it, she didn't see any conceivable way to cross the dam on foot. The current ran fairly fast through the canal, so if she tried to swim across, she might be swept into security camera range, or over the top. She was resolute in her decision to continue moving downstream and determined to get some sleep, and then tonight, after dark, she'd start moving again. Hopefully, if she made it far enough downstream, past the dam, she might discover some other options.

Lauren settled back and used the still-damp chart to cover her face in an effort to ward off the ever-present insects. She'd crossed her arms across her chest and closed her eyes when she heard the faint purr from an outboard motor. Lauren sat up, drew the pistol she'd taken from the pilot, and waited, holding her breath. The motor stopped and Lauren turned and peeked over the edge of the embankment, but she couldn't see the boat or how many were aboard. She heard voices but couldn't understand the words, though quickly the volume escalated, and she couldn't miss the angry tone. Crouching as low as she could, Lauren quietly moved closer to the river. Whoever was yelling wasn't far; a dozen more steps and she stopped and took cover behind a tree. Only a few yards below where she stood was an older man, a fisherman, sitting in his wooden boat, the bow pushed up on a small sandbank, the oars still in the water. Standing in another boat was the man yelling—he was better dressed than the men she'd seen so far, and as he pulled his own boat up onto the sand and stepped out, Lauren could see that his street shoes and creased slacks were way out of place in the woods. The man strode purposefully toward the fisherman and pointed a gun at the old man, apparently not happy with the conversation. From a pocket, the gunman removed some papers and held them up for the fisherman to inspect. Lauren was close enough to spot the passport pictures of her and Daniel. The fisherman shrugged and shook his head. Lauren could see the fear in the old man's eyes.

The gunman swung his pistol and clipped the defenseless man across the side of the head, instantly drawing blood, and then leveled his pistol and cocked the hammer.

The gunshot was loud, seeming to reverberate through the trees. A crane, startled by the sound, took flight, squawked, and screeched as it flew away. Lauren was about to fire again, but the gunman had collapsed, his gun in the sand, both hands grasping his shattered knee as he thrashed on the ground in pain. The fisherman, his face filled with shock and surprise, turned to look up at her. Lauren held her pistol barrel up, as if she were not a threat. An instant later, the fisherman was out of his boat, knife in hand, standing over the gunman. There were two quick exchanges of words that Lauren didn't understand, and then the fisherman slashed the knife across the gunman's throat. The gunman's death wasn't quick or easy, and finally he lay motionless on the sandbar.

Lauren gripped her gun tightly as she came down the incline to the sandbar. "Do you speak any English?"

"A little, thank you." The fisherman leaned down and picked up the pictures of Lauren and Daniel. He handed them to her. "You saved my life."

"I need help," Lauren said. "These men have been hunting me."

"You were in plane crash?" The fisherman passed Lauren what looked to be a bottle of wine.

Lauren nodded as she opened the cork and put her lips to the opening and drank what turned out to be water.

"What did you ask him before you finished him?" Lauren asked.

"I ask him how many were here with him." The fisherman knelt and washed the blood from the blade of his knife. "He said he was alone—he lied. People are searching, many men. Where is the man traveling with you?"

"We split up. We will meet later." Lauren handed the bottle back to the fisherman, knelt and took the dead man's gun and stuffed it beneath her belt. She searched his pockets and found more cash, but nothing else. No wallet, no papers of any kind. She turned to the fisherman. "Any idea who he is?"

"I do not know, but he is not with the others. He is German or maybe Polish, from a city. He did not know very much about what is happening on the river."

"What is happening?" Lauren asked.

"The Slovakian military is looking for you, as are some other men. You damaged their helicopter, yes?"

Lauren nodded.

"You are very clever. I've heard they are Ukrainian—very bad. This man wanted answers to questions the others already know."

"Like what?" Lauren asked.

"He did not know about the bodies or that the airplane has been found."

"What bodies?" Lauren asked, the news of the Learjet being found was not surprising, but she wanted Daniel's death to remain undiscovered.

"Inside the plane were two bodies, a pilot and one passenger."

"Will you help me?" Lauren said as she took out her map.

The fisherman nodded.

"My name is Lauren. What's yours?"

"Gusztav."

Lauren opened the map and held it for Gusztav to see. "What is the safest way for me to get to a large city?"

Gusztav went to his boat and reached for a battered lunch box and pulled out a sandwich wrapped in a paper towel and handed it to Lauren.

"Thank you so much," Lauren said as she relished the salami, hard cheese, and butter between two slices of rye. She tried to chew slowly, to make it last, but in moments it was gone. Gusztav handed her the water bottle, and when she'd washed the food down, she again thanked him before turning her attention to the map.

"Take his boat and follow this channel." Gusztav traced a calloused finger along the chart. "Here, there are summer houses, many have boathouses."

"Then what?" Lauren lowered the chart. Where he'd pointed was at the edge of the paper, she'd have to memorize the rest.

"Steal a fast boat. Get as far away from this area as possible. Do not go by road, there are checkpoints. If you go downstream fifteen kilometers, you will come to another river on your right. Twelve kilometers upstream will take you to Győr, Hungary. You won't be safe very long, the police are corrupt, but you maybe call for help."

"You're going to be in trouble for helping me. I want you to tell them I shot the man and did that to your head." Lauren pulled out the wad of bills she'd taken, nearly two hundred Euros, then handed Gusztav the stack.

"Go now, the men looking for you are looking too far upstream. They could be in this area by later today."

"Thank you, Gusztav," Lauren squeezed his hand. "You saved me."

"We're even." Gusztav retrieved another bottle of water and handed it to Lauren. He held the gunman's boat steady as he helped her get aboard.

Lauren moved to the rear seat. She pulled on the rope and the small gasoline engine sparked to life. She backed off the sand, straightened the bow, and twisted the throttle until the boat chugged down the channel. She secured both pistols next to one of the oars. The river eventually wound through the trees and grew to be every bit of a hundred yards wide. She was fully exposed, but buoyed by Gusztav's words that the people looking for her were searching too far upstream. She urged the little outboard to propel her faster and hoped she could make it to the summer homes without being seen.

She looked down at both pistols. The Glock she'd taken from the man Gusztav killed looked brand new compared to the Warsaw Pact-designed Makarov. Both were equally deadly, but it further implicated that the guy with the Glock was a new player, one with more resources. Lauren felt no remorse for the man she'd shot. By all outward appearances he would have killed Gusztav, an innocent fisherman, because of her. Or for that matter, he would have probably killed her if given a chance. She'd maybe bought herself some time, but Gusztav was right, she needed to get away from this area entirely or they would find her.

On impulse, she checked to make sure she still had the flash drive Daniel had entrusted to her. It was still safely tucked into her front pants pocket. The reality that far more lives than her own were at stake was never very far from her thoughts. For everyone's sake she needed to get somewhere so she could open the drive, and then she needed a way to reach someone who could do something with the information she suspected it held.

CHAPTER TWELVE

THEY'D CHECKED INTO the hotel and each gone to their own rooms to shower. Afterwards, they'd assembled in Donovan's room, and Montero handed out their weapons. With the precision of a military operation, she made sure everyone understood their role, and if they went off book to stay in touch. The last part of her briefing was to make sure everyone knew where the American Embassy was located and told them to snap a photograph of anyone acting even remotely suspicious. Then as planned, she and Donovan left Michael behind and went down to rejoin their hired driver.

"It's been a while since I've seen you in full battle mode," Donovan remarked as the Mercedes pulled away from the hotel. Within minutes they'd merged onto the A-4 and were speeding into town.

"To be honest, I never thought I'd be back in the field."

"How does it feel?"

"Good, like an old pair of jeans."

"Do we have an appointment with this guy?" Donovan was pleased that Montero seemed relaxed and loose.

"No, it doesn't work like that." Montero raised her phone and opened an email that just arrived, and then handed the phone over so Donovan could read.

Donovan read the text:

—Klaus Mikos is presently in Vienna. He accepts clients by referral only and has cut back his work due to a contested divorce from wife number three (Sophia). He was recently photographed at a hotel in Venice with a young Italian model, see attachment. I ran facial recognition on the girl, she's fifteen years old, part of a sex trafficking ring under investigation by the Italian authorities. I hope that's useful.

—KX

"I think we'll get the information we want if we can just get to him," Montero said as Donovan passed her the phone.

"Who's KX," Donovan asked. "And how did you get this?"

"KX is a source I have in Florida. I want to call him a private detective, but he's so much more. My guess is he's a former detective of some kind, but his abilities as a world-class computer hacker, with a legal background, are what set him apart from any researcher I've ever known. I've used him over the years to help me track down missing children, girls at risk, sometimes even the parent who kidnapped their own child. He works miracles and never charges me for that kind of help. Don't get me wrong, he doesn't always do pro bono work. In fact, I went ahead and put him on retainer. Between KX in Florida and my contact in Interpol, we have round-the-clock data mining capability."

"How do you plan to get us a referral?"

"You leave that to me."

Donovan's phone rang with a number he didn't recognize. He showed it to Montero who shook her head in puzzlement. He took the call.

"Good morning, sir, it's Trevor. I just wanted to let you know that I've arrived in Salzburg, and I've just gone over the machine, it's in tip-top shape. The paperwork seems in order, and I'm looking for your final authorization to transfer the funds, as per your man in Washington."

Donovan appreciated how much information was being transmitted without the use of any last names, or an actual description of the transaction. "I'm sure all the appropriate insurance binders, registrations, and taxes are in the works, and you'll be free to leave once the funds arrive."

"Yes, sir. They're topping off the petrol as we speak. Though there's another reason I called. When I landed, I had a rather urgent email from our mutual friend in London. Seems he's come across some information that another player has entered the game and may already be on the field. They would be a larger team looking to clean up a specific situation. Our friend was a bit distressed by this news and, of course, wanted me to inform you of this development."

"We expected that move," Donovan said as his jaw hardened. "Get to Vienna as soon as possible."

"Right," Trevor said. "I'll finish up here and get on with it then."

"I'm texting you contact information for Vienna. His name is Michael, and he knows you're coming. Rendezvous with him. He'll give you the full briefing. I'll see you later today." Donovan ended the call, put his head back, and exhaled.

"What's happening?" Montero asked.

"Our man in London passed on some information. You were right, we're going to have more competition that we thought, in fact, it sounds like they may already be on the scene."

Montero pursed her lips and nodded, the determination in her eyes intensifying. She glanced outside at a road sign. "We're almost there. Follow my lead."

The Mercedes exited the autobahn and maneuvered into the heart of Vienna. After several turns the driver eased to the curb on a quieter side street in a very elegant neighborhood. The buildings appeared to be older, but very well maintained. There were trees, flower boxes, a scattering of small shops sprinkled amongst ornate entryways marking the portals to luxurious residences.

Montero got out and Donovan followed after instructing the driver to stay put, that they were going to take a look around the neighborhood.

"Right there in that building." Montero pointed as they walked. "There's a penthouse we're going to buy, or at least act like we're going to buy. I phoned the realtor's office and left a message that the only way we'd even look at the property was if Klaus Mikos would redesign the interior. We'll see how eager they are to sell. Oh, if anyone asks, we're the Davidsons out of Chicago. I'm Laurie and you're Robert."

"That just never gets old for you, does it?" Donovan shook off his annoyance at Montero giving his actual first name as a cover. This wasn't the first time. It made sense on a procedural level, less confusion, but she enjoyed it a little too much.

"It'll never get old. Oh, and the apartment is on the market for a little less than five million dollars."

Donovan heard his phone and silently thanked whoever it was that was calling. "Hello."

"It's me," William said. "Can you talk?"

"Yeah, what's up? It's early, even for you."

"I just got a call from Calvin," William said. "The Slovakian authorities have found the Learjet. There are a total of three bodies recovered, none of them Lauren. It looks like the emergency exit was opened."

Donovan dared hope that Lauren had somehow survived.

"There's another report from Slovakia, a woman shot and killed a man who has yet to be identified. She then assaulted a fisherman."

"Do we have any official confirmation that this woman is Lauren? Why would this woman kill one guy and assault another?"

"Word is that the fisherman seems to have tentatively identified Lauren from her passport picture, but he's not a young man and has suffered a possible concussion. Nothing he says is making much sense so it's not official."

"Where did the shooting take place?"

"Slovakia, on the Danube River, near the Gabčíkova Dam. It's about fifty kilometers south of Bratislava. Not all that far from the Learjet. The military has ramped up their search efforts as well as cordoned off the entire area to anyone but military personnel, which means they've put up a no-fly zone. The media is just now picking up on this story, but it won't take them long before it goes front page. The jet has been missing for days, and no one has reported it missing. It's raising all kinds of flags. The CIA is maintaining their distance, though there has already been a report leaked through the British media about the plane being part of a possible European arms deal. The misdirection is classic CIA."

"Keep me posted, William, and thank you." Donovan ended the call just as Montero motioned for him to follow her to an outside café. They were seated in a group of tables under a tree away from other patrons. They ordered coffee and Donovan brought Montero up to speed on the new developments in Bratislava.

"Do you know what bothers me?" Montero said. "The photo William mentioned, the one they showed the fisherman. Where did it come from?"

"Her passport must have been recovered from the Learjet." Donovan said after quick consideration.

"I know, that makes sense, but still, it seems a little fast for me. The military is involved in the recovery, and while they can be thorough, I've never known them to be especially speedy." Montero pursed her lips. "I can't help but wonder if the CIA supplied Lauren's photo to the men it contracted to clean up their mess."

"You know I don't much like sitting here doing nothing," Donovan said as he let Montero ponder the issue of the photograph. "How do we know this designer, Klaus, will meet with us?"

"Because he's greedy, and this is like money falling into his backyard."

"How long do we give him to show up?" Donovan said, feeling his impatience getting the better of him. "Why can't we go find the bastard and get the information we want?"

"You're not far off on the tactical aspects," Montero replied. "We are going to shake him down. We will straight up get in his face and threaten him with unspeakable consequences. But we need to do it slowly, and make it seem like he has no other options."

"We don't have many chances at this. I doubt we get very far going house to house asking for Archangel. I know him. I'll recognize him if I see him, but as far as he knows I've been dead for over twenty years. I can make him understand, but I need to be close enough so he can look into my eyes and hear the sound of my voice."

Montero glanced down as her phone beeped. "Klaus Mikos will be here in a few minutes."

Donovan searched the sidewalk as Montero finished sending a text. Ten minutes later, rounding the corner, he spotted a tall, tanned, graceful-looking man who walked up to the hostess. Montero recognized Mikos and waved.

Donovan disliked the man instantly, gracious only because it benefited him, arrogant, privileged, without a trace of humility or sincerity. Donovan shook his hand and there was no eye contact—Klaus Mikos was already eyeing Montero.

"Please sit," Montero offered her hand which Klaus leaned in and kissed.

Donovan sat, impatient for this process to be over.

"So nice of you to meet us on such short notice," Montero said. "I'm assuming the realtor told you we're ready to make an offer on an apartment here in the First District, but not unless you'll agree to redesign the entire space."

"Yes, it was all explained to me. I am rather booked at the moment," Klaus replied. "What time frame did you have in mind?"

"Yes, we heard you're busy going through an especially complicated divorce from Sophia," Montero said as she slid her phone in front of Klaus so he could see the picture of him and the underage girl that had been taken in Italy.

"You do know she's only fifteen?" Donovan asked. "Does Sophia, or her attorney, know about your appetites?"

"How dare you!"

Donovan was startled at how fast Klaus dropped his façade and his temper flared. His fists clenched, his eyes became narrow slits radiating hatred. Donovan casually dropped his hand to the butt of his pistol.

"What do you want?" Klaus tried to recover with a smile, to backtrack and give the impression he was unaffected by the images.

"You know you're guilty. The Italian authorities are investigating the man who appropriated these girls for you. It might take months, you know the Italians, but we could make sure the news broke before your divorce was final."

Klaus tried to maintain his composure, he unclenched his fists and his hands shook. Donovan was enjoying how quickly

Montero had found his vulnerability and was now applying the necessary pressure.

"This property," Montero selected the photo of Kristof Szanto's Hungarian home on her phone and turned it to face Klaus. "Who authorized you to work on this house? Was it the same person who commissioned you to work on the chalet in Innsbruck?"

Donovan saw the color drain from Klaus' face. His expression of anger fell away into obvious fear.

"We know who owns the properties, so do you," Donovan said. "Tell me who you dealt with, or I'll go straight to Interpol. You'll be disgraced by nightfall and bankrupt by the end of the month."

"I uh, can't," Klaus mumbled, his eyes darting back and forth like a cornered animal.

Under the small table, Donovan saw Montero reach out and place her shoe into Klaus' crotch and push.

"Try harder," Montero said.

"The whole world hates pedophiles, especially her," Donovan said. "I'd suggest you start talking."

Klaus jumped, his Adam's apple bobbed nervously as Montero increased the pressure. "There was a young woman. I only met her twice—when she hired me, and when we closed on the houses. Everything else was done via email or overnight mail."

"Where is she from?" Donovan asked, his fading patience evident.

"I don't know for sure. For a while we mailed correspondence or fabric choices to an address in downtown Budapest, but eventually everything was sent to Austria."

"Where in Austria?" Donovan demanded. "How long ago?"

"Three weeks ago, sent to an address not far from Innsbruck."

"Give it to me." Donovan said.

With shaking hands, Klaus retrieved his phone and handed

the instrument to Donovan who with one glance realized he had
no need to copy the address. He knew exactly where the house
was located. He returned Klaus' phone, leaned in, and whispered,
"What you need to be thinking about is who you're most afraid
of, your wife's lawyers, the Italian police, or Archangel."

Donovan stood, and Montero followed his lead. They walked
from the café leaving the frightened designer sitting at the table,
his face buried in his hands. Donovan spotted the Mercedes and
signaled their driver, who sat unmoving, his head tilted forward
as if asleep.

"We have a problem," Montero said. She instantly clutched
Donovan's arm and turned to walk in the opposite direction.

"Two men in a car parked at the curb. I think they're waiting
for us, and it's possible they took out our driver. When we get to
the corner, we're going to turn right and start running. Once they
commit, we'll reverse direction and surprise them."

"Who are they?" Donovan turned his head just enough to see
the Audi pulling away from the curb.

"Take your pick," Montero said. "Maybe Klaus was hotter than
we thought. Get ready."

Donovan turned to look, the car was almost on them when
they reached the crosswalk and without warning, Montero bolted
to her right with Donovan close behind. The Audi made the turn
into traffic, and the moment it did, he and Montero stopped and
ran in the opposite direction. Trapped in the flow of traffic, the
Audi didn't have the space to do a U-turn and was forced to turn
to the left and make a messy three point turn amidst angry motorists and a barrage of honking horns.

"Back to the car," Montero called out as she turned to judge
their distance from their pursuers.

Racing down the sidewalk, Donovan saw that Klaus was gone.

Montero was behind him as he reached the Mercedes. There was a small, neat bullet hole in the side window. He threw open the driver's door and shoved the body of their driver aside as he forced himself behind the wheel, started the engine, and with his foot on the brake, put the Mercedes in gear. The Audi was barreling down the street towards them when Montero, Glock drawn, ducked behind the car parked in front of the Mercedes.

"Ram them!" Montero called out.

Donovan's foot flew to the gas pedal and the powerful car roared away from the curb. Still accelerating, hands on the wheel at four and eight to help brace himself, he slammed the heavy Mercedes head-on into the grill of the far lighter Audi. The Mercedes bucked, the airbag deployed and quickly deflated.

Through the cracked windshield, he saw Montero was already at the Audi's side door, pulling a stunned man out by his shirt. Donovan put his shoulder against the door, threw it open, drew his Sig, and headed for the Audi's passenger door. The man seated there was bleeding from his nose, his seat belt unfastened.

Donovan followed Montero's lead, opened the door and pulled the still dazed man out onto the street where a pistol clattered to the asphalt.

"I'm pretty sure I know who these guys are," Montero yelled as she came running around the back of the car. She knelt and took a picture of the second stranger's face with her phone. "Let's go! We need to keep moving."

Once again they sprinted down the street, making two turns until they intersected a busy boulevard. Donovan raised his arms and whistled in the direction of a taxi that swerved to pick them up.

"Michelbeuern Metro Station," Montero told the driver.

They rode in silence, and ten minutes later, they pulled up to the Metro station. Donovan peeled off some bills and handed them to the driver as he and Montero stepped to the curb.

"Nice job," Donovan said. "You haven't lost your touch."

"Not having any rules certainly makes it easier than working for the FBI."

"Like you ever followed the rules," Donovan said. "Who were those guys?"

"I pulled this from the driver." Montero handed Donovan a smartphone. As he studied the screen he recognized the Gulfstream he'd chartered. He and Michael were clearly visible as they walked across the ramp. From the setting and the angle, he knew exactly which parking lot at Dulles Airport the photo was snapped.

"Scroll to the next one." Montero said, her arms folded across her chest and an angry expression locked on her face.

Donovan did as instructed and found Lauren's passport photo. Overhead, Donovan's attention was drawn to a familiar sound and he looked up and caught sight of a low-flying bright red EC-130 helicopter. Their ride had just arrived.

"The images were sent from a four-one-zero area code." Montero said. "The CIA routinely routes calls through Maryland."

"We shouldn't stay in Vienna." Donovan said.

"Roaring into Innsbruck looking for Archangel is a bad idea," Montero said. "Especially if Michael is with us."

"Suggestions?"

"Up those stairs is the heliport. Michael should have our bags onboard. I need to make some calls before we join up with them. Give me five minutes."

Donovan nodded as Montero drew out her phone. He watched as she spoke while keeping her eyes focused on her surroundings. In an easy, practiced manner she was her own best defense, maybe his best weapon to find Lauren. No one expected the attractive black-haired woman to be the most lethal person in the room.

Donovan thought about Kristof and what they'd learned. Was his old friend even alive? He tried to process all of the current possibilities regarding Kristof and what their next move would be beyond getting to Innsbruck.

Montero pocketed her phone and they walked up two flights where they found Michael waiting at a chain-link gate. Behind him was his latest purchase. The bright red helicopter was neatly parked, the skids lined up perfectly with the white H, its rotor blades spinning in the sun. He took a moment to admire the sleek lines, the shrouded tail rotor, and the tinted Plexiglas. Michael opened the door to the cockpit.

"Trevor, this is Donovan. Donovan, meet Trevor."

The two men shook hands. Trevor was an ordinary-looking man somewhere between thirty and forty years old. He wore a relaxed smile in contrast to serious gray eyes. His brown hair, cut short, was curly. Donovan patted the former SAS pilot on the shoulder. "Thanks for getting here in such a hurry."

"No problem," Trevor's eyes moved to Montero as she climbed into the rear row of seats.

"Trevor, I'm Montero. We need to get to Budapest."

"What's in Budapest?" Michael asked as he fastened his seat belt.

"I gather we're not announcing our arrival?" Trevor asked.

"No, that's not our first choice," Donovan said. "I think we take our bright red chopper and fly in like we own the place."

"I'm thinking that'll work," Montero said. "I'll give you the full story once we're airborne. Dr. McKenna may be alive, but we've learned the Slovakian authorities have shut down the entire area."

"What about a nighttime extraction?" Trevor asked. "I mean, if we had the equipment, it might be possible."

"I like how you think, but no," Montero shook her head. "The Slovak army is more than capable of taking out an unidentified helicopter in their no-fly zone," Montero pulled out her phone and read an incoming message. She held the phone so Donovan could see as well.

Donovan scanned the text. It was confirmation that their chartered Gulfstream would be positioned to Budapest.

She stowed her phone and looked back toward the cockpit. "We think she's trying to make it down the Danube River out of Slovakia. When she does, we'll be in Hungary ready to pull her out. We're staying at the Presidential Hotel in Downtown Budapest."

"Ma'am," Trevor said, "if we're going to avoid the authorities, I'm not sure a downtown hotel is quite the way to go."

"Call me Montero, and the President Hotel has a heliport on the roof, so it's exactly where we should go—we'll hide in plain sight."

Trevor, a sly grin spread across his face, turned toward the instrument panel and moments later they lifted off, pivoted crisply, and accelerated to the southwest.

CHAPTER THIRTEEN

LAUREN SPOTTED THE channel that Gusztav had shown her on the map, relieved she'd made it the short distance without seeing any other boats. So far, Gusztav had been right, far upstream she occasionally caught sight of a helicopter working back and forth.

The quiet inlet was narrow and tree covered. Lauren killed the engine, and the boat drifted toward the shore. She picked up the lone paddle and silently maneuvered the boat deeper into the channel. The waterway was about a half mile long, shaped like a horseshoe, and if she followed it all the way around, it would eventually lead back to the river. She estimated she'd traveled nearly a third of the distance when a wooden dock slowly came into view. It was connected to a boathouse. The main house was set back from the shore, nearly concealed in the lush foliage. Next to it was another boathouse. Lauren kept rowing until she could see that there were at least eight of them. It reminded her of cabins she'd seen in northern Maine. These were probably summer homes owned by wealthy people in Bratislava.

Lauren stopped rowing and allowed the boat to drift ashore. She stepped out and pulled the bow as far up onto the bank as she could. She removed her boots and rubbed her tired feet, then tied the laces together and looped them over her head so that they'd stay in place around her neck while she swam. She grabbed the binoculars and water bottle, secured both pistols firmly under her belt and waded into the water. She kept close to the bank, using the shadows cast by the overhanging trees for concealment as she came to the first boathouse. She stopped and listened, hearing only the songs of birds and the sound of insects.

Lauren took a breath and sank beneath the surface. Using her hands to guide her in the muddy water, she surfaced inside an empty slip. She pushed off and swam underwater until she came to the next boathouse, coming up to take a breath alongside the structure. Blinking the water from her eyes, she peeked around the edge and scanned the shoreline to make sure she wasn't being observed. Satisfied, she submerged, coming up inside the boat-house. She realized she was only inches from a varnished wooden hull, a waterline painted deep green. The paint looked fresh, which she took as a good sign that the boat was well maintained. She hoisted herself up on the dock.

Her eyes first shot to the ignition which held a key attached to a wooden float. She took in the graceful lines of the runabout; the mahogany deck gleamed as if newly redone. It looked similar to the vintage Chris Craft inboard her father had restored when she was a girl. She jumped down into the cockpit. The vinyl uphol-stery was the same rich green color as the waterline. She climbed over the back seat and opened the hinged doors to reveal the en-gine. It didn't look new, but it was relatively clean. There was both a battery and a fuel tank. The gauge on the tank showed half-full. As her father had taught her, she counted sparkplug wires to de-termine how many cylinders. There were four and she frowned, a boat like this could have easily accommodated a six-cylinder en-gine. Still, if it started, it would work perfectly.

Lauren threw off the bowline, turned and studied the door. It was a common door with tension springs, not unlike a garage door. She reached down and lifted, but it didn't budge.

Casting off the stern line, Lauren double checked that the run-about was now floating freely. She slid behind the wheel, found the throttle and gear levers. She cranked the key and to her great relief, the motor rumbled to life. She quickly shut it off, climbed out and rummaged around a small work bench until she found a screwdriver. She held her breath and dropped back into the water. Lauren popped up outside of the boathouse and moved to the main door. About two feet up from the bottom was a metal hasp fastened with a rusted padlock. Lauren took the screwdriver to the hasp, prying it from the soft wood. The sound of bending metal screeched briefly before it ultimately snapped free. Lauren submerged, and pulled herself up on the dock. Once again she tugged on the door and this time it opened and rumbled up the rails to its full height.

Lauren slid into the cockpit, double checked she had it in neutral, turned the key, and moments later the engine fired, shattering the silence. She clicked the lever into reverse and eased the runabout out into the channel. She cranked on the wheel until it was pointed downstream, eased the shifter into forward, and nudged the throttle.

She resisted the impulse to go to full throttle and get away as fast as possible, but with all the boathouses, it was a sure bet that this was a no-wake area. If she went flying out of there, anyone who was home was going to look out the window. She was exposed enough without drawing attention to what she was doing.

Lauren rounded the bend and could finally see where the channel fed into the main river. She glanced in the mirror and saw that the cluster of boathouses was finally well behind her. She inched the throttle forward, and the four-cylinder dug in and the bow rose. She burst out into the main river and snapped her head back and forth looking for other boats, thankfully finding the river deserted. The Danube was over a hundred yards wide, and she pushed the throttle as far as it would travel. The bow flattened out as the runabout roared onto the step and accelerated quickly. Her hair whipped by the wind, Lauren leaned back and welcomed the brief, but cherished, memories of being out on the water with her father. After what seemed like days of trying to be quiet and moving slowly, the sensation of speed was exhilarating.

Off the port bow and through the trees, Lauren spotted houses, dozens of them, as well as a road that paralleled the river. This was the first road she'd seen that looked to be paved. Moments later she flew by a boat ramp. Several people looked up as she roared past.

Lauren smiled and waved with her entire arm, as though she were having the time of her life. A few of the onlookers waved in return.

Lauren turned left, away from the shore, and studied the river. She stood, bracing herself on the windshield frame and searched for the main channel, looking for the deepest water. Satisfied, she turned the boat slightly to the right and sat back down, but as she did, she caught sight of an object in the mirror. She looked over her shoulder and in the distance spotted a helicopter flying in her direction.

Lauren made another turn to stay in the center of the channel and put the helicopter square in her mirror. At this distance it looked different than the one she'd damaged yesterday. If she had to guess, she'd say it was military.

She thought about the guns and knew she had little chance of defending herself against a helicopter with two pistols. She was an American citizen who survived the crash of a jet that was operating illegally in their country. She'd shot a man and she thought of what might happen when they opened the jump drive and found plans for a stealth fighter with nuclear capability, or a target list, or God knows what else Daniel saw fit to download. She couldn't be captured, too much rested on her escaping. If she were caught, she'd find either a firing squad or a prison cell.

Lauren glanced in the mirror again, the helicopter was still behind her, but closing. She knew that one helicopter, short of firing on her, couldn't stop the boat. The helicopter would have a radio, and troops were probably already being ordered to intercept her. An idea formed as she made another wide sweeping turn at a bend in the river until she could no longer see the helicopter.

She slammed the throttle into neutral and killed the engine. As the stern rode up in the wake, Lauren grabbed her water bottle, took the cork out with her teeth and drank the remaining liquid. She stepped to the stern, opened the engine compartment, leaned down and unscrewed the filler cap on the gas can. She tipped the can and half poured, half splashed gasoline in the bottle. Once it was two-thirds full she stopped, secured the cap on the can, careful to leave the hatch open, and made her way back to the cockpit. The helicopter was still nowhere to be seen, so she slipped back behind the wheel, wedged the bottle between her thighs, cranked the engine. The second it caught, she slammed the throttle forward until once again she was at full speed.

Straight ahead, this section merged into the canal downstream from the hydroelectric dam, and once again became a single large river. With that thought, Lauren started searching the cockpit for some dry cloth, something she could use as a fuse.

Lauren looked back. The sun was in her eyes, but she finally spotted the helicopter about a mile away. It had changed course when she did and was set to intercept. Ahead, she saw where the channel joined the main shipping channel, it was wider, the waves bigger. She was going to make a hard ninety-degree turn downstream and hug the shoreline.

Lauren felt the sleeve of her shirt. The wind had dried out the material. She used her fingernails to work at a small rip near her elbow. When she had a strong enough grip, she yanked and a section of cloth pulled free in her hand. She had two parts of her bomb, but she didn't dare put the fabric into the gasoline until she had it lit. Lauren looked up at the helicopter in the sky behind her. They'd descended, erasing all doubt of their intentions. Her turn was coming up fast. Lauren gripped the wheel and wedged the bottle of gasoline firmly between her knees.

She set her feet and was about to lean into the turn when the bow of a barge nosed in the channel dead ahead. The barge was moving upstream against the current, spray thrown up as the long, narrow hull was pushed forward by the tugboat connected to its stern. Lauren swore, recalculated her options, judged the distance, reset her feet and yanked the runabout hard to the left. The little boat tipped dangerously on its side and knifed in front of the barge's bow with only feet to spare. The second she was clear of an impact, Lauren slammed the throttle closed, smashed the binoculars into the floor of the cockpit until the plastic case separated and the lenses popped out and rolled around. She snatched one, examined it and held the lens above the section of rolled-up cloth until the sunlight was focused into a tiny dot. The cloth instantly began to turn brown and smoke.

Lauren rammed the engine into reverse and backed toward the barge until wood scraped metal. She held her position snug against the hull, as the runabout bounced and scuffed down the side of the barge. She was close enough to the hull she couldn't see the bridge, which meant they couldn't see her. The helicopter wasn't in sight yet, either.

Lauren held the lens steady until the material was burning with an open flame. She used her body to protect the fire from the wind.

She stood on her seat and used her foot on the steering wheel to keep the runabout against the hull. She stuffed the burning fuse into the neck of the bottle and tossed the Molotov cocktail into the open engine compartment. Lauren dove headfirst into the water and clawed as deep as she could to put precious distance between herself and the propellers of the tug.

When she finally surfaced, the barge had continued to surge forward before it could finally come to a complete stop. The helicopter was circling the column of black smoke rising from the starboard side of the barge. The runabout was still burning.

Lauren took several deep breaths and disappeared beneath the surface of the turbulent water.

CHAPTER FOURTEEN

DONOVAN FELT HIS leg muscles tense as Trevor banked steeply over downtown Budapest. At the moment, Donovan ignored one of the most dramatic and storied riverfronts in Eastern Europe. Though well educated on the sound aerodynamic principles of helicopter flight, Donovan didn't enjoy them. As an airplane pilot, once in a helicopter, nothing translated. All of his experience as an aviator went out the window, and he didn't particularly care for the sensation.

"Hotel security will meet us on the roof," Montero said over the intercom.

Trevor set the helicopter down gently in the center of the yellow circle. Michael jumped out and helped Montero and Donovan to the ground, then pulled their luggage from the baggage compartment. Leaving Trevor to deal with the helicopter, the three of them joined the small entourage of hotel staff waiting for them at a doorway.

Donovan followed the group through the doors just as Trevor shut down the engine and the rotor blades began to slow.

"Good afternoon, I'm Benjamin, chief of security, but everyone calls me Ben. Welcome to the President Hotel. Please, allow us to take your luggage."

"Thank you Ben, I'm sorry for the last-minute reservations," Montero replied. "Are the accommodations ready?"

"Yes, please follow me." Ben held the door open while they stepped in an elevator. "The VIP floor is designed with a larger group in mind, but I've taken the liberty of blocking out the entire floor for the three of you. You each have a view of the river, and just so you can enjoy our spectacular city, all of the glass is bulletproof. Your room key must be used in the elevator to access your floor. Myself or my staff are available twenty-four hours a day should you have a concern or a question. The employees are fully vetted by me, personally. Feel free to order room service, or the concierge will be more than happy to make other arrangements with your continued security in mind."

Donovan caught a look from Michael that told him he might be mildly impressed. They came to Michael's room first.

"I have some phone calls to make," Montero glanced at her watch. "Drinks in the bar at six?"

"Sure," Michael said.

"I will see to it that a table is reserved for you," Ben said the moment Donovan nodded his approval.

"See you then," Michael followed the bellman into the room.

Donovan's room was across the hallway from Michael's. He dug in his pocket and slid two one-hundred-dollar bills from his neatly folded stack. As he was led into the spacious suite he pressed the cash in Ben's hand. "Thank you for taking such good care of us, I appreciate the effort."

"Very well, sir," Ben smiled, bowed, slipped the bills into his pocket, and handed Donovan a business card.

Donovan closed the door. He reached for his phone, saw that he had no messages, then scrolled through his contacts until he found the number he wanted. As he waited for the call to go through, he looked out the window at the Danube River, thought of Lauren, and hoped she was somewhere safe.

"Hi, it's me," Donovan said at the sound of Lauren's mother's voice. "How are things going?"

"We're having a wonderful time. Are you with Lauren? Do you have any idea yet when you'll be coming home?"

"We're still working on that," Donovan said, he hadn't told his mother-in-law anything about what had happened to Lauren. For the moment he needed containment. "We'll let you know. Is Abigail awake?"

"She's right here, hang on."

"Daddy!" Abigail cried out. "Where are you?"

"I'm in Europe. What have you and Grandma been doing?"

"We made breakfast. It wasn't pancakes. They were crepes. Later we're going to the park, maybe the aquarium, and then we're going to come home and bake a cherry pie."

Donovan smiled, his daughter's voice was easily the best thing he'd heard since he'd left home. Abigail loved her Grandma time.

"Can I talk to Mommy?"

Her words immediately sent his spirits plummeting. "Mommy is still working, but now that Daddy is here, I can help her finish so we can come home."

"Oh, okay." Abigail replied. "When *are* you coming home?"

"In a few days, I'll call and let you and Grandma know for sure, how's that?"

"Daddy, remember, you promised you'd take me to my riding lesson with Halley."

Donovan clearly recalled his words. "You'll see Halley next Saturday, I promise."

"Okay, Daddy, I love you, tell Mommy too. Grandma wants to talk to you again."

"I love you, too," Donovan said and waited for Lauren's mother to come on the line.

"She's so energetic. I just want you to know that if you and Lauren aren't back in a few days, I might take Abigail and go stay at your house. I swear all she talks about is that horse Halley and how much she misses him."

"That's fine, whatever you like. If you need a break, remember, you can always call Susan, Michael's wife, she'd be delighted to watch Abigail."

"I never need a break from my granddaughter. You take care. Call when you can."

Donovan ended the call and tried to channel his fear and frustration into something he could use, something positive. Once again he picked up his phone, only this time he dialed his voice mail at work. He grabbed a pen as he listened to several messages. It was the last message that prompted him to write down a number. He dialed immediately, hopeful that this was one problem he could fix.

He heard a small tap behind him and he turned to find a door he hadn't noticed. He and Montero had connecting rooms. He opened the door so she could see that he was on the phone. "Hello, Mrs. Spencer. This is Donovan Nash. I just got your message."

"Oh yes, Mr. Nash, thank you for calling. As I said in my message, we're undergoing some possible changes, and as such, we are accepting offers for our horses. I wanted to give you some advance warning that we're looking to sell Halley, and already have several interested parties. I understand your daughter is very attached to that particular horse, so as a courtesy, I wanted to let you know that Halley may not be here for Abigail's Saturday lesson. But rest assured, we have another horse in mind that we're sure Abigail will enjoy."

"Really?" Donovan processed what he'd heard but also what wasn't being said. "Why the changes?"

"There's a real estate developer interested in our property. We only lease this land, and the family that owns it stands to make a great deal of money if they sell."

"How much do you want for Halley?" Donovan asked.

"I don't think you understand, Mr. Nash. Halley is a Black Welsh Pony of the highest pedigree."

"You haven't answered my question."

"We're asking twenty-eight thousand dollars."

"It's a deal. Can you draw up the paperwork?"

"Are you serious?"

"Yes, Mrs. Spencer. Do we have a deal?"

"Why, of course, I'll get everything started."

"Can I also arrange for Halley to continue to be stabled and cared for at your facility? I'm interested in a seamless transition, and I want the best for Halley. Also, if it's not too much trouble, I'd like for Abigail to be unaware that Daddy bought her a pony."

"No problem. You're not the first parent to ask me for that favor."

"Perfect. I'm in Europe at the moment, but if you email the paperwork to my associate, William VanGelder, he can finalize the purchase and transfer the funds."

"I see here we have Mr. VanGelder's information in our files as an emergency contact. He should see the papers in the next hour or so."

"Thank you, Mrs. Spencer. Take care of Halley, and I'll see you soon. Oh, and before you go, could you tell me the name of the developer?"

"It's the Fleming Group, they're friends with the Butler family who we lease the land from."

"Thank you so much." Donovan ended the call and felt better than he had in days.

"You just bought Abigail a twenty-eight thousand dollar pony?" Montero shook her head in disbelief, though a tiny smile came to her face.

"It felt good," Donovan said, and then his smile evaporated. "What time are you and I leaving to fly to Innsbruck?"

"I'm working on that, but I want to talk to you about something else."

"I'm listening..."

"We've never worked together when we weren't adversaries. We seem to have changed the dynamics of our relationship when you asked me to come with you on this mission. I'm not exactly certain where the lines are, so I'm just going to come and say what's on my mind," Montero squared up to him. "You're so quiet, reserved, almost withdrawn, and I'm not sure why."

"You're right, our relationship has changed. Before now, you were always pushing someone else's agenda, not mine. We had a long way to come from you as my blackmailer, to you as my protector and tactician, but here you are, and I couldn't be happier with the job you're doing."

"But—"

"Here, let's both sit down," Donovan motioned toward the sofa. "You're not wrong. What you're seeing in me is the freedom to not have to watch each and everything I say. I don't have to try to maneuver you. We're on the same side."

"Thank you, I appreciate that, but I can tell this is moving too slowly for you," Montero's tone softened. "I know you're impatient to find your wife. The fastest way to find her is dangerous, you know that. If we find Archangel, you'll be revealing yourself to someone you left behind, and now you show up decades later and ask for his help."

"I know. I turn up now and he'll have every right to be furious, maybe to the point of telling the world who I am—or shooting me on the spot."

"It's a risk," Montero said, "but you keep coming back to him as our best solution. I say we go to Innsbruck and we'll make the rest up as we go. It's what we seem to do best."

"It's what Lauren does best, too. She's always ten steps ahead of everyone else. If she's alive, she has to know I'm coming, and she's doing everything she can to survive until I get to her. I just don't know if I'm holding up my end of the bargain. Right now I feel like I should be loading up a boat-full of mercenaries and going upriver to find her. Shoot my way in and out if I have to."

"I know, she's ahead of everyone, which includes the people after her. We just stay on our game, get the help we need, then find her, quietly and quickly. If we start drawing the kind of attention we did in Vienna, we'll have bigger problems on our hands. But we'll deal with that later." Montero slapped her hands on her thighs and stood. "Now, I'm ready for that drink."

Donovan threw on a sport coat and they went down to the bar. Montero was quick to step out of the elevator ahead of him and scan the hallway. Over her shoulder, Donovan could see Michael waiting for them. As he and Montero neared the doorway to the bar, Donovan surveyed the interior. It was on the small side, dark, almost cave-like. "How about a walk instead? I could use a little fresh air before dinner."

"After what happened in Vienna, are we sure we want to walk around outside and play target?" Michael asked.

"Does everyone have their weapons?" Montero asked. They both nodded. "We might as well go find out if we have a problem in Budapest. I saw what looks like a park between here and the river. Let's check it out, maybe find a bar with a view?"

Michael produced a cigar. "Perfect, I don't know about fresh air, but since my wife won't let me smoke these anywhere in North America, my goal at some point this evening is to have a quiet smoke."

"Let's go. I hope you brought two of those." Donovan held out his hand.

Michael reached inside his jacket and produced two more cigars. "I brought three. I wouldn't dream of leaving anyone out."

"Thank you, but no thanks," Montero said.

They left the hotel and walked out into the early evening sunlight. It was rush hour and traffic was heavy. Cars honked while motorcycles weaved in and out of the gridlock. Donovan led the way, cutting in and out among frustrated drivers until the three of them were across the avenue. They strolled down a quieter, tree-lined street, toward a large park.

"This is Liberty Park," Montero said. "The American Embassy is just down there on the right. See the barricades? Somewhere around here there's a statue of Ronald Reagan." Montero turned to the left, then to the right, as if searching for the monument.

"You're a regular tour guide," Donovan said.

"Not really, I wanted to double check that we're being followed. Don't anyone turn around and look, but we've picked up a tail. He's wearing jeans, a black windbreaker, dark glasses, and he has long blond hair, tied in a frizzy ponytail. He's probably not alone. Let's see if we can force their hand."

"What's the play?" Donovan asked.

"Let's turn right. See that bench that backs up to the steel fence? I'm going to act like I have a phone call and step away, out into the grassy area. You two act normal, continue to talk, light your cigars, but stay beside the fence so no one can come up from that direction. I can talk on the phone and move around, maybe pick out the others."

Michael handed Donovan a cigar, and they casually leaned against the wrought iron while Montero put her phone to her ear and wandered away from them. Donovan removed the cellophane and inhaled the fragrant leaf. He waited as Michael did the same, produced clippers and snipped off the end. Donovan huddled around Michael's lighter, eyes scanning the immediate area for any sign of a threat and finding several candidates.

Michael drew heavily and then let the smoke drift away slowly, savoring the taste and aroma. "She doesn't seem even slightly concerned."

"I've seen her in action. She has no reason to be concerned." Donovan checked the lit end of the cigar and studied the burn. Montero was twenty yards further into the park, wandering as if lost in conversation. "I watched her take out two bouncers in a strip club. They were big guys, spoiling for a fight, and they never stood a chance."

"You'll have to expand on that story one of these days."

Over Michael's shoulder Donovan saw Montero abruptly change course and explode into a man who tried too late to fend off the attack. With two jabs to his midsection, and then a game-ending knee to his chin, she dropped him. She spun as another man began to run away. Montero let him go and knelt over her victim, patted him down, and took his picture. Donovan was still watching when her head snapped up, and she yelled something in their direction, but the sound of her voice was lost by the high-rpm whine of a speeding motorcycle.

Donovan turned—a motorcycle was bearing down on them, the driver held a baseball bat in perfect position to swing it at Michael. Donovan reached for his Sig as two puffs of blood erupted from the center of the driver's chest. Montero's slugs slammed him backwards, the bat slipped from his hand, and he started to lose control. The motorcycle wavered and began to fall, catching Michael flatfooted. He put out his hands in a reflexive motion to ward off the collision as the driver began to tip sideways from the motorcycle.

Donovan took two steps, driving with his legs, and dove. With outstretched arms, he tackled Michael, both of them careening to the side as the motorcycle's handlebars dug into the dirt. In an explosion of sod and wrecked parts, the motorcycle cartwheeled up and over both men, hit hard, and then crashed as it impacted the ground. Donovan and Michael rolled away on the grass as the motorcycle's engine revved and then mercifully fell silent. Donovan felt Montero at his side and she helped him off of Michael who grimaced with pain, holding his right hand protectively.

"He's hurt," Montero said to Donovan. "Help him up."

Donovan eased Michael to his feet and saw that his friend's shirtsleeve was ripped, his forearm scraped and bleeding. When Michael finally opened his right hand, Donovan could see that the index and middle fingers were bent sideways.

"Wow, that's not good," Michael said between clenched teeth and then looked at Donovan and tried to smile. "Thanks, though, I'm sure getting hit by a motorcycle hurts even worse."

Montero pulled out her phone and took a picture of the lifeless motorcycle driver and then stood. "Let's get out of here."

Donovan led the way as they left the park, taking a different side road back to the hotel.

"We'll get you back to the hotel," Montero said as she inspected Michael's injuries. "They have a resident physician."

They escorted Michael through the lobby. As they headed for the elevator, Montero asked the woman behind the desk to send Ben and the house doctor up to Mr. Ross' suite. The clerk nodded and immediately picked up the phone.

Michael produced his key and they opened the door to his room, closing the door behind them. He grimaced as Montero removed his pistol and holster and stashed the weapon in the top drawer of the nightstand. Donovan helped him ease out of his shirt and carried the ripped and bloody garment into the bathroom where he wadded it up and stuffed it into the plastic-lined trashcan. He ran water on a washcloth and grabbed two hand towels.

"The cuts are a little deeper than I thought," Michael said as Donovan used the wet washcloth to dab away the blood on Michael's arm.

"A few stitches probably wouldn't hurt," Montero said.

"And a drink," Michael said, "a drink would be good as well."

A light knock from someone in the hallway produced a Glock in Montero's hand. She went to the door, confirmed it was Ben and another man, then swung it open.

"This is Vladimir," Ben announced. "What happened?"

"An unfortunate accident," Montero replied. "Michael tripped and fell."

The doctor was in his mid-fifties with thinning gray hair and round facial features. He sat Michael on a chair and positioned him so that the desk light would illuminate the wound.

Donovan watched intently as the Russian worked. First he selected a syringe, checked the contents and made several strategic injections. When he finished he sat back. "We'll let the painkiller go to work, and then I'll fix you up. All very routine, I assure you."

Montero glanced at the screen on her phone then turned toward Donovan. "I need to go make some calls. Can you watch over Michael? When you're done, knock on my door."

"No problem," Donovan said as the doctor began stitching Michael's wound.

A few minutes later, Vladimir had set both of Michael's fingers, then selected a curved aluminum brace and began to position the fingers together. With the splint in place, he wrapped Michael's hand with an elastic bandage.

"Is that it?" Michael asked as he carefully tested his arm.

"Do you have any drug allergies?"

"No."

Vladimir reached in and removed two bottles of pills from his case, opened a bottle of water that was sitting on the table, and tumbled two pills into Michael's good hand. "Take two of these now, they're for the pain, but watch your alcohol intake, no more than two drinks tonight. The other medication is an antibiotic— the instructions are on the bottle. Take two more pain pills before bedtime, and then tomorrow every four hours as needed. Keep the dressing dry and take it easy. Your hand and arm are going to be swollen and sore for a day or two. I'll check on you late morning, and we'll see if the dressing needs to be changed."

Ben gathered up all of the bloody towels and stuffed them into several plastic bags. "These are all going to the incinerator. I'll send housekeeping up with fresh towels. Is there anything else?"

"I think that'll be it for now. Thank you, Ben." Donovan shook his hand and led him to the door. Once the locks were thrown, Donovan went straight to the minibar, pulled four miniatures of whiskey from the rack, collected two glasses, poured two bottles into Michael's glass and two into his own.

"Does this count as one or two?" Michael asked as he took the glass from Donovan.

"You're an adult," Donovan said as he held up his glass. "Do your own math."

"To still being aboveground," Michael said, his words slurring slightly, as the two friends clinked glasses. "We'll find Lauren. I'll be better tomorrow and we'll go help her."

"I believe you," Donovan was touched that his friend's thoughts were about Lauren. "Get some rest, I'll check on you later."

"You don't think Montero screwed up, do you?" Michael said right before he closed his eyes.

Donovan found Michael's room key and then let himself out and went to his own room. The door connecting his room with Montero's was still wide open. She stepped into view, her Glock in one hand, a laptop in the other.

"How is he?" Montero holstered her weapon.

"Out." Donovan went to the bar and discovered a bucket filled with ice. He glanced at Montero who nodded and he set out a second glass. "You like a little water and ice in yours, right?"

"Not tonight, make it neat."

He handed her a whiskey and took a pull on his own. "Whatever those pills were, they really did a number on him. He had two sips of whiskey and could hardly talk."

"I'm sorry he was hurt," Montero said.

"He asked if I thought you blew the call," Donovan said evenly, curious how Montero would handle the prospect of having misjudged the situation.

"Is that what you think?"

"What's important is what you think," Donovan said.

"I stand by my actions. Given the same set of circumstances, I'd do it again."

"I agree," Donovan raised his glass, putting the moment behind them. "Back to business. Do we know yet who the guys were?"

"No, I sent the pictures to my person at Interpol, as well as KX in Florida. It might take some time. They could be working for anyone."

"As you said on the plane, we can't trust anyone." Donovan tossed back the last of his drink and set down his glass. "Regardless of what happened today, we still have to try and get to Archangel."

"The Gulfstream has arrived from Vienna. It's an hour flight from here to Innsbruck. We take off at six o'clock in the morning."

Donovan's phone rang. It was a Northern Virginia area code. "Calvin," he said to Montero.

"Answer it and put it on speaker," Montero said, moving closer, "and tell him I'm here."

"Hello," Donovan answered.

"It's me," Calvin replied. "Can you talk?"

"Yeah, I'm here with Montero. I'm going to put you on speaker."

"I can't talk long, but I'm getting some troubling intelligence from your part of the world. A dead driver and two injured motorists in Vienna, and just a few minutes ago, near the U.S. Embassy in Budapest, a man on a motorcycle was shot and killed. I have no idea if they're connected, but my sources at Langley seem to think these are related, and some people are unhappy."

"The two events could be related," Montero said. "Have your source at Langley keep track of who's upset. That information could prove useful."

"You'd tell me if this thing was getting messy already—wouldn't you?" Calvin asked.

"Of course," Donovan said. "We're sitting here having a nightcap, discussing our plans for tomorrow."

"There is one more thing. There's some military chatter out of Slovakia. It seems that a motorboat was stolen and then subsequently crashed and sunk in the Danube while being pursued by a Slovakian Air Force helicopter."

"Where?" Montero asked.

"The closest town is Ňárad, Slovakia. We can't confirm anything beyond a column of smoke in the area spotted via satellite, but I wanted you to know. If it's her, then she's still on the move."

"Keep us posted." As before, Donovan had no way to successfully process the information. An uneasy frustration crept into his chest and then spread out from there, a general self-defense mechanism against the unknown. The only thing he knew for sure was if Lauren were still alive—she was running out of time.

CHAPTER FIFTEEN

LAUREN GASPED AS her face broke the surface of the water. She treaded water and pivoted to get her bearings. Far down the river, the helicopter was still orbiting the column of smoke coming from the burning runabout. She turned and spotted her next concern. What she had in mind was going to take some effort. She made a quick check that she still had the jump drive, then drew in a deep breath and once again submerged.

In the murky water she couldn't determine a course. All she could do was swim and try to keep the force of the current along her left side and let it push her downstream. Her ears buzzed with the sounds of engines and propellers, though underwater she had no sense how close the ship was, only that something was getting closer. She swam until her lungs burned, the mechanical whine growing louder as she did. She carefully eased her head above the water and took in a much-needed breath, keeping her silhouette as small as possible.

Bearing down on her was a different barge, one she'd spotted earlier. The huge craft churned downstream, a bow wave cascading up the low-hulled craft. Lauren could finally identify the cargo. In two narrow levels were cars, brand-new German automobiles being shipped east.

Lauren took two more full breaths, exhaled fully, and then drew in as much air as possible, and slipped back underwater.

Diving deeper this time, the water became cooler. Lauren kicked and dug hard with each shoulder pull. The noise of the approaching barge was nearly deafening, and she had the terrible image that she'd misjudged, hadn't swum fast enough, or gone as deep as she needed. If not, then the huge spinning propeller blades were closing on her. She stroked faster and kicked harder, her oxygen depleting with every second. She opened her eyes and tried to see upward in the muddy water, hoping she could at least make out the shadow of the barge.

She needed to breathe and finally had no choice but to kick toward the surface. She kept her eyes open, frantically trying to spot the barge. The engines were ringing in her ears and growing closer. The deeper dive had made the trip to the surface longer. She slowly exhaled, releasing the air in her lungs in preparation for reaching the surface and began to feel the panic of running out of air. As she struggled the last ten feet, a great dark shape filled the space above her. The turbulence from the bow wave pushed her aside and tumbled her sideways in a series of flailing summersaults.

Lauren would have screamed but she had no air. She was disoriented when her face burst to the surface. She gasped a mixture of air and water and was then thrown downward in the corkscrew current created by the heavy ship. She felt rough steel scrape the back of her leg, and she found the strength to kick away. She shot to the surface, gagged on the water that came up from her lungs, took in a ragged breath, and began swimming, parallel to the aging black hull, looking for something to grab.

The ship was traveling far faster than she could swim. Even with the current, she was going to be left behind in a matter of seconds. This close to the hull, she couldn't see anything but the scarred metal racing past. Above the waves, she could see the stern of the barge coming fast. Directly behind would be the far narrower tugboat, its bow attached to the stern of the barge. She'd formed a mental picture of the barge and tugboat. The hull of the tug was a faded green, and she'd paid particular attention to where she imagined the propellers would be. Once more Lauren plunged under the surface and fought to reach the bend in the hull that would put her beneath the giant. As she did, the pounding of the engines punished her ears and resonated through her entire body.

Eyes open, she found that her outstretched hand was only inches from the keel. She spotted the stern of the barge and the smaller rectangle that marked the hull of the tugboat. Her window for success would be on her in seconds. Lauren timed her burst and began kicking upward. She grazed the stern of the barge with her heel and came to the surface only feet from the side of the tug.

Three stories above her towered the massive glass-enclosed bridge. She could see the antenna that bristled up into the sky. The noise from the diesel engines was loud, but not as deafening as underwater. Two powerful strokes forward, and she reached out to grasp an old tire hanging from the deck. She clutched onto the rubber fender and was jerked forward out of the water. Using her last reserve of energy, she pulled herself above the waterline. Free from the drag of the water, she climbed onto the tire. Visible to anyone on shore, Lauren knew she couldn't stay there for very long. From her new vantage point, crouched precariously on top of the tire, she evaluated her options.

The wooden deck was completely dry. If she tried to run to safety, her wet footprints would give her away. She only had one option, to use the edge of the deck as a handhold and carefully inch her way from one tire to the next. Below her feet, the water boiled up from the wake. Lauren stepped over a heavy steel cable running from the tug and stretching to the stern of the barge, the first of two such obstacles. She made it to the second cable, this one shorter in length, but higher. She crouched beneath the cable when a shadow fell across her eyes. She looked up to see two thick forearms. Above her, someone was leaning on the deck railing.

The roar from the engines and the wake beating against the hull made it impossible to know if he was alone. She pressed herself even closer to the hull, hoping he wouldn't glance down. Her eyes were locked on his arms when without warning, the ship rocked heavily, bow to stern. Lauren nearly lost her balance as the cable she was holding tightened against the load. She could see the symmetrical waves fanning out toward the shore. They'd crossed the wake of another barge. When she pivoted and looked up, she found that the arms were gone. Despite pitching against the waves, Lauren was able to scurry over the railing of the cargo barge and climb aboard.

She crouched between two cars and watched the tug. Had anyone seen her? She couldn't do anything about the water pooling at her feet except brush it toward the edge to disguise the footprints. The lower deck of the car carrier was about ten feet tall and looked like an underground parking lot. Facing the tug were ten neat rows of brand-new automobiles parked bumper to bumper, no more than eighteen inches apart.

Lauren made her way toward the bow, putting as much distance as possible between her and the crew of the tug. She counted as she moved. Ten cars in a row, ten across, two levels: two hundred cars. Crouched near the bow, between two black sedans, Lauren let the breeze pour over her. She put out her arms against the door handles to steady herself. She checked to see whether the car was locked. It was.

She slumped against the car door, physically and emotionally spent. She was isolated and exhausted. She'd shot a man today, yet

she felt so removed from reality, as if it had happened to someone else. In that moment the first tear formed, trickled down her
cheek, and was followed by more. Lauren tried to fight them, to
keep her focus, not give in to her emotions, but the images of
Abigail and Donovan, and what they would go through if she
didn't survive, pushed her over the edge. She gave in, slid down
the side of the car until she was curled up on the deck where she
covered her face with her hands and sobbed.

* * *

Lauren awoke abruptly as she was yanked to her feet. Unsure
where she was, confused by the darkness, she had no time to react
as strong hands gripped her by her wrists. With her hands pinned
behind her, she was propelled aft. On one side of the river, there
were signs of civilization. Towns cast their glow into the night sky,
but she had no idea where she was and she was furious at herself
for falling asleep.

She'd yet to see the face of the man who had her, but he was
solid and strong. His grip cut off the circulation in her hands. He
forced her through a door, up a flight of steps, yanked her to the
side, and pushed her toward another set of steps. She was being
taken to the bridge.

As he propelled her through the door, she could see a panel of
instruments. She was in a place that reeked of cigarettes and ancient coffee. A gray-haired man in a padded chair turned to face
her as her captor brought her to a halt. The two men spoke rapidly, their voices raised, but the older man was clearly in charge. If
she were to guess, the language was Hungarian, which she had no
hope of understanding.

"Who are you?" The gray-haired man finally said in halting English as her captor cupped her chin and held her face up to the light.

Lauren remained silent despite the rough, calloused hands on her skin.

"What are you doing on my ship? How did you get aboard?"

Lauren stared at him blankly, refusing to answer.

"You have committed a crime," he said. "You'll be turned over to authorities when we reach Budapest."

With that, her captor pulled Lauren sideways through the door and marched down the stairs back into the tug's galley. Lauren planted a foot, dug in, and tried to twist away. She was able to wrest one hand away and turned to face the sailor who held her. He was young, in his mid-twenties, husky build, and clean shaven with a crew cut, but with a cruel look in his eyes. Lauren used her hand to simulate that she needed a drink.

He grunted and turned on the spigot to the faucet above a dirty sink. She leaned over, cupped her hands and began to drink the tepid water. Using her body to block her actions, she reached down and grabbed a paring knife she'd seen lying amongst the dishes and slipped it up her one remaining sleeve. When she nodded that she was finished, he turned off the water then grabbed both of her hands and held them out in front of her, as he deftly wrapped her wrists together with duct tape. He ripped the section from the roll, spun her around, and pushed her aft toward a narrow door. With her wrists taped together she was powerless, and she couldn't use the knife. She started to panic when she could smell the sweat on him as he threw open the door, set her down heavily on a closed toilet, and slammed the door shut. The stench in the head was overwhelming as Lauren sat, trembling in the dark.

She stood and tried to compose herself. Using her hands, she probed in the pitch-black space for a light. Finally, she found a switch, and above her a low-wattage recessed light snapped to life, illuminating the tiny space. She tried the door, but it was secured. There was a toilet, a saucer-sized steel sink, a plunger, and a mirror. She caught sight of herself and even in the dim light she was appalled. Her face was drawn and dirty, marred by small cuts from running through the bushes.

Lauren brushed her hair from her face as best she could, then pulled at the mirror and discovered it was polished metal and fastened firmly to the wall, not glass, and therefore of no use in cutting the tape. Disheartened, Lauren sat and forced herself to focus, to find a solution. She studied the tape, located the edge, but couldn't reach it with her teeth. As she struggled to unearth a way to free herself, Lauren tried not to think what would happen when the captain turned her over to the police—but most of all, she tried not to think of what the crew might do to her before they reached Budapest.

Lauren had been trying to free the knife taped under the sleeve of her shirt without success when she heard the diesel engines slow. The vibration under her feet diminished and she felt her adrenaline surge at the thought she might have only one more chance. Her eyes darted around the tiny lavatory as she tried to find something she could use to rip at her tape. In a flash, she had an idea. She flew to her feet, turned and knelt in front of the toilet. She raised the lid and carefully positioned the hilt of the knife between the lid and the bowl and pressed, holding the knife in place. She worked her arms back and forth until the blade severed the material of her shirt and fell into the bowl.

Lauren was able to pick up the knife with her right hand, cup it toward her, and began to saw against the thick tape. Moments later her wrists were free. She quickly removed a slice of tape from what used to be her handcuffs, pulled the jump drive from her pocket, and secured the rubberized unit snugly in a recess far underneath the sink. If the police found the drive, she'd be instantly guilty of whatever they wanted to believe, a spy, a co-conspirator to a possible terrorist nuclear attack, even a murderer. Without it, she held a small window of deniability.

She slid the knife into her boot, adjusting the blade to where it felt most comfortable and readily available. Then, she positioned a section of the tape over her wrists so she'd still appear bound, the sliced section out of sight underneath. She blew out a tension-filled breath, sat down, and waited.

The engines made so much noise that she never heard the footsteps. All she saw was the door abruptly swing open. Startled, she shot to her feet. Instead of the stocky sailor, she was face to face with a man she'd seen before—from the helicopter, the severe-looking bald man she'd pegged as the leader of the group searching for her.

Saying nothing, he grabbed her by the front of her shirt and yanked her from the lavatory, pushing her into the arms of his accomplice. The second man pressed his hands into her upper arms holding her completely still.

"You're resourceful, I'll give you that, Dr. McKenna."

"I have no idea what you're talking about," Lauren replied, her voice sounding more defiant than she felt.

"You assaulted my pilot, damaged my helicopter. I'm also assuming it was either you or Daniel Pope who broke the collarbone of one of my men." His eyes narrowed and with his right hand, he slapped Lauren hard across the cheek.

She recoiled from the stinging blow, leaving her eyes watering and her hair hanging in a tangle over her face.

"Where's Daniel Pope?" The man pushed the hair from her eyes, letting the skin on the back of his hand linger on her cheek.

Lauren glowered at him, unblinking.

"I don't have time for your tactics," he said as he removed a folded piece of paper from his shirt pocket. He unfolded it and held it up for her to see.

Lauren saw the familiar pictures from her and Daniel's passports. She remained resolute in her desire to say as little as possible.

"You're with the CIA. You were on the plane. You and he escaped. Where is he?"

"We were separated," Lauren said, realizing how much they wanted Daniel. The moment they realized he was dead, she was of no use to them. "We're going to meet in Budapest."

"Doubtful. Now where's Daniel?" he said, then waited several seconds before he punched Lauren in the stomach.

Lauren folded over and retched.

"Get her up on deck!" the bald man said.

Lauren was pushed roughly through the door out into the early morning twilight. Having spent hours in the tug's head, she drank in the fresh air. The leader stood to her right. His accomplice was directly behind her but had loosened his grip. Still bent over as if in pain, she pulled the knife from her boot, yanked her wrists apart and in one continuous sweeping arc slashed the blade across the face of the man who'd hit her. He cried out in pain and spun backward, his hands instinctively covering his face. Lauren kept turning until she faced him, and buried the knife to the hilt in the side of his neck. The stunned expression on his face went slack as he crumpled to the deck.

Lauren released the knife, turned, and bolted for the stern. Running as fast as she could, she reached the end of the deck and leaped headfirst over the railing, diving into the dark water and swimming deep to avoid any bullets. She swam as long as her air allowed. When she surfaced, she was alone. The tug was far away, still churning downriver. Beyond, sat a dome of lights threatening to wash out the remaining stars—Budapest.

CHAPTER SIXTEEN

"I NEED TO call Trevor," Montero said as the Austrian Customs officer handed them their passports and signaled they could deplane.

Donovan got up from his seat in the Gulfstream. As he stood in the open doorway, he took in the beauty of the Innsbruck Airport nestled between two steep mountains. He'd flown in here many times, and each approach had been an adventure, winding down the valley, perilously close to granite towering on both sides. Now, at seven in the morning, there was a chill in the air even though it was summer. He told the pilots they'd be gone at least an hour, maybe more. He'd call when he had a firm departure time. Behind him Donovan heard Montero talking to Trevor and he ducked back into the cabin to listen.

"He's fine," Montero explained. "The doctor fixed him up and then knocked him out with some meds. We checked on him last night. He's probably still sleeping. Mr. Nash and I are chasing down some leads and won't be back until later. Can you keep an eye on him?"

Donovan was relieved when Montero shot him a thumbs-up.

"I can't thank you enough. The floor of the hotel is secure, but I instructed Ben, the hotel security director, to give you access to Michael's room. I'm also sending you some pictures of the guys who attacked us. Take a look and be on alert for anything out of the ordinary."

"Michael's going to wonder where we are," Donovan said as Montero pocketed her phone and he led the way forward.

"We've got time to figure out our story."

Donovan slid behind the wheel of their rented sedan and waited until Montero fastened her seat belt. "Are you ready?"

"The question is, are you ready?" Montero said. "I understand the direct approach, but are you certain that driving up and knocking on the front door is the best idea?"

"I don't know if he's here, or if he's even alive, and if I do find him, what to expect," Donovan turned the key to start the engine. "But Lauren's out there, and he's the one man I know can help us get to her. So yeah, I'm ready, and I'll deal with the damage control later."

"You remember how to get to this place?" Montero asked as she found a map folded between the seats.

"We're going to the village of Seefeld. I could drive there in my sleep." Donovan maneuvered out of the airport and merged onto a highway to travel west along the Inn River. The mist hung just above the valley floor and thickened as they climbed up into the mountains.

"This place is beautiful," Montero said as they exited the highway and began the climb up the mountain. "You came here as a boy?"

"Every winter, for years," Donovan said, the memories of that simpler time flooding his thoughts, thankful that he was with Montero, so he could freely relish his past. "Kristof and I used to ski every day. We were maniacs. When I look back, it's a miracle we didn't kill ourselves."

"Tell me more about the two of you."

"We met when I was probably eight, he was twelve. Our families would get together here in the winter. In the summer, his family would travel to see us in the States. Sometimes Kristof would come a few weeks before his parents, and we'd stay at the farm in Virginia. We fished, swam, and sometimes slept in a tent out back. Dad would put us to work helping him with different projects. Mom would take us to the Smithsonian or the zoo. We'd go to baseball games in Baltimore. God, we had such a great time. We drifted apart after my parents died, but William, bless his heart, tried to maintain some of those ties. It was in college when Kristof and I reconnected. Those were some wild times."

"I can imagine. When did you last see him?" Montero asked.

"It's been a while." Donovan's thoughts raced back over twenty-five years, not long after Kristof had sold his family oil interests to Huntington Oil. His friend had taken his fortune and spent almost all of it. Nearly bankrupt, he'd gambled the last of his resources on an arms deal that went poorly. Kristof had been arrested, and Donovan had used his wealth and connections to bail him out, literally and figuratively. But after Donovan had propped up his friend, Kristof used his second chance to delve back into a life of crime. There had been a huge argument one night in Corfu, and the two came to blows. The next morning Kristof left Greece and never looked back, evading authorities, creating an empire and a legend.

Donovan knew the man behind the Archangel myth, and as much as he was hurt by Kristof's path, he never exposed Archangel. He and Kristof never really spoke again, though Kristof had tried shortly after Meredith had been murdered in Costa Rica, reaching out to offer whatever help he could. Donovan declined, he'd already decided to end one history and start another. He knew through William that Kristof had been devastated at the news of Robert Huntington's death.

"I didn't mean to pry," Montero said.

"No, sorry, you weren't." Donovan shot her a brief smile. "I was a little lost in thought. So much has happened over the years."

"There's still time to abort." Montero's concern was evident. "We can turn around and find another way to do this."

"I'm good. Besides, we're here." Donovan nodded as if to reconfirm his commitment when he turned into a driveway surrounded by landscaped foliage, the house nowhere to be seen amidst the manicured grounds. "Let's just hope in the long run, friendship trumps anger."

Montero looked up and then snapped her head around to look behind them. Donovan knew the look on her face. They had a problem. Donovan hit the brakes as a van pulled out in front of them, another van coming to a stop inches from the rear bumper. Donovan and Montero were trapped. Moments later, the door of both vans slid open and armed men poured out, surrounding them. With automatic weapons shouldered and aimed, he and Montero were ordered out of the car. They saw a woman jogging down the driveway towards them. She was in her mid-twenties, slender, attractive in a natural way, with startling turquoise green eyes and her black hair tied in a ponytail. She wore dark tights with a white sleeveless top. She looked fit and muscular.

"They just want to talk," Montero said. "Do as they say."

Donovan's door was flung open and he was seized by the upper arm and physically pulled out of the sedan, slammed against the side of the car, and frisked. His wallet and passport were lifted and brought to the woman. On the opposite side Montero endured the same treatment, and he wondered how much self-restraint she had to summon not to drop the first guy who put his hands on her.

Donovan got a closer look at the jogger-woman who had now stopped just out of earshot. She held a pistol and was talking with one of the armed men who presented Donovan's and Montero's identification. She leafed through Donovan's credentials, then Montero's. She motioned for her men to bring Donovan over to where she stood.

"Okay, talk," the woman said to Donovan as she handed him his wallet and passport. "I don't know who you are, or why you're at my house, but I recognize former FBI agent Ms. Montero. Just so you know—I'm not in the mood for anything but the truth."

"I'm impressed you recognized her," Donovan tried to sound casual despite being surrounded by armed men. "Most don't."

"Right this moment I want to know who you are, what you want, and why you're here. Again, I would suggest you not lie to me."

"I'm here to make amends with an old friend." Donovan locked eyes with the young woman. "I came to see Kristof."

"What makes you think this Kristof lives here?"

"He used to. I was here every winter when we were kids," Donovan said. "Look, I don't even know if he's still alive—I know I'm intruding, but I need his help."

"I know all of Kristof's friends from the past, and Donovan Nash is not one of them." She pulled the hammer back on her pistol. The distinct click transmitted that her patience was growing thin.

Donovan remained calm, relieved that she'd just confirmed that she knew Kristof. "My name wasn't Donovan Nash back then. Kristof used to call me Bobbie."

"Bobbie?"

"Yes, we were best friends."

"Bullshit!" the woman snapped. "The man you're talking about is dead, just like you're about to be."

"Kristof will remember," Donovan replied evenly.

She looked at him hard, as if trying to determine if there was an element of truth to what she was hearing. "I know a great deal about Bobbie—and you're not him. I'll ask you one more time. Who in the hell are you?"

"You have Kristof's eyes." Donovan was past the point he'd feared most, having to reveal his identity to a stranger.

"Take them up to the house," the woman told her men as she released the hammer and lowered the gun.

Donovan had never been to the house during the summer. The trees seemed bigger, though as all memories from childhood, the house seemed smaller now. Montero joined him and together they were escorted up the driveway to the front door, which opened before they made it to the first step.

A forty-something man with short gray stubble for hair stood in the doorway. He wore a black suit, and Donovan spotted the bulge at his hip, announcing he was armed. The armed man motioned them into the foyer, and as soon as the main door closed behind them, the woman ordered them to stop.

"Eric." The woman spoke to the man in black as she leveled her pistol at Donovan. "Bring me the framed picture on the piano, the one with my father and his old friend. Ms. Montero, if you don't behave, my first bullet kills Bobbie here."

Eric left the room and returned moments later with a picture in a polished wooden frame and handed it to the woman.

"Thank you, Eric. Now keep an eye on Ms. Montero. She's extremely dangerous."

Eric flexed his fingers and stared at Montero.

When Donovan caught a brief glimpse of the photograph, he was jolted by memories. The flashbacks came flooding back as he remembered the day like it was yesterday. Taken by Kristof's mother, not far from where he stood now, only months before he lost his parents. Donovan had been fourteen at the time. He and Kristof had just raced down the mountain for the last run of the day. They were all pink skin and smiles, ski googles pushed up on their foreheads, each with an arm over the other's shoulders. Donovan was caught off guard by the emotion a simple photo evoked.

The woman held the picture up, her eyes darting from the photograph to Donovan's face, and she moved until she duplicated the exact angle in the image.

"In your wallet, there's a picture. You have a daughter? How old is she?"

"She's five."

The woman stepped forward as she continued to closely examine Donovan's face. "Let's pretend for a moment that I believe you. Kristof used to tell me stories, the expensive cars, the money, you and your airplanes. You were at Cambridge, right?"

"Oxford," Donovan knew he was being tested.

"Oh, that's right."

"What's Kristof's middle name?"

Donovan smiled at the thought. "He made me swear I'd never repeat it, but under the circumstances I can tell you his middle name is Dewitt."

"God, he hates that name. I'm told you had a fight once. Where were the two of you when this occurred?"

"Corfu, Greece."

"The fight left him with a permanent reminder, what was it?"

"A missing tooth. Upper left side."

"He left you something as well?"

"Inside lower lip, an inch-long scar."

"Who won the fight?" she asked.

"When friends fight, nobody wins, everyone loses," Donovan said as he looked directly into her eyes. "Kristof said that, and he was right."

"He still says that." She lowered her weapon and looked Donovan up and down one final time. "My name is Marta. I'm Kristof's daughter."

"Your mother, did she live in Warsaw?" Donovan asked as the spark of an ancient memory flickered.

"Yes, her name was Natalia."

"I met her when she was traveling with Kristof. I liked her. You look like her."

"She was very sweet, but she's gone now," Marta said, and then abruptly changed the subject. "I have to tell you, this is a little surreal. I mean, for God's sake, you've fooled the entire world for nearly twenty-five years, and now you're standing in my foyer. I warn you, the second I learn that you're not him, that you've lied, and this is some sort of elaborate scheme, you're a dead man."

"I understand," Donovan nodded. "Family is everything, which is why I'm here after all these years. I know my showing up comes as a shock. Obviously I've had some work done, and I would have never come asking Kristof for anything for myself. It's my wife. She's missing and needs help—Kristof's help."

"Eric, where's my father?" Marta said. "We'll see if he remembers you, but I have to warn you. He's not well."

"He's in the sunroom," Eric said.

"Eric, these people are our guests. We'll need some privacy."

"Yes, ma'am." Eric turned and vanished into the house.

"If you are Robert Huntington, the irony is remarkable," Marta said as she slid her pistol beneath the elastic of her pants in the small of her back, the grip readily accessible. "Two boyhood friends, both heirs to vast fortunes in the oil business, both who turned their backs on their destiny and vanished."

"That's one way to look at it," Donovan replied. Clearly, Kristof had talked to his daughter about his friend Robert Huntington. He wondered what version she knew.

"Do you remember my grandfather?" Marta asked. "Dad's father?"

"Of course, our families were close."

"Then you remember how my grandfather died?"

"Oh, no," Donovan whispered as he remembered the rapid decline of Kristof's father from cancer.

"My father has prostate cancer, and it's metastasized to the bones in his legs. He's recovering from surgery and in a great deal of pain. He takes a mountain of pain medication, and he also drinks heavily. He's been quiet this morning, so I'm not sure what his state of mind is right now. He oscillates between sedate and calm, and very angry and agitated. I can't remember the last time he left the house to go anywhere except to see the doctor. He's depressed, volatile, and I have no way to predict how he's going to react."

Donovan felt the air leave his chest. "I'm glad he has you to care for him," he said, unprepared for the emotional upheaval at hearing the condition of his old friend. Through a doorway he spotted a gaunt man seated in a recliner, reading a newspaper. All of the furniture he'd seen inside the house had been updated, but Donovan remembered the room. The dramatic view of the mountains had always been one of Kristof's favorites. The room was warm, but Kristof wore khaki slacks and a sweater. Donovan was shocked to see that Kristof was nearly forty pounds lighter than Donovan remembered. His old friend had gray whiskers on his face, but his head was shaved clean.

As they approached Kristof, he lowered the paper, and without a flicker of recognition, studied his visitors. A wave of regret and sorrow descended over Donovan. In his mind, he and Kristof were both young and vital, the world at their beck and call.

"Dad," Marta said, waiting until her father looked at her. "Someone is here to see you. It's Bobbie."

"The hell it is! What's going on here?" Kristof threw down the newspaper and with an expression of pain on his face, a vein pulsing in his neck and sweat popping out on his forehead, he struggled to his feet and balled up his fists.

"Kristof, it's me, Bobbie." Donovan locked eyes with the clearly confused Kristof. "I'm sorry to barge in like this. Please, sit down. Let's talk."

Kristof hit Donovan in the jaw. "You can go back to hell."

Donovan could have avoided the punch, but didn't. Kristof needed to lash out, inflict pain. Donovan winced, but found the swing was without energy, the blow benign.

"Why?" Kristof asked.

"It's complicated. Please, let's sit and talk."

"It's always complicated with you, isn't it?" Kristof said as he began to sway. Marta reached out and steadied him, guided him back into his chair. "Just go, Bobbie. I don't want to hear it anymore. That you faked your death speaks volumes. After that night in Corfu, all of your talk to me about integrity—complete bullshit! The only reason to run and hide would be the reality that you actually did kill Meredith Barnes. Now get out. You were dead to me when I woke up this morning, and you're still dead to me."

Kristof's final blow stung the most. In all of the scenarios Donovan had run in his head, outright rejection hadn't entered his mind. He imagined anger, disbelief, but not being thrown out of the house.

"I said, go." Kristof growled. "Don't make me send for Eric."

"I'll show you out," Marta said.

Donovan turned to follow Montero out as Marta stayed, speaking quietly to her father. He had just failed Lauren, maybe even jeopardized her survival. Once they were in the foyer, they stopped, waiting for Marta. When she finally joined them, she was brushing away the tears in her eyes.

"Your car is being brought around front," Marta said.

"Why did he bring up Meredith?" Donovan asked. "As far as I know, the two never met."

"They did meet, once. He told me she was in Europe, shooting her documentary about overfishing in the Mediterranean. Like most of the world, he was smitten with her and contributed to her foundation for years. He told me how happy he'd been for the two of you. Did you know she reached out to him about reconciliation? It was shortly after your engagement. I think she wanted for the two of you to resolve your differences so my father could be at your wedding."

"I didn't know that." Donovan lowered his head. "She was gone not long after."

"I know, and Father was heartsick. He told me he called you . . . afterwards."

"He did, but I'd already made up my mind." Donovan felt the full crushing weight of his past press down on him. "Is there anything I can do for him, for you?"

"No, thank you, I'll try and talk with him later, when he's had some time to process everything that just happened. But I think I can help you. You came here to ask Archangel to help you find your wife."

"Yes."

"I'm Archangel now. I'll help you, on one condition."

"Name it."

"Be in our life, his life, don't give up on him. Promise me you'll come back and visit once he's feeling better. I can tell he's in a great deal of pain this morning. He has a nurse who tries to control him, but he does as he likes. He may just need some time to absorb all of this."

"I'd like that." Donovan gratefully nodded his acceptance.

"Is your wife the woman the authorities are looking for in Slovakia?"

"Yes."

"She's a spy, isn't she? That's the reason the CIA is involved?"

"She's an analyst. She works for the Defense Intelligence Agency. She was on a mission for the CIA—it went sideways."

"How many are there in this group of yours?" Marta asked.

"Two others," Montero said. "Though we have contacts inside Interpol, as well as the State Department. Plus, we have a helicopter at our disposal in Budapest."

"How did you get to Innsbruck?"

"We have a chartered Gulfstream at the airport," Montero replied.

Marta slid a phone from her pocket and pressed a single button. "It's me. I'm headed your way. I'll be on the ground in an hour and a half. Pick me up at the private terminal. It'll be me, plus two others. We have a job, highest priority. By the time I arrive, I'll want everything you can find on—"

"Dr. Lauren McKenna," Donovan said. "CIA code name, Pegasus."

"There was also an assault in Liberty Park yesterday, near the President Hotel," Montero added. "A man was killed, another escaped, but he may have been arrested. I have pictures."

Marta repeated all the information and then hung up. "Let me throw a few things together. Once we're on our way, we'll send the pictures you have to my man in Budapest, and then you can give me the full briefing."

"I'll call the pilots and let them know we're on our way," Donovan said.

"I do need to confirm one detail," Marta said. "Who told you we were here?"

"An interior designer, who has a taste for underage girls. He's terrified of going to jail or facing his ex-wife," Montero said with a shrug. "He was easy to squeeze."

"Klaus, in Vienna," Marta shook her head as if learning about an errant child. "You threatened him into telling you what he knew, didn't you?"

"It wasn't difficult." Montero replied.

Marta called for Eric who hurried into the room. "I'm leaving for a few days. Tell the others. Call me if anything changes with my father. Oh, and have our people in Vienna find Klaus Mikos, and make sure Klaus understands confidentiality. Remind him that despite his personal and legal problems, the person he needs to fear most is Archangel."

"Yes, ma'am."

Donovan felt physically energized, but emotionally wrung out. Seeing Kristof brought back cherished, fleeting memories of the old days, setting off a wellspring of emotions. Not the least being that he and Montero had just enlisted the support of a woman who was one of the most powerful arms dealers in the world. In an instant Donovan felt as if everything had transformed into a far more complicated equation than he could immediately contemplate. Whatever rules of engagement had been in place when he and Montero had driven up to the house, had now been irrevocably altered. Maybe Kristof was right, everything he did was complicated.

Montero, as if reading his thoughts, leaned in and whispered, "I hope you know what you're doing."

CHAPTER SEVENTEEN

LAUREN COULD FINALLY touch the bottom of the river and she slogged through the mud toward shore. Her shoulders felt limp from the exertion of swimming. The sun was almost above the horizon, and if she stayed in the water any longer, she'd be easy to spot. The shore was lined with trees. In the distance, she could see several tall antennae, as well as a single smokestack, the only real clues about the area surrounding her.

She crouched, hidden among bushes, to rest and listen. Tiny gnats swarmed her and waving them away only seemed to invite more. The tenacious insects flew into her ears and nose, forcing her to move. Shaking her head against the onslaught, she stood, pushed through the underbrush, and stepped onto a narrow asphalt path. She spun when a voice cried out behind her and a bicyclist slammed on his brakes and skidded to the ground to avoid a collision. His hands shot to a bloodied knee, and he began yelling at her. Lauren didn't answer, her English would only identify her as a foreigner. Instead, she picked up his bicycle, hopped on, and began to pedal. The injured rider hobbled to his feet, limping, gesturing, and yelling. When she took one last glimpse, she saw he was already on his mobile phone.

Moving fast, Lauren passed some other bicyclists going in the opposite direction. The riders were dressed in tights, gloves, and helmets. With matted hair and soaked street clothes, she was the antithesis of a recreational bicyclist. As she whizzed past, people turned and stared at her suspiciously. As she swerved around two joggers, she knew she had to get off the path. She squeezed the handbrakes, put down a foot for balance and made a hard right turn. What began as a quiet street turned busy. Tennis courts paralleled one side, a small park on the other. She realized she was gathering even more attention. People stopped and pointed. She heard a police siren and began pumping to build speed.

When she came to an intersection she leaned hard right, a bus blew its horn, and a car swerved to miss her, honking savagely. Lauren felt trapped. The police siren seemed to be getting closer and traffic was increasing. On impulse, she turned back toward the river. The streets weren't safe and the police could easily spot her. She made another turn, the rear tire skidding on sand. She lost speed, regained it quickly, and made another turn that took her back to the bike path. Free of street traffic, Lauren continued downriver. She passed numerous joggers, walkers, and other bicyclists. Several blocks to her right, the police siren wailed and then silence. She caught flashes of buildings through the trees to her right, the Danube to her left. Ahead of her stretched the bike path and she pedaled harder.

Lauren's mind raced. She had to ditch the bike. From what she could see through the trees, a combination of residences and businesses filled the area. She could go back into the river, but the increased boat traffic around Budapest seemed to make that a poor choice. Lauren heard a roar behind her and turned to look. Closing fast was a police motorcycle, red-and-blue lights flashing. Lauren turned forward and found a gold-and-blue police car nosing onto the path.

Lauren squeezed both brakes and tried to slow and turn. She skidded, and the fragile front tire bent as it slammed into the bumper of the police vehicle. Lauren went over sideways, and ended up on her back, stunned as the two policemen surrounded her, yelling in Hungarian, their guns pointed at her chest. They rolled her over, face down, and handcuffed her, the steel biting into the skin of her already raw wrists.

She was pulled to her feet and bent over the hood of the car as a crowd gathered to watch. Lauren clenched her jaw as she was thoroughly frisked, then guided to the rear door of the police car, and placed into the back seat. That's when she got her first look at the policeman who had searched her, a lean, square-jawed young man, with short hair beneath his hat. He glared at her, the expression on his face told her he didn't consider her a petty bike thief. The door slammed closed and she remembered her mission briefing from the CIA. Don't get caught. Now here she was a possible foreign agent captured in Hungary, wanted in Slovakia. The officer slid behind the wheel and pulled away from the stolen bike, siren blaring once again. Lauren hung her head as onlookers took in the excitement.

The trip wasn't a long one. The driver killed the siren the last few blocks, and Lauren looked up to see busy streets as well as buildings, most no taller than three or four stories. Official flags flying in front of one building told her they'd reached their destination. The officer wheeled around back and pulled into a concrete garage. The door closed behind them and they were plunged into darkness. Lauren wondered if she'd see the sunlight anytime soon.

Lauren was eased out of the backseat by two officers who seemed to be waiting for her arrival. Wordlessly she was pushed through an open steel door. She held her head up and met the inquisitive stares with as little emotion as possible. Marched down a sterile corridor, through two more doorways, she came to the end of her short walk. The final door led to a cell. A single bench and a toilet bowl, the air smelling much like her prison on the tug. Her handcuffs removed, she was pushed the rest of the way into the cell. When the door slid shut behind her, she flinched as steel met steel. The distinct sound of the heavy lock falling into place echoed around her, and Lauren felt as if all of her options had just abandoned her.

CHAPTER EIGHTEEN

AS THE CHARTERED Gulfstream leveled off on the short flight back to Budapest, Montero and Donovan briefed Marta on everything that had transpired since Lauren had gone missing. Watching Marta, Donovan began to see Kristof in his daughter. She had his mannerisms and expressions. They were subtle, but they were there. Montero on the other hand, unbridled by the FBI, had become a force. She spoke to Marta about assets, both human and tactical. What weapons were available, traceable or untraceable? They discussed larger weapons, what would they have if this became a shooting war?

"How did you finally find your father?" Donovan asked once the talk of war seemed complete.

"I did what you did. I held my breath and hoped I wouldn't be killed. I was seventeen. My mother was an addict, and pretty far gone by then, but she finally told me who my father was. My father was Archangel. In my mind I figured he'd just as soon kill an unwanted child than invite me into his life. I cried for days. I'd lied about my age and I worked in a bar. There was a regular who would whisper about knowing Archangel. I found a photograph of my mother and me, taken years ago. I wrote our names and birthdays on the back, and handed it over, hoping that it would somehow reach my father."

"I gather Kristof got the message?" Donovan asked.

"He came himself," Marta said. "I'll never forget that moment. He and his men walked into the bar, and his men cleared the place out, the owner was asked to disappear. Everyone but me. He was larger than life—sent from above to rescue me and my mother. He remembered my mother and explained that he never knew about me. He took out a small kit and we both swabbed our cheeks and sealed them in tubes. He put them in an envelope and told me that the results would take several days. He said that if I was his daughter he'd be back and things would change, for both me and for my mother. If there wasn't a match, he'd never return. He slid me an envelope filled with bills and asked that I pass it along to my mother. On his way out, he stopped and turned and asked me my name. When I told him, he smiled and left."

"The waiting must have been difficult." Montero said.

"It was, but ten days later, his men showed up and asked me to come with them. You have to understand that at that point in my life nothing good had ever happened. I went, waiting for the next bad thing to happen. It was all very businesslike. I was taken to an office where his attorney was waiting. Archangel smiled when I arrived, and I was seated next to him in front of this huge desk. He took my hand, and the lawyer announced that the DNA results were a perfect match, I was indeed his daughter. The rest was a whirlwind. Father took immediate custody of me and had my mother entered into rehab. That afternoon I went from living in a dirty walk-up apartment to a penthouse downtown. I was taken into a world I couldn't have imagined. A designer took me shopping, a mountain of new clothes appeared. I spent an entire day at a spa. My hair styled, my first manicure, pedicure. I felt like a princess. During all of this, my father and I began the delicate task of getting to know each other."

"When were you brought into the family business?" Donovan asked.

"I had street smarts, but the hardest part of my transition was my lack of education. I'd done well in school, but in my early teens lost any motivation to keep going. I'd dropped out, and Father would have none it. Instantly, there were tutors, tests, certifications, and then college."

"Where?" Donovan asked, not surprised by Kristof's actions.

"Cambridge. I studied psychology, plus social and political sciences. In the summer I was sent to a villa in Scotland, where, under the tutelage of a former Mossad agent, I studied weaponry and tactics, martial arts, and perhaps my favorite subject, poker."

Donovan smiled at the thought. Kristof was an obsessive poker player, though never as good or as lucky as he needed to be. It was part of his early financial downfall.

"Why the smile?" Marta asked Donovan.

"I remember playing cards with him. He was . . . how do I say this . . . passionate. He loved to play, though he wasn't ever very good. But I fully understand why he wanted you to learn the game properly. He valued the game, but he was never very much fun to be around when he lost."

"You're right. He's a terrible card player, and an even worse loser. He had more tells than a nervous schoolboy." Marta shook her head at the thought. "I was about nineteen when he included me in one of his games. I was allowed twice—I won big both times, and was never asked back. I wasn't sure if he was angry or embarrassed."

"Probably both," Donovan said. "So you departed England with more education than the usual Cambridge graduate."

"He had seized a business opportunity in Hungary. We spent most of our time in Budapest. For the most part I oversaw logistics, calculated economics, but eventually I stepped into more of the day-to-day operations. Thanks to his foresight, I was able to prove myself early, and from then on I was known as the little Archangel."

"Your mother?" Montero asked.

"She died when I was at Cambridge. We did all we could, but she was lost to us by then. She's finally at peace."

Montero looked out the window and then at her watch. "Marta, before we land, I have a request for you."

"Yes."

"As I explained earlier, there is Michael and Trevor. They don't know anything about Donovan's past, and we'd like to keep it that way."

"How many of us are there keeping this secret?" Marta asked.

"As of today, there are nine."

"A well-kept secret, I admire your caution. I can assure you my interests aren't served by ruining close relationships, or by inciting a media frenzy surrounding you, me, or my father. I can only imagine what would happen if the world knew you were still alive. There would be a media firestorm."

"Exactly, which is why we both thank you for your discretion," Montero added.

"I understand why you have her." Marta directed her comment to Donovan. "She's smart, capable, and she allows you more freedom. Though I'm surprised you chose a high-profile former FBI agent to be in your group."

"That's one of her many strengths. I operate in her shadow, plus, she can open a great many doors I can't."

"Ms. Montero. Earlier, when we were in the foyer of the house, I could tell how uncomfortable you were as I examined the photo in relation to Bobbie. What would you have done if I had pulled the trigger?"

"I could have easily taken Eric's gun and killed you where you stood."

Marta thought about it for a moment then shrugged. "Perhaps. Either way, I like you. Neither of you have to worry. I'll call you Donovan or Mr. Nash. Your secret will be safe. Donovan, I do need to ask you something in reference to my father's earlier remarks. Were you an accessory in the death of Meredith Barnes?"

"No." Donovan's reply was immediate and he held eye contact with Marta until she finally looked away. "I think Kristof's intention was to hurt me, and it had nothing to do with Meredith, but with Corfu. We both said things that night before the first punch was thrown. I questioned, and then attacked, his integrity, his courage, and his character in an attempt to keep him from turning his back on his loved ones."

"Corfu. He threw the first punch, didn't he?"

"Yes, just like he did today," Donovan said with a firm nod. "It hurt more back then."

"Are you sure about that?" Marta asked, the inflection in her voice leaving no doubt that she'd meant her words to hit at multiple levels, and then she picked up her tablet as if to signal that the topic was closed.

"I have a question," Montero said. "Do you traffic in girls?"

Marta's eyes scanned back and forth as she scrolled through several pages. She never looked up as she replied. "What would you do if I told you yes?"

"Right now—nothing."

Marta continued to read her tablet. "Here's what I was looking for. Of course, it says Veronica Montero currently sits on the board of a group of women's shelters in the southeast United States. The answer, not that it's any of your business, is no. I was once a lost girl on the streets of Warsaw. I knew girls who ran off in hopes of a better life, and I knew what became of them. I can assure you, the human traffickers that show up on my turf don't last very long. Still, it's a multifaceted problem that consists of both economic and societal complexities. But I deal harshly with those that steal children or sell them drugs, so I can assure you we're on common ground."

"Thank you for being forthright."

"Make no mistake," Marta said as she locked eyes with Montero. "I am involved in a great many illegal activities. The majority of our business deals in state-of-the-art military hardware. We don't sell obsolete junk. We inventory everything from the latest automatic weapons, to customized armor-plated vehicles, to secure global communications, to modern helicopters and even small coastal gunships. Most of our methods, as well as clients, would probably conflict with your buttoned-down FBI sensibilities."

"Of course," Montero said. "Anything we see or hear is strictly between us."

"While we're exchanging favors," Marta added. "I expect the same level of secrecy about my dealings that you've asked of me."

"Everything remains confidential," Donovan said. "Montero doesn't have typical FBI sensibilities."

"Really, sounds as if there's an interesting story there," Marta remarked as a tiny smile came to her lips.

"When Donovan and I first met, I was still with the FBI," Montero said. "And then I blackmailed him. But we don't need to get all wrapped up in those details right now. I do appreciate what you're doing to help us, and I'm confident my sensibilities will be fine."

"Tell me that after we're finished," Marta said. "What I'm about to do is throw a grenade into a room and see what happens."

"That's a perfect metaphor," Montero replied.

"That's what I fear you don't understand. I'm not talking metaphorically."

As the landing gear came down, signaling their final approach, Donovan marveled how one minute, Marta could talk so lovingly about her father, and then a moment later talk calmly about the harsh world of arms dealing, as well as killing.

"We'll be met by Karl," Marta said as she pulled her seat belt snug. "He'll have already reached out to our immediate resources in Western Hungary. Aside from the network of our illegal pursuits, there are a great many government officials we can access. We may get lucky, but if we don't, then we'll need to accelerate our efforts immediately. Considering how long Lauren's been missing, I'll be honest, we're running out of time."

The main gear kissed the runway, and the Gulfstream made a left turn and fell in behind a yellow vehicle that would marshal them to the General Aviation area. The ramp was busy with the morning freight arrivals. FedEx, UPS, DHL, and a handful of other regional airliners were lined up, being unloaded. Once they came to a halt, Donovan thanked the crew and the three of them were taken inside via passenger van where they were quickly processed by Customs and Immigration.

Marta passed through the automatic doors and waved at a familiar car. A full-sized black Mercedes Benz 600 sedan wheeled up to the curb. The driver, a muscular man dressed in a suit and tie, wearing dark glasses and sporting thinning white hair, hurried around and opened the rear door.

"I'll sit up front," Marta said. "Karl, this is Mr. Nash and Ms. Montero. We are to take utmost care of them both."

"Yes, ma'am." Karl dipped his chin at Donovan and Montero, and once everyone was seated in the car, he gently closed the door and took his place behind the wheel.

"What have you found?" Marta asked.

Karl handed her a thin file, put the car in gear, and drove off the airport property, merging onto the thoroughfare that led downtown.

Marta quickly scanned the file and began to read. "A fisherman was interviewed who positively identified Dr. Lauren McKenna. He claims to have witnessed her shoot a man and then slit his throat and steal a boat. From our friends in the Slovakian army, it's now been determined that there were no bodies in the destroyed runabout."

"This witness," Montero said. "Was the runabout his?"

"No, he had a small boat powered by an outboard," Marta continued reading. "The fishing boat that Lauren reportedly took was found intact not far from where the runabout was stolen. All of that was at least twelve hours ago. She could be anywhere by now."

"If she were safe, we'd hear about it, so we have to assume she's still on the run," Donovan said. "But I'm having a hard time believing she slit a man's throat after shooting him."

"I agree," Montero offered.

"We never know what we can do until forced. She doesn't know who's safe and who isn't," Marta remarked and kept reading. "The last detail that Karl pulled up was from the Hungarian police. It concerns the man who was arrested yesterday in connection with the attack in the park. We're very familiar with him. He's a contract player who works for Western intelligence concerns, including the CIA. We're taking steps to have him released, and then we'll pick him up for a chat."

A phone rang and Karl answered. He listened for a moment, then handed his mobile across to Marta.

"Are you sure? How long ago? Do we have anyone on the inside to confirm?" Marta waited as her questions were addressed. "I see.

Call when you find some answers. In the meantime, send a crew over to investigate."

"What's happened?" Donovan asked, fearing the answer.

Marta turned in her seat. "Nothing's been confirmed. We've learned that a Jane Doe was just brought to the city morgue. The initial description matches Lauren, but it's vague. I'm sending people to get eyes on the body. We'll get a photo."

"No, not like that," Donovan said between clenched teeth. He fought his rising panic as he spoke. "I'm not identifying my wife via email. Take me there."

"I'm not sure it's in our best interests," Montero said. "It could be a trap, or a distraction."

"Now," Donovan said in a voice he hardly recognized as his own. His hands balled into tight fists, as a white-hot rage flushed outward from his chest. He thought of nothing except getting there and learning the truth.

Marta gestured for Karl's phone and hit redial. "It's me, change of plans, we're on our way there now."

Karl drove fast, but with precision, smoothly changing lanes frequently, glancing in all three mirrors. Donovan stared out the side window; they were headed south. Beyond that he had no real sense of where they were. There was a ringing in his ears as if the pressure had suddenly dropped. His world seemed to shrink, as if he'd tumbled down a well, the sounds around him muted and distorted. Honking horns in the street sounded as if they were far in the distance.

"It's around the next corner," Marta said. "My people aren't here yet. Both of you stay in the car until I say it's safe."

Donovan nodded absently, his hands were shaking.

"Where are we?" Montero asked.

"Semmelweis Medical University. Karl, take us down that alley, we'll go around to the back of the building."

The Mercedes came to a gentle stop. Karl stepped out of the car, his hand rested inside his sport coat as he surveyed the people scattered about the tree-lined sidewalks that connected the separate buildings. Satisfied, he signaled for everyone to get out of the car. They walked to a set of double doors, and Karl held one open.

Donovan was struck by the immediate smell of disinfectant, and something else, heavier and unpleasant, that he didn't want to consider. An older gentleman in a white lab coat met them. He and Marta spoke and then the man turned to Donovan.

"Mr. Nash. I am Dr. Janos. If you'll follow me, please."

Marta began speaking Hungarian, and she and Dr. Janos had an extended conversation as they walked down a waxed corridor, down a flight of steps, and finally to a heavy door that was locked. Janos swiped his card and the lock clicked open.

"He says she was found early this morning on the bank of the Danube. She had no identification, no immediate cause of death. The police brought her here for forensic analysis."

Donovan felt lightheaded as they pushed through a final door into a chamber with stainless steel drawers along one wall. In his entire life he'd never stood in a place like this, waiting for his world to shatter.

Marta glanced at Montero who nodded and then placed her hand on his back to let him know she was close. The door was opened and the sheet-draped body rolled out. Dr. Janos took the edge, but stopped short of pulling the sheet back.

"Do it," Donovan said.

Dr. Janos pulled back the sheet, folding the fabric respectfully over her breasts.

It all happened at once. Donovan saw the auburn hair and stiffened, the chalk-white skin pulled over similar bone structure, and then it was all wrong, the lips, chin, the forehead—it wasn't Lauren. Donovan couldn't speak. He slowly shook his head that it wasn't her, then turned away and walked from the room. His emotions were frayed, but more than anything, he felt immense relief, followed by anger. A woman who bore more than a passing resemblance to his wife had died. Was it accidental or a carefully planned execution?

"Let's go," Montero and Marta caught up with him, walking him up the stairs from the morgue. At the top of the stairs Montero's and Donovan's phones beeped, Donovan's began ringing.

Donovan saw that it was Calvin; it was early in D.C. "Nash here."

"Thank God I found you!" Calvin's voice left no doubt that something had happened. "Lauren was arrested near the river north of Budapest. She's being held at the District III police station. The chatter we picked up says she's going to be transferred to Police Headquarters in Budapest. I already spoke to William, he says the embassy in Budapest is stalling, which you and I know is by design. You need to get to her, do everything you can to make this as public as you can. We need reporters taking pictures, start a riot, anything! The fear at this end is she'll be turned over to the Hungarian Secret Police; if the TEK have her, she'll be swept off into the shadows, and we'll never see her again."

"I'm on it." Donovan ended the call.

Montero had just finished reading the email Calvin had sent. "Marta, she's at the District III Police Station, but they're transporting her to Police Headquarters. How do we get to her?"

"Follow me." Marta hurried for the door. "Karl!"

Donovan heard what sounded like muffled gunshots the same moment that Marta reached the double doors. He heard a car door slam and an engine rev.

Marta took one look through the glass, turned and yelled, "Get back!"

Donovan grabbed Montero and pulled her with him as the doors exploded inward, the space filled by the trunk of the Mercedes 600. More gunshots sounded.

Marta was the first to reach the car. She opened the front door and motioned for Donovan and Montero to get in the back as before. Once they were inside, Donovan could see where bullets had peppered the side window and windshield leaving opaque divots, but none had penetrated the interior.

"Go!" Marta shouted the instant they were all in the car. "It's an old trap. Kill someone who looks like a missing family member and then kill everyone who shows up at the morgue."

Karl slammed the gas and the tires spun on the smooth waxed floor as they pushed through the remains of the wooden door out into the open. He cranked the wheel to the right and not so much as winced as two slugs hit the glass next to his head. The Mercedes screeched as Karl swerved down the alley where at the far end, a white van pulled across the entrance to block them.

"Brace yourselves!" Marta yelled as she pulled her seat belt across her body in one fluid motion.

"We've got a car behind us," Donovan said as he turned and spotted a burgundy Volkswagen in pursuit.

Donovan and Montero secured themselves as Karl accelerated down the narrow corridor. The heavily armored Mercedes slammed into the side of the van, nearly slicing it in half as both vehicles rolled out onto the boulevard, shedding tires, glass, and debris as they went. Karl jerked the Mercedes to the right, slammed on the brakes, threw the Mercedes into reverse, and collided with the Volkswagen the moment it emerged from the alley. Donovan barely felt the impact, and as he spun in his seat to look, he could see the second car pinned against the corner of the building. The front airbags had deployed, steam and dark smoke from hot oil poured out from under the buckled hood.

"Stay in the car," Marta ordered Donovan and Montero as she produced a pistol and opened her door. Karl threw the Mercedes into park and exited quickly to catch up with his boss. Donovan watched as Marta, gun first, leaned in through the shattered passenger window. Moments later, Marta and Karl jumped away from the vehicle as the whoosh of igniting gasoline enveloped the wrecked car. Both of them ran to hurriedly slide back into the Mercedes. When Donovan took one last look out the rear window, the sound of the first sirens could be heard echoing through the buildings. The car that they'd T-boned was blocking traffic and the few onlookers began to flee as Karl pushed on the gas and they sped away from the growing funeral pyre.

Montero looked up from her phone. "A motorcade just left the District III police station. Calvin thinks they're transporting Lauren."

"Idiots!" Marta snapped. "Hungarians are afraid of police, so they think if they show force and flash their lights they're safe. But all they've done is advertise their intentions."

"How far are we?"

"Too far. We'll never get to her before they reach Headquarters."

Donovan already had his phone to his ear. "Trevor! Where are you?"

"Mr. Nash, I'm at the hotel with Michael. Where are you?"

"In trouble," Donovan said. "Get the helicopter ready to fly. We're going to be there as fast as we can."

Marta turned to face Donovan. "If you're talking about the President Hotel, we're twenty minutes away in this traffic."

"I heard that," Trevor said. "Let me come to you. Where are you?"

"I'm handing you off to someone who knows the city." Donovan put the phone into Marta's outstretched hand.

"Take off from the hotel, fly west. When you reach the river turn south. You'll cross three bridges. When you get to the fourth, we'll be on the east side."

Marta handed the phone back to Donovan. "Trevor, you got that? Let's keep this line open."

"We're on the roof now," Trevor reported. "I see smoke to the south and I hear lots of sirens. Does that have anything to do with us?"

"Yes. And hurry." Karl accelerated through a yellow light and made a tight turn, pressing Donovan hard against the door.

"We'll be airborne in three minutes," Trevor said.

"We might have a problem. I don't think this will work," Karl said as they rounded the corner that put them next to river. "He can't land a chopper here, the park is full of kids." He quickly raced the length of the busy park and then slammed on the brakes, put the Mercedes into a U-turn, and sped back the way they came.

Donovan desperately searched each open area in the park, but there was no place for the helicopter to land safely.

"Up there, just this side of the bridge." Montero pointed as she spoke. "A tour boat just departed."

Karl nodded and gunned the big engine. Through the trees, Donovan spotted what they needed—an empty dock without obstacles.

Donovan picked up the phone. "Trevor, are you still there?"

"It's Michael. Trevor's flying. We'll be there in thirty seconds. We see the bridge. Where are you?"

"Do you see the tour boat pulling away from a dock next to the bridge?"

"Yeah," Michael said.

"We're headed for the dock."

"Trevor says that's perfect."

Donovan pocketed the phone as Karl pulled the Mercedes to a stop next to the gangway that led to the dock. There was a fence prohibiting entry.

"Stay put." Karl swung the car around and used the grill as a battering ram. The chain snapped and the fence buckled and twisted to the ground. "Now you're good."

"Thanks, Karl," Donovan said as he and Montero stepped out—as did Marta, who reached back in, took a pistol from Karl, and handed it to Montero. Behind them the bright red helicopter roared down the river, slowed at seemingly the last second, raised its nose, and gently touched down on the floating dock.

Karl peeled away the moment the three of them reached the helicopter. Michael was out and holding the door open against the downwash. Protecting his bandaged hand, he helped Donovan, Marta, and Montero climb into the helicopter.

"I just spoke to William," Michael shouted. "He briefed me on Lauren's situation and he wanted me to tell you that the Hungarians are ignoring the Ambassador's request to release Lauren into American custody."

Donovan nodded his appreciation for the update and piled into a seat next to Montero, strapping in as Michael hurried back up front to join Trevor.

"Where to?" Trevor turned and asked.

"North. Follow the river," Marta said as she found her harness and clicked it into place.

Without hesitation, Trevor lifted off, and in a smooth turn to the left, they accelerated, the helicopter only a few scant feet above the muddy Danube. They gained altitude and passed over a twin span suspension bridge and continued to climb until they were clear of any obstacles as they followed the river. They made a gentle right turn abeam the Hungarian Parliament, the massive dome and ornate spires dominating the horizon. Donovan pulled a set of headphones for himself, then handed a set to both Marta and Montero and saw that everyone was connected.

Michael turned to Marta. "Who are you?"

"My name is Marta, I'm a consultant. A private detective, if you will. I know my way around this part of the world. We need to get to the north end of Margaret Island. From there we'll backtrack toward the District III police station. There's only one route the motorcade can travel, which is over the Árpád bridge. I'm sure we can spot them."

"Then what?" Michael asked.

"Most big city media outlets monitor the aviation frequencies," Donovan said. "Calvin suggested we draw some attention to the fact that Lauren is being held. I'm pretty sure we can provide some news, so that reporters will start moving in the right direction."

Trevor nodded as they cruised down the river at nearly 150 miles per hour, a city map of Budapest on his knee. He finally pointed out the tip of the island and the Árpád Bridge that spanned the Danube.

Donovan leaned forward, and peering over Michael's shoulder, scanned the river ahead. "What in the hell is going on over there?"

CHAPTER NINETEEN

LAUREN, WEARING A bulletproof vest, sat in the back of a police car, her hands cuffed behind her. The motorcade whisking her toward the center of town consisted of three squad cars and two motorcycles. Off to her right, she spotted a small blue-and-white helicopter with Police painted on the side. The entire time she'd been in the cell, she'd asked for the American Embassy, explaining over and over that she was the victim of a robbery, that she'd been thrown from a bridge in the dark. The only comfort was the fact that she'd been given water, a hardboiled egg, and some cheese. It was the first food she'd had in nearly twenty-four hours.

They sped down the thoroughfare, three lanes in each direction. She had no idea where they were, but sensed they were headed south. They passed cement-gray apartment buildings, leftovers from Stalin-era construction. A cemetery flashed past, as did more modern office buildings. En route, drivers had been forced to pull over, turning to look as the procession sped past. The road made a curve to the left, and Lauren caught sight of the half-mile wide Danube, a sliver of an island and a marina to her left, a larger island to her right. Ahead, she could see two modern office buildings, easily fifteen stories tall, straddling each side of the bridge.

Lauren looked up as the police chopper once again flew over-head. An instant later the helicopter transformed into an orange ball of fire, rotor blades and burning debris tumbling uselessly in the sky as the burning aircraft began a sickening corkscrew descent into the river below. Lauren flinched as the shock wave from the explosion enveloped the convoy. She spotted the smoke trail from a missile diffusing and fragmenting in the sky.

The driver slammed on the brakes, and Lauren was thrown forward. She hunched her shoulder and tried to get low as the sound of automatic weapons filled the air. Ahead, through the steel mesh partition, she saw the lead car raked with gunfire. Then it burst into flames. None of the doors ever opened. Behind her, policemen leapt from the vehicle and began shooting. Lauren looked to where they were aiming and she caught sight of two speeding white BMW X5s. A man's torso protruded from the sunroof of the lead car, the missile launcher on his shoulder erupted, and the police car behind her exploded.

The side window of the police car exploded inward and Lauren sank as low as she could in her seat as the officer on the passenger side slouched forward, his chin resting on his chest. With the next burst of automatic weapons fire, the windshield dissolved into tiny fragments that bounced wildly, showering Lauren with pieces of glass. The lead BMW ground to a halt, and a man jumped to the road. Leading with an automatic weapon, he came straight for her. As he neared, she recognized him—the sharp features, dark eyes, and now he wore a heavy gauze bandage taped to his cheek.

He yanked her door open, leaned in, and dragged her out of the car by her hair. Lauren screamed from the pain and shock as her feet hit the asphalt hard. She tried to gain purchase with her boots to keep up with the man who had her, but she kept falling. The sound of rotor blades filled the air, and the man with the missile launcher was looking upward, twisting in all directions to spot an incoming craft. A second later, a red helicopter raced across the

bridge no more than ten feet above the concrete. Startled, everyone ducked. With tears streaming down her cheeks, Lauren was
dragged the last few feet, picked up, and tossed into the back seat
of the one of the white BMWs. Before the door slammed shut,
she thought she heard the sound of the helicopter coming back
around.

CHAPTER TWENTY

"BLOODY HELL, THAT helicopter just exploded!" Trevor yelled over the intercom.

"There was a missile. I can still see the smoke trail," Michael said.

Donovan leaned to get an unobstructed look out the front just in time to see burning debris raining down into the river. Another flash and a car on the bridge exploded.

"Can you bring us in close without ending up like the other helicopter?" Montero asked.

"You bet," Trevor transmitted.

Donovan tightened his seat belt as Trevor dropped down until they were eye level with the modern concrete-and-steel bridge. He eased the helicopter to the left and hugged the shore of the island, the treetops just below the skids. In a flash they sped over the Grand Budapest Hotel. Donovan could see the startled onlookers who'd been drawn outside by the sound of the explosions. They were suddenly past the hotel, and Trevor banked away from what looked like a hospital. As they approached the bridge, Donovan saw a white SUV with a man standing up through the sunroof, the unmistakable shape of a Stinger missile tube on his shoulder. Three police cars were stopped on the bridge, two were burning.

"I see the guy with the launch tube, he's looking up, he can't find us," Trevor's voice came through the intercom. "We're coming in low and fast. I want everyone to hang on."

Donovan leaned forward. As they drew closer, he spotted two SUVs, BMW X5s. They were converging on the remaining police car. A figure stood at the rear door. He leaned in, yanked a woman out of the car, and began pulling her across the pavement. As the helicopter flashed overhead, Donovan recognized Lauren; she was being dragged by her hair. His anger flared beyond all comprehension, and he was about to yell for Trevor to land, when the bottom seemed to drop out of the helicopter.

As they crossed the bridge span, Trevor made a hard descending turn, nearly touching the water. He slowed dramatically, raising the nose as they flew under the bridge and came to a hover.

"They have no clue where we are," Trevor said. "but that fellow with the missile launcher bothers me. If I pop us up real quick, is there someone who can put a bullet in him?"

"I can," Montero offered at the exact same time as Marta. Both women gripped pistols.

"We can't shoot, they have Lauren," Michael said and looked back at Donovan. "I saw her."

"I did too," Donovan said. "Those men have her. We can't attack. We need to follow them."

"Bloody hell," Trevor said as he exhaled. "I can't follow up high, he'll shoot us down. This will have to be low and dirty. We're going to break a bunch of laws and generally piss off the whole lot of Hungarian police. Understand that we're not going to be able to go back to the President Hotel, or any civil airport in Hungary . . . ever."

"Make it happen," Donovan said.

"Here goes, then," Trevor moved the stick and they slid sideways out from under the bridge. The second he had rotor clearance, Trevor climbed them straight up to take a quick look. The two BMWs were gone.

"There they are, headed west!" Marta shouted as she spotted them. "There's no one standing in the sunroof."

Trevor pivoted the helicopter smartly, and staying low, gave chase. Donovan couldn't get the image of his wife out of his head. Handcuffed, wearing a vest, a man with a bandaged face pulling her by her hair. Donovan vowed to make them all pay. The advantage of giving chase in a helicopter was they were twice as fast and could maneuver in three dimensions, but Trevor was right, if they climbed to the optimum altitude for observation, they'd no doubt get a missile. He kept his eye on the twin BMWs and realized he had no idea which one held his wife. If the vehicles split up, they'd be screwed.

The BMWs exited the main road and merged on a road that led south, toward central city, on the Buda side of the river. Donovan pulled out his cell phone, found the number, and sent the call. He ripped off his headphones and held the phone close to his ear, using his free hand to cover his opposite ear to try to block out the noise. Donovan let out a silent thank you when Calvin answered. "It's Donovan! Can you hear me?"

"Yes, barely, there's a lot of background noise."

"Lauren's alive, I saw her! She was just abducted from a police motorcade. We're in pursuit via helicopter. The kidnappers are driving two identical BMW X5 SUVs, and I don't know which one is Lauren's? Calvin, I need your help!"

"Give me your position!"

"We're in Budapest, north end of Margaret Island, flying south along the river."

"Which side of the river?"

"East."

"Standby," Calvin replied. "No matter what—stay with her."

"We're trying," He could picture Calvin in one of the sophisticated Defense Intelligence Agency control rooms. Donovan had been in one years ago. There were a dozen high-definition flat screen panels around a central control station. The room was kept cold to keep the solid-state computer equipment from overheating. There were direct links to the National Reconnaissance Office, as well as the Pentagon. Calvin would be calling out orders and the half dozen analysts, and technicians, most of them friends of Lauren, would be doing everything they could. Donovan braced himself with his feet as Trevor banked sharply to the left and cut between two buildings no more than twenty feet above the ground. Trevor then banked to the right and shot between two apartment buildings and crossed the thoroughfare just behind the speeding BMWs.

"We're getting assets moved into position," Calvin said. "Stay with her, we'll never find her without you acting as a spotter."

"Calvin," Donovan said. They've got surface-to-air missiles and they've already shot down one helicopter."

In a sudden maneuver, Trevor whipped the helicopter around and dropped down toward the road. They built speed and shot the gap between two more concrete high-rises, using the structures to block any kind of a clear missile shot from the X5s. Trevor climbed until they were just above roof level of a series of six-story brick buildings, leapfrogging from roof to roof while keeping the vehicles in sight.

Michael pointed out something to Trevor. Without his headphones, Donovan had no idea what he meant, but straining to look, Donovan spotted the concern. The sunroof on the tail vehicle was open. Trevor accelerated past the SUVs, dived back to street level, hovered between two glass-clad structures, and waited for the vehicles to pass. When they did, he started forward as if he were going to follow, then he pivoted the helicopter and darted back behind the closest building.

Donovan saw the flash from the missile followed by an explosion along the side of the building. Fragments from the building's heavy plate glass peppered the side of the helicopter like a shotgun. Trevor banked steeply around the corner and climbed.

"Are you still there?" Calvin asked.

"Yes, what's happening?"

"We're re-tasking an asset, but it's going to take some time."

"She doesn't have time." Donovan knew that re-tasking meant they had to make adjustments to a satellite. "If they split up, we're going to have to make a choice, and I don't want to be wrong."

"I need six minutes," Calvin said.

Donovan understood that six minutes was quick in terms of reorienting a satellite, but as Trevor darted from one building to another, six minutes seemed like an eternity.

Trevor made a steep banking turn around a tall antenna, narrowly missing the guy wires that stretched down to the ground. By manipulating their speed and altitude, Trevor also banked the helicopter left and right, giving the guy with the missile launcher nothing more than a fleeting target. A steeple flashed past. Trevor flew up and over a building, and then Donovan realized that ahead of them was an open area and they were about to be exposed. Instantly, Trevor banked hard and cut directly over the top of the speeding SUVs, heading for the safety of a series of concrete-and-steel structures on the other side of the thoroughfare. As they neared a narrow gap, Trevor was forced to slow, or they'd overshoot, and run the risk of their rotor blades clipping a wall.

Donovan turned as the man in the BMW shouldered the Stinger missile launcher, swung it in their direction, and fired. In the close confines between the structures, the missile couldn't maneuver with the helicopter and impacted the edge of the building behind them, exploding huge chunks out of the masonry which tumbled to the sidewalk below.

Trevor climbed, reached the roofline, then banked hard to parallel the road. He then eased the helicopter over slightly until they could all see the road to try to reacquire the vehicles.

"We saw that one," Calvin said. "The satellite's infrared systems become effective before the optics. We're trying to use the heat signature from the missile's exhaust to pinpoint the source, the more missiles, the better."

Trevor set his jaw, nosed the helicopter down, and made an abrupt turn to the right and cut diagonally over the vehicles. As the helicopter flashed overhead, both SUVs made an abrupt left turn away from them down an alley.

Donovan nearly dropped the phone as Trevor slammed the helicopter into a punishing turn and brought them back around. They raced down a side street to try to intercept the BMWs, but they had vanished.

Marta, leaning in her seat, pointed to her left and spoke rapidly into her microphone. Trevor reacted immediately by pivoting to the right, climbing until the helicopter was skimming the rooftops. He darted away from the safety of one building to take a look below. Both SUVs were speeding south along the river's edge. The road next to the Danube only gave Trevor one side of the street to negotiate. Trevor swung out in the open and the man with the missile launcher was ready.

Trevor slammed the controls and climbed as the missile exploded directly below them. The sound of the warhead detonating rose above the noise of the beating rotor blades. The shock wave staggered the helicopter as Trevor banked away. He was able to stabilize the helicopter just as another missile arced toward them, flying wide before penetrating the window of a close-by building and exploding inside. Trevor immediately dropped back down to street level and accelerated down a side street, leaving the SUVs behind.

Phone still pressed to his ear, Donovan watched as Trevor came back around to jump ahead of the SUVs. Trevor slowed, cut off traffic by hovering directly in the middle of the three-lane thoroughfare. He descended lower as if intending to land. At the sight of the helicopter, drivers began slamming on their brakes, bringing southbound traffic to a swift halt.

Trevor climbed and Donovan saw both SUVs had come to a stop in the gridlock. Just as quickly, the BMWs wheeled to their right, jumped the curb, and tore across the grassy lawn of a park, scattering pedestrians in their wake. Further down the road Donovan spotted the flashing lights of police cars in pursuit of the BMWs. Donovan could see up ahead. Directly in front of them were the hills on the west side of the Danube. Perched at the top, the sprawling Buda Castle dominated the skyline.

"We'll be in position in thirty seconds," Calvin's voice sounded through the phone. "Give me your exact location."

Donovan pressed his hand tight over his ear to hear Calvin, as Trevor pivoted sharply above an intersection just as the two SUVs sped through.

"Donovan!" Marta shouted. "I think they're headed for the tunnel at Castle Hill. It's where the road off the Chain Bridge funnels traffic underneath the castle."

"Did you hear any of that?" Donovan asked Calvin. "We're headed toward the Chain Bridge."

"Yes, we're almost in position."

Trevor skimmed the roofs of the small structures not far from the river's edge. To their right, the mountain and the castle towered five hundred feet above them, and dead ahead, the Chain Bridge loomed large, its two massive concrete towers, the foundation for the girders and cables, supporting the famous structure.

"We have you, but I don't see the SUVs," Calvin said. "We have another problem. There's a Budapest police helicopter lifting off from their base at the airport. Radio intercepts are telling us that he's going to direct two military helicopter gunships in an effort to stop the BMWs. Donovan, you need to break off pursuit the moment we lock on to them with the satellite. The gunships will close on you the moment they spot your red helicopter. You'll lead them straight to Lauren."

"You think they'll fire at the BMWs?" Donovan asked.

"As far as the Hungarian police are concerned, a prisoner was taken from custody, and fellow officers were killed in the process. Lauren is considered one of them. Make no mistake, they're going to shoot."

"Where are they?" Donovan yelled to Montero. "Calvin says we're going to have company real soon. Gunships are headed this way."

"They're on a narrow road between those buildings. We should see them in seconds," Montero said.

Trevor eased the helicopter into a hover. Donovan could see the large open space, a convergence of the roadways as the cars entered the roundabout before being funneled into the tunnel. The SUVs would be here in seconds, and Trevor had no place to hide.

"Calvin, the two SUVs are just about to arrive at the roundabout on this side of the tunnel," Donovan repeated. "Give me another option besides abandoning the chase. What if there's a window to try and save Lauren? We need to be there."

"There's no other option," Calvin said. "She's dead in ten minutes if the gunships find her. Donovan, listen. The people who have her could have killed her earlier; instead, they kidnapped her. She has value to them."

The two SUVs burst from the side street and careened around the rotary. The man standing up through the sunroof spotted them, turned, shouldered the Stinger missile launcher, tracked them through the sights of the launcher, and fired.

"They're on the rotary now!" Donovan shouted into the phone just as a jet of smoke poured from the rear of the launcher, and a microsecond later, the missile leapt from the tube. Donovan's eyes were locked on the accelerating missile when the enormous wall of the Chain Bridge's west tower filled the windows. Trevor had darted behind the massive structure, and so thick was the edifice, Donovan never saw or heard the explosion of the warhead on the other side.

"We have them both," Calvin said. "I repeat, we have satellite lock on both vehicles. Suggest you exit the area, low, over the river, and head south."

"Trevor. Get us out of here." Donovan relayed Calvin's instructions. "Low and fast, to the south. There are gunships coming."

Trevor moved them away from the bridge, pivoted, and accelerated as he dived to wave-top level.

"I promise we won't lose them," Calvin replied.

"Thank you, Calvin," Donovan said. "I want to know exactly what's happening, when we can make our move. I'll talk to you soon."

"Can everyone hear me?" Trevor asked. "Like I explained earlier, everyone in bloody Budapest has a smartphone and probably recorded footage of our pursuit. The authorities will be looking for us. We need to lay low, go somewhere and hide for a bit. I also need to check the machine over, make sure there isn't any damage."

"I know a spot," Marta said. "Keep following the river. It's a little ways, but up ahead, on the left, will be a set of train tracks. Follow the tracks east, they'll take us to a deserted warehouse amidst the railroad yard. We'll be safe there."

Donovan held the phone in his hand, poised to answer it the instant Calvin called. He hoped that Calvin was right, that the fact that whoever it was who had kidnapped Lauren needed her, which might give him time to rescue her. His only hope at this point was that the men in the BMWs would be unaware that they were being tracked by satellite.

Trevor flew just above the water as they roared under three bridges in quick succession, visible only to people in the immediate vicinity. When Marta pointed out the tracks, Trevor banked left and followed the rails as they wound through industrialized Budapest. Up ahead they spotted a freight train, and Trevor slowed to fall in behind the last freight car, the helicopter's skids barely above the shiny steel tracks.

"I'll use the racket from the train to mask the noise we're making," Trevor announced. "People who live near train tracks generally learn to tune it out."

They quickly flew into an area of older warehouses, where side tracks held derelict boxcars, and rusted machinery littered the area. Marta pointed toward the building she had in mind, and Trevor slowed, allowing the train to pull away from them. He brought the helicopter to a hover and then inched inside the building through open doors not much wider than the diameter of their rotor blades. He pivoted one hundred eighty degrees so the nose was pointed toward the door, and then descended the last few inches, gently touching the skids to the concrete floor.

CHAPTER TWENTY-ONE

THEY'D DRIVEN FOR what seemed like hours. Leaving Budapest, they'd put a black hood over her head and forced her to stay low and out of sight in the vehicle. Her captors spoke little, and when they did, she couldn't understand a word. When they finally came to a stop, the hood was removed, as was the bulletproof vest. She blinked, surprised to see the sun low on the horizon.

The driver grabbed her roughly by the arm, pulled her from the BMW, and marched her toward an old farmhouse. All Lauren could see in every direction was plowed ground. She was shepherded through the door into the kitchen and was hit by how musty the house smelled, as if a hundred years of wood smoke clung to the walls around a cast iron stove. The man who had her by the arm took her to a back room and placed her in a chair. Her hands were still cuffed behind her back, and he used zip-ties to secure her ankles to the legs of the sturdy chair. He then walked from the room, closing the door behind him.

Lauren was alone for the first time since she'd been arrested by the police. She twisted around to examine the dingy room, finding a narrow bed pushed up against the wall, the mattress ripped and stained. There was one small window, grimy with dirt, but she could see it was growing dark. Lauren tested the handcuffs until the metal bit into her flesh. She strained with each foot to free herself from the zip-ties, and in an uncharacteristic moment of

pure frustration, she exploded into a frenzy of pulling and pushing to try to free herself. She attempted to stand, but the chair,
fastened to her legs, threw her off balance and she crashed sideways onto the dirty wood floor. She pushed and twisted to no
avail, until she lay there, panting, realizing she couldn't get herself
back up. Finally, she gave up trying.

Questions flooded her brain. She thought of the men who had
kidnapped her and wondered how they'd known where she was.
Where were the police taking her? The American embassy perhaps? Who was in the red helicopter? Was it friend or foe?

She tried to settle her mind, to think clearly, but she knew she
didn't have enough facts. She had no idea what the Budapest police
knew about her or whom they might have told about her arrest.
As far as she knew, her demands to talk to the embassy had been
ignored. As many times as she ran the scenarios in her head, the
slim hope that anyone knew where she was seemed improbable.

As if to emphasize the point, if anyone did know, where were
they? She felt desperation and fear threaten to take over her log-
ical, scientific mind. She focused on her breathing, in and out,
slowly, calmly, but it reminded her of giving birth to Abigail, and
the sorrow pounded at her far worse than anything else. A sob
escaped her throat and she clamped down, refusing to cry. She
was not going to allow these men to think they'd broken her. She
would show no weakness.

Lauren swallowed hard as she heard the heavy footfalls approaching and the door to her room opened. Still on the floor, she
looked up and tried to mask her fear. It was the man she'd cut with
a knife on the tug, the man who'd dragged her by her hair. She'd
heard his men call him Aleksander. Judging by his demeanor, he
was the man in charge, and because of the bandage on his face, he
was easy to spot.

He bent down, put his hands under her arms, and pulled both Lauren and the chair upright. Rubbing his hands together, he moved until he was directly in front of her, then slapped her hard across the face. Lauren was taken by surprise, her cheek stung and then grew warm, her eyes watered from the pain.

"I underestimated you once, and you slashed me with a knife," he said in accented English.

"I was defending myself," Lauren said defiantly.

"You also stabbed my colleague, and he bled out on the deck of that tug." He walked behind her and put his hands on her shoulders, leaned in, and whispered, "Where is Daniel Pope? I hope you know that if your positions were reversed, he would have already told me what I want to know. He's not very tough."

"So, you're the tough one?" Lauren said as she did her best to pull away. "You hit defenseless women."

He came around and stood in front of her, sliding an object from the pocket of his windbreaker. A simple push of a latch and a blade unfolded and locked into place. He touched the steel to Lauren's cheek. "Because it's a war, I'll do whatever it takes. Now, where is Daniel? Where are the two of you going to rendezvous?"

Lauren was under no illusions. This man would carve her apart piece by piece unless she gave him a reason to spare her. "Daniel was hurt in the crash, it was his ankle, he had trouble putting weight on it to walk. He insisted he was slowing me down, that we needed to split up."

"You're lying." He pressed the point of the knife until blood began to pool in the indentation on Lauren's cheek. "We searched everywhere."

"I went downstream, fast and dirty, getting everyone to chase me. He went upstream."

"What did he tell you about the airplane?"

"Nothing. We picked him up and then we crashed. The debriefing hadn't gone beyond verifying that he was indeed Daniel Pope. You and your missiles, you're the one who shot us down, aren't you?" Lauren felt the pressure from the knife vanish.

"I was following Daniel after he ran." He showed Lauren the tip of his knife, a single drop of her blood balanced on the point. "He stupidly went straight to the airport and boarded your Learjet. My men were waiting, and we destroyed it after it departed. You're lucky to have survived."

"I can take you to him," Lauren said, as the tip of his knife moved closer to her other cheek.

"Tell me what he did to sabotage the airplane he built, and I'll kill you now, quickly. Dying the slow way is brutal, even by wartime standards."

Lauren felt her fear expand. The look in his eyes left no doubt that he spoke the truth.

"He'll only show himself to me," Lauren said, her eyes locked on his as she tried to ignore the blade hovering only inches from her face.

Aleksander backed away, whipped a vibrating cellphone from his pocket, checked the screen then pressed it to his ear. "Oui?"

Lauren was surprised that he switched from English to French and she listened intently.

"Are you sure? You tested it thoroughly?" Aleksander paused, listening. "Good work. I'm on my way. We'll go tonight. How's the weather? How fast is the line moving? How high are the tops?"

Even with her rudimentary knowledge of French, she knew meteorological dialogue when she heard it, and he was asking for answers to the questions pilots would want to know.

"That could work in our favor. Start loading and fill it with

fuel. I'll be there as fast as I can." He ended the call and turned
to Lauren, a smile on his face. "You just opted for the slow way to
die. I don't need you *or* Daniel anymore."

Lauren tried to look brave, but she understood that the *Phoenix*,
the stealth airplane Daniel had built and then sabotaged was now
flyable, and any negotiating strength she had was now gone. With
that one phone call, she'd become nothing more than a loose end.

He opened the door and called for one of his men. They stood
in the doorway and spoke briefly in Ukrainian, then Aleksander
hurried off, leaving his man standing there, lingering. He looked
Lauren up and down, making no effort to disguise what he was
thinking. He finally walked away, leaving the door wide open. She
heard more talking, heard a door slam. Then there was more conversation, laughter, the noise of pots and pans, dishes, then finally
the smell of food. They were preparing a meal. Lauren knew that
after they ate—they would come for her.

CHAPTER TWENTY-TWO

"I CAN'T TELL you what's happening," Calvin said to Donovan. "We've lost satellite coverage. Another asset will be above the horizon in twelve minutes."

"That's too long." Donovan glanced at his watch as he paced. Calvin had tracked both BMWs to a remote farmhouse west of the city. As far as anyone knew, she was alive and there, but he was doing nothing.

"I'm sorry," Calvin said. "It's the best I can do. Are you positive you don't want me to send in a tactical team? I can have assets from SEAL Team Two in position for a pre-dawn raid."

"Tactical isn't my problem," Donovan replied. "Not knowing what's been happening at that house is my problem."

"I'll send you an image in twelve minutes, that's the most I can manage."

"Thank you, Calvin." Donovan had no business being frustrated with any of the people around him. They were all doing their best to free his wife. "I'm sorry, it's been a rough day."

"Don't worry, we'll get her back."

"I wish I could believe you."

"Think about it," Calvin said. "They kidnapped her when they could have killed her. She has something they want. She'll use it to buy time. Lauren's smart, she understands how this works, and she'll milk it for all it's worth."

Donovan respected Calvin's slant on the situation, it made sense. "Thank you for that."

"You'll hear from me in twelve minutes."

A familiar Mercedes 600 sedan pulled around the corner and slowly drove in through the open door and parked in front of the helicopter.

"It's okay. It's Karl," Marta said as she started toward the car.

Donovan hung back and watched as Karl jumped out and moved to the rear door of the Mercedes where he swung it open and stepped aside. Despite the summer heat, a head wearing a watch cap emerged and turned to face them. Kristof. He was dressed smartly in black slacks and a V-neck pullover shirt. Dark glasses masked his eyes, and he leaned heavily on a polished wooden cane.

"What the—?" Marta said as she changed course and headed for her father. "You're not supposed to be—how did you even get here?"

"I had no idea you planned to leave Innsbruck with him," Kristof said as he slid off his sunglasses, letting them hang from the neck of his shirt. He leaned his hip against the trunk of the car for support. "I had to hear it from Eric."

Donovan had motioned for everyone else to hang back. He approached the car and stood next to Marta, noticing that Kristof's eyes appeared more alert. His pallor had improved, but the fatigue was still there, carved deeply into the lines on his face.

"I'm a big girl, I can do what I please," Marta said with conviction. "You turned down Mr. Nash's request for help. I accepted. It's as simple as that."

Kristof's eyes went from his daughter to Donovan. "Like I said before, it's never simple with this man. I thought about what you whispered to me after I demanded Nash leave. I tried to catch you, to explain, but you'd already taken off for Budapest. Now I'm here."

"Explain what?" Marta said as she cocked her hip.

"I wanted to tell you that you were right. I only saw the situation through my lens. I didn't look at it from your perspective," Kristof said. "But after everything I've seen and heard since I've been in Budapest, I also need to tell you that this situation with Nash and his wife is more dangerous than you know."

"In what way?" Marta asked. "From what I've seen so far, we're dealing with a small terrorist group, either Slovakian or Ukrainian, and they're not all that well trained."

"It's not them that worry me, though we both know better than to underestimate anyone with a blind passion and an AK-47. I'm talking about the Americans. Karl was telling me about a man who was arrested last night after an attack in the park near the President Hotel, a man who you arranged to be released into our custody."

"Yes. Has he decided to talk?" Marta replied.

"From what we're told, he was working for the CIA, sent to slow down Mr. Nash and company, so they could find his wife before he did."

"To what end?" Marta asked.

"Are you sure they weren't sent to kill us, instead of merely slowing us down?" Donovan asked.

"I'm sure," Kristof replied. "Another team was working on finding your wife. They were found killed in Slovakia, probably by the people who now have your wife. They were murdered in a way that allows the Slovakian authorities to suspect your wife of the murders. I would strongly suggest she never return to Slovakia—ever."

"We know where she's being held, and once we have her, we're headed straight for Vienna," Marta said. "It's a simple in and out."

"There's more." Kristof raised his hand. "Before he stopped talking, the man from the park gave us the name of his contact here in Budapest. Our associates, in turn, spoke with that individual. A name did come from that interview. Does the name Kirkpatrick mean anything to either of you?"

"I know that name. He's CIA at Langley, and he's mine." Donovan remembered his thoughts of dealing with Kirkpatrick after all of this was finished. Kristof's words poured gasoline on that particular fire and now that task became a vow.

"The United States government has a long reach," Kristof warned. "I followed most of your antics today by seeing it on television. A running battle between a civilian helicopter and two SUVs through downtown Budapest made for spectacular footage, and it's being played and replayed globally. I promise you've got the attention of the entire world. I'd remove the word simple from anything you plan to do."

"Dad," Marta said frowning. "Did you take your medication today?"

"No, I needed to travel, and have my wits about me. It'll wait."

"You know how much pain you're going to end up in later." An expression of sympathy came to Marta's face. "Why don't you have Karl take you to the apartment? I promise I can handle the rest of this, and then Mr. Nash can be on his way, and you and I can talk."

"The pain helps me focus," Kristof gestured to Karl and stepped away from the trunk. "I brought a few things you'll need."

Donovan heard the latch release and the armor-plated trunk opened hydraulically. The space was full of various wooden boxes, high-impact plastic cases, and a white paper bag that smelled like food.

Kristof leaned in and handed Karl the food and then motioned

Michael, Trevor, and Montero to come closer. "We'll get to dinner in a minute."

As Marta sprung the lids on two metal cases, Donovan leaned closer and saw a cache of weapons. There were at least six assault rifles, two long rifles fitted with scopes, an assortment of handguns, and several sawed-off twelve-gauge shotguns. In the second case was box after box of ammunition.

"What's in those smaller cases?" Montero asked.

"Kristof," Donovan stepped back to make introductions. "This is Montero, Michael, and our pilot, Trevor. Everyone, this is Marta's father, Kristof, our benefactor."

"Nice to meet you," Michael said, as he and Trevor both shook Kristof's hand.

"Holy crap," Montero said as she flashed a knowing smile at Kristof, and then leaned in, picked up one of the assault rifles. She turned to give Marta a perplexed look. "The Israelis are still developing this model. How did you get these?"

"Around. Check these out." With a shrug, Marta removed a small black case from one of the ammunition boxes, held it flat in her hand, and opened it for Montero.

"You are shitting me!" Montero said, wide-eyed. "Government-grade Blackphones? These aren't—I mean, most people don't even know they exist. How did you?"

"I'm glad you're familiar with them. They're active, encrypted, satellite capable, and if you need them to, they'll scramble themselves and short out. Take this one. We'll need to stay in touch. As for the weapons, I believe you still have the one we borrowed from Karl. Feel free to take another one for yourself." To the group, Marta said, "I want everyone to be well armed. Pick what feels right, load it, and be ready. They're all untraceable. If you fire it, feel free to dump it anywhere."

Donovan picked out a .45 caliber Colt 1911. He liked how it fit his hand. He shot a glance at Kristof who was fully engaged in discussion with Montero.

"Nice choice." Marta placed a box of bullets in Donovan's hand. "This model is one of Dad's favorites. He has several in his personal collection."

"I know," Donovan said quietly. "He's the one who let me shoot one for the first time. I have to ask—the fact that he's here is re-markable. What did you whisper to him this morning?"

"I told him if something happened to him, you were going to be all that I had—the only link to the man my father had been, a link that could extend to his yet unborn grandchildren." Marta stood on her tiptoes and kissed Donovan on both cheeks. "Dad and I have to go now. We've been over the plan, and you know exactly what's going to happen."

"I'll update you as soon as Calvin has another satellite in place." Donovan hated being left behind, but at this point, he had no other option.

"Perfect, but regardless of what Calvin finds, my men and I are going in as soon as it's dark. I'll see you as soon as the farmhouse is secured." Marta stepped away and Donovan glanced out the open warehouse door at the sun perched in the western sky. Waiting for nightfall was going to feel like an eternity. He heard Montero and Trevor confirming the few remaining details with Marta as she powered up the secure phones. Donovan took the opportunity to approach Kristof who was standing next to the open rear door of the Mercedes waiting for his daughter to join him.

"I just wanted to say thank you," Donovan told Kristof, wish-ing he could read his friend's thoughts.

"I didn't do any of this for you," Kristof said. "I did it for Marta. If you let anything happen to her, I'll kill you—are we clear?"

Donovan felt his jaw clench, he didn't like to be threatened, he didn't care who it came from. "One dead man killing another dead man? That should prove interesting."

"I'm not dead yet."

"I'm sorry I deserted you all those years ago. I'm sorry that I appeared out of nowhere and made you so angry. It was never my intention, and if it means anything—I have missed you, Kristof. Again, I'm sorry, and once this is over I'll vanish again if that's your wish."

"We'll see how all of this turns out, won't we? In my experience, people around you seem to suffer."

"Are you ready?" Marta came around and helped her father into the car. She kissed Donovan on the cheek once again, then they sped out of the warehouse.

Michael, Trevor, and Montero were already opening up the grocery bags. Karl had brought a huge selection of deli sandwiches, energy bars, and bottled water. Everyone but Donovan ate.

"I haven't really had a chance to talk to you since yesterday. I know there's a lot going on, some of it I don't understand," Michael said with his mouth full. "Maybe you could start by telling us about Marta. Our twenty-something consultant who looks like a pop star, and might be a tad on the overly aggressive side."

"Don't underestimate her," Donovan said. "When she told you she was the equivalent of a private investigator, she was stretching the truth a little. She's a specially trained undercover operative. I know very little about her, and if the truth be known, I'd prefer not to know any more. I reached out to her father, who as you all could see has been ill, and as a favor, she volunteered to help me find Lauren. To be honest, I didn't ask a lot of questions, and I think it's best if none of us do. I want my wife back, and they seem to be making that happen."

"Fair enough. I'm not sure we could break any more Hungarian laws after today," Michael said. "I, for one, am ready to get out of here, and knowing you, I'm impressed how you're holding up under the stress of having to sit and wait."

"I don't seem to have a choice," Donovan said, feeling an upwelling of affection for his closest friend. "I am glad you're here. How's the hand? Can you shoot left handed?"

"I can with the sawed-off shotgun I found in the trunk."

"Trevor," Donovan asked. "Talk to me about jumping the border and flying to Vienna."

"It's a piece of cake," Trevor said using his hands to illustrate. "We fly low over the border, then pop up over a small airport as if we just took off, and then proceed like we own the joint. But I hate to tell you, your helicopter is far too hot for us to land at any commercial airport. I was thinking we wipe it for prints and leave it somewhere remote, preferably on fire. I hope you're insured, because you're going to want to report it stolen."

"I like the fire idea," Montero offered. "It'll destroy any DNA evidence."

"Fire it is," Donovan nodded, unconcerned about the helicopter. "What are the provisions if we have wounded?"

"Two options," Trevor explained. "If it's really serious, we can drop off and go. There are three different hospitals in Budapest that have helipads. Then we alert the embassy on our way out and head for Austria. If it's not so serious, being it's dark, we maybe could pull off a drop and go at the President hotel. They did a nice job on Michael."

"How are you set for fuel?" Michael asked.

"I'm going to say we've got two hours and forty-five minutes until dry tanks. We've more than enough to get to the pick-up point, and then off to Vienna. But I suggest we stick to that program. I haven't seen the telly, but I doubt there's anywhere in Eastern Europe we can stop and buy fuel. So, at this point, our chopper is like one of those disposable lighters. When it's out of fuel you throw it in the bin."

Donovan's phone rang. Calvin. "Tell me we're back in business."

"We're in position," Calvin announced. "But there's bad news. One of the BMW's is gone."

"I was afraid of that." Donovan closed his eyes, the jolt felt as if he'd just been stabbed. "Infrared? Can you tell us how many people are in the house?"

"No, not yet. Though, it's possible later, as the house cools."

"How long is this satellite overhead?" Donovan asked.

"We'll have a four-hour window, a ninety minute gap, and then another four hour window."

"I would have thought there'd be twenty-four hour coverage of this part of the world," Donovan said, more thinking out loud than asking an actual question.

"Oh, there is, but these are the only ones I can personally re-task without asking permission. Even so, I'm taking some risks."

"Thank you, Calvin. We wouldn't be anywhere if it weren't for you." Donovan didn't know what else to say.

"Do me a favor," Calvin asked. "When you get her, let me know."

Donovan turned to the others. "That was Calvin. We have satellite coverage again. One of the BMWs is gone—and we don't know where it went."

CHAPTER TWENTY-THREE

LAUREN HEARD CHAIR legs scooting against the wooden floor accompanied by the sound of clattering dishes. Dinner was over. There was more conversation, laughter. As best Lauren could figure, there were seven of them. She stiffened when she heard the footfalls coming down the hall. A light switch was flipped, and a single bulb illuminated the shabby room. Lauren blinked at the sudden change in brightness. Leaning in the doorway was the driver, the man who'd zip-tied her ankles to the chair. He drew his knife from its scabbard and held the blade up to the light, as if admiring the edge.

"Aleksander left me in charge, and he asked me to do him a favor," the man said in halting but passable English. "He wanted me to begin your, how did he say it? Your slow death, by returning the favor for the wound you inflicted on him."

Lauren pushed down her terror as he smiled and came toward her. As he closed the distance, Lauren, only secured to the chair by her feet, sprang upward from her knees and drove the top of her head into the unsuspecting man's face. With her hands cuffed behind her back, she lost her balance and toppled sideways, unable to break her fall. He staggered backward. His free hand shot to his bleeding nose. Furious, he shook his head as if to clear his vision and then came for her.

Above and behind her, Lauren heard the soft tinkle of glass falling from a pane in the window, and a round hole formed in the man's forehead just above the bridge of his nose. His eyes rolled up in his head and his forward momentum carried him onto Lauren's chair before he crashed headfirst into the wall. He slid down the faded wallpaper, leaving a streak of blood, then lay motionless in a misshapen heap.

Lauren snapped her head from the broken window to the doorway as she heard heavy boots coming down the hall. A large man rounded the doorway with a drawn pistol. Two more muted gunshots were fired through the window and the man collapsed in a heap.

"Lauren," a voice whispered. "Close your eyes!"

Lauren did, just before an intense white flash emanated from somewhere down the hall, followed by a deafening boom that rattled the frame of the house. Her ears rang, but she was far enough away from the blast to still be able to hear. There were men yelling and screaming, more shots were fired, and seconds later it was over.

A gun barrel was used to clear the remaining glass from the window and a lithe form dressed in black slithered through the opening and landed catlike on the floor. A knife was drawn and made quick work of the zip-ties securing Lauren's ankles.

"Who are you?" Lauren said as she struggled to her knees.

"Are you okay?" the figure asked as she removed her mask and shook her black hair free.

"I'm fine. How did you find me? Who are you?"

"It's a long story. I'm Marta Szanto. My father and your husband were once friends."

"Archangel," Lauren whispered, remembering the stories Donovan had told her about his past. The implications came flooding through. "Donovan found him—to get to me?"

"Yes." Marta smiled and nodded, "Don't worry. Everyone's secrets are safe."

"All clear?" A voice called out from the hall.

"All clear in here! Anyone hurt?"

"We're all good," A man stood in the hallway, his mask still in place. "I don't think they got off a single shot."

"Did any of them survive?" Marta asked.

"We left one of the bastards breathing, just like you asked."

"Take him outside to the garage, find out what he knows," Marta ordered. "Someone else bring me the medical kit and some bolt cutters."

"My husband and daughter," Lauren asked. "Are they safe?"

Marta tilted her head at the sound of an approaching helicopter. "You can ask Donovan yourself in a few minutes. How's your head? I was outside and we were about to breach the main part of the house when the light in this room came on. I got to the window in time to see what you did to that guy. Quick thinking."

"Do I hear a helicopter?" Lauren asked. "Earlier today, a red one flew over the bridge just as I was being taken. Was that you?"

"All your husband's doing," Marta said with a smile. "He loves you very much."

"Where are we?" Lauren asked, her confusion clearing and her priorities gaining traction.

"About thirty miles east of Budapest."

"The guy in charge of all . . . this." Lauren gestured to the bodies in the room. "His name is Aleksander. He's the one who kidnapped me. He was here earlier, but he left in a hurry."

"We were afraid of that happening. We've had satellite surveillance on this place for most of the day, but we didn't see who drove off." Marta said, then turned to yell down the hallway. "Where's my bolt cutters!"

A man hurried through the door, and Lauren held her wrists apart as each handcuff was snapped in two. She immediately began massaging her tortured skin.

"Any luck in the garage?" Marta asked her man as she dug some antiseptic ointment from the medical kit.

"He's talking, but he doesn't seem to know much."

"Ask him where Aleksander went in such a hurry," Marta said as she dabbed salve to the worst of Lauren's cuts.

As the man hurried off with his instructions, Lauren heard the growing sound of the helicopter change as the spinning rotor altered pitch, and she knew Donovan was on the ground.

This time, the sound of running footsteps coming down the hallway was the sweetest sound Lauren had ever heard. She turned as Donovan filled the doorway, and his eyes told her everything she would ever need to know about the man she'd married. There was fear mixed with relief, plus anger and fatigue. He'd done what she knew he'd do, which was to do whatever he could to get to her. He wrapped her in his arms and held her tight, as if he would never again let her go. Lauren felt her eyes flood with tears and she pulled away and kissed him and touched his face; there were no words yet.

"Are you okay?" Donovan whispered.

Lauren nodded. "Are you?"

"Not yet." He pulled her against his chest and held her close.

"We need to go," Marta interrupted. "The gunfire as well as the helicopter are going to draw some interest."

"I gather you two have met," Donovan said as he lowered his arms. "Marta, I can't thank you enough."

"It wasn't a favor," Marta said. "It was a deal, remember?"

More people could be heard hurrying down the hallway. Michael, followed by Montero, entered the room. Michael grabbed Lauren and hugged her, as did Montero. Lauren was nearly overcome. Two of her favorite people had stood by her husband to come find her.

"We need to move this reunion out to the helicopter," Donovan said as he took Lauren by the hand.

"I need a phone." Lauren wiped the tears from her eyes. "I need to call Calvin."

"Let's get out of here first," Donovan said. "We'll call him on the way to Vienna."

"No," Lauren said as she pulled up short. "Before Daniel died, he told me he'd been forced to build a stealth aircraft. He thinks they have a nuclear weapon and the aircraft is the delivery system."

"An attack?" Donovan asked. "Where? When?"

"I heard Aleksander on the phone earlier. I think the when is tonight," Lauren said as Marta handed her a phone. Lauren did a double take as she took the mobile, and then punched in Calvin's number. As it rang, Lauren glanced at Marta. "Nice phone."

"Calvin, it's Lauren, I'm okay. Listen, we have a big problem." Lauren took a breath. "A nuclear problem."

"I'm listening," Calvin said.

"Daniel was forced to build a stealth aircraft. He thinks the people who held him plan to use it to deliver a nuclear warhead."

"That's a little thin, Lauren. Where's Daniel now?"

"Daniel's dead. Before he died he gave me a jump drive. It may or may not have details of this attack stored inside."

"May or may not?" Calvin said.

"I don't have it, but I know where it is." Lauren said. "I was on a tugboat headed downstream, pushing a barge full of Mercedes Benzes. The name of the tug was something *Kirov*."

Montero drew her phone and hit a button. "Yeah, it's me. I need a priority search for a tug named something *Kirov*. It's pushing a load of new German automobiles down the Danube, most likely in the Budapest area. I need a location and I need it now. Call me back."

One of Marta's men came up to her and whispered into her ear. "Anything we should know?" Donovan asked.

"The man we were questioning about Aleksander was unable to help us, and it seems he's passed away from his injuries."

"Let's go," Michael said as he led the way out the door.

"Where to?" Marta asked.

"That tugboat is somewhere on the Danube," Michael said. "The folks aboard the *Kirov* are about to have company."

"Lauren," Calvin said through the phone. "Find out what's on Daniel's jump drive, I need more before I can move on this. A lot more."

"I understand," Lauren said, refusing to second-guess herself for stashing the drive. "Calvin, is there by chance a line of thunderstorms in my part of the world?"

"Yeah, as a matter of fact, we just issued a weather warning to NATO Europe. There's a fast-moving cold front connected with a deep low pressure area sitting over the Baltics. We're looking at severe weather from Estonia to Northern France, why?"

"It might mean something," Lauren said as they cleared the house and sprinted toward a red helicopter sitting with no exterior lights illuminated, though its rotor blades were turning. "Calvin, I know you had to have been helping Donovan find me, thank you. I'll talk to you soon."

"Lauren, up front with Donovan," Michael called out. "You know what this barge looks like. I'll sit in back with Montero and Marta."

"Nice to see you again, Dr. McKenna." Trevor nodded from the pilot's seat. "It's been a while since a certain Paris rooftop."

"My guardian angel." Lauren leaned over to give Trevor a quick hug.

"He's your angel." Trevor pointed toward Donovan. "I'm just

the guy that gets him there. Now, what's this I hear about a barge? And what exactly are we going to do when we find this thing?"

"Retrieve my property," Lauren replied. "And maybe exact a little revenge."

Montero, her cell phone still up to her ear, leaned forward. "The barge is the *Nastasha Kirov*, and she's cruising on the river beyond Budapest, sixty nautical miles south of our current position."

"ETA thirty minutes," Trevor said as he spooled the eight-hundred-and-fifty horsepower turbine engine, stabilized the rpm, and then with a gentle pull on the collective, the skids lifted free of the grass and he swung the helicopter to the south and accelerated.

Lauren located her headset and slipped it on, Donovan's hand found hers and she intertwined her fingers in his, knowing his aversion to helicopters. After being alone and on the run in a foreign country, the feeling of being around people she loved was almost overpowering.

"We do have a computer on board, don't we?" Michael asked. "I mean, we are off to retrieve a jump drive, and it would be nice to be able to open the files."

"I have mine," Montero said. "Lauren, do you have any idea what's on this drive?"

"No, we'd just gotten Daniel on the plane and taken off when we were hit. He and I survived the crash landing and managed to escape the sinking Learjet. He told me what happened, what he'd built, and then gave me the drive before he died."

"I'm sorry Daniel died," Donovan said, and gave her hand a reassuring squeeze. "I know the two of you had a history. For what it's worth, I liked him."

"Thanks," Lauren replied. "He told me he sabotaged the airplane before he escaped, but from what I heard tonight, they might have found the problem. I'm hoping that the jump drive will give us something to stop this attack before it even starts."

"Did Daniel know where he was being held?" Donovan asked.

"No, it's somewhere close to Bratislava, which was the first town he was able to contact us from."

"So there's a stealth aircraft with possible nuclear capability somewhere near Bratislava?" Michael said. "Shouldn't we alert the Slovakian military, or NATO, or someone?"

"We have nothing to tell them, plus, if we do, they'll no doubt connect it to the crashed Learjet, which brings them to Daniel and me," Lauren said. "We'll need hard evidence that it isn't an American-engineered threat before we say anything."

"Where exactly on the tug is this drive?" Montero asked.

"In the lavatory near the galley. I taped it under the sink. I was captured and held on the barge. The captain used the bathroom as a cell and told me I was going to be turned over to the authorities. I thought if they found the jump drive, I'd have zero deniability, and be treated as a spy. So, I stashed it knowing it could be found again."

"Good thinking," Marta said.

"You said something earlier about revenge," Donovan said. "What did the tug crew do to you?"

"They sold me out. Instead of the police, they turned me over to Aleksander and one of his thugs. I managed to escape, but I pissed off this Aleksander guy in the process."

"He's the guy we saw on the bridge? Dragging you from the police car," Michael said. "I remember him. He had a bandage on his face."

"That's him, though the bandage is new. He and I had a difference of opinion." She felt Donovan give her hand another squeeze.

In the cockpit, lit only by the instrument lights, Lauren could see the set of Donovan's jaw, and the hardened, determined look in his eyes. He was with her in heart and spirit, but mentally, she knew he was already thinking ahead to the barge and what he'd do when they arrived.

CHAPTER TWENTY-FOUR

"ARE YOU SURE that's the tug?" Donovan asked as Lauren lowered the binoculars. The vessel was steaming down the river using a bright searchlight to sweep the water in front of the barge.

"Yes." She handed him the binoculars. "See the white navigation light on the stern? You can just make out the letters that spell *Kirov*. It's what I saw when I went overboard."

"Okay, everyone," Donovan said. "We all know what happens next."

Trevor approached high and from the rear of the tug with all of the helicopter's external lights extinguished. The rotor noise hopefully mixed with the growl from the diesel engines. As they closed in, Trevor started a steep descent. The sailors aboard the tug might hear the helicopter, but unless they looked straight up into the night sky they would not spot them. At what felt to Donovan like the last second, Trevor checked the descent and slowed to a hover directly above the highest point on the tug, at the roof of the bridge. Gun in hand, Donovan threw off his harness and jumped down onto the metal surface, stepped to the edge, and pointed his gun into the surprised face of the captain as he burst from the bridge.

Montero, Marta, and Michael followed and quickly killed the intense searchlight. Lauren stepped out last and Trevor lifted off and climbed into the night sky. Donovan jumped from the roof and seized the captain by the front of his shirt and pushed him roughly into the railing. The barrel of the Colt never left the captain's forehead.

The captain's eyes darted from the barrel of the gun to the helicopter as Trevor swung around, turned on his landing light and expertly set the helicopter down on top of two Mercedes sedans, the skids resting on the roofs and then brought the engine to idle.

As Trevor brought the helicopter to idle, Donovan, his fury barely contained, tightened his grip on the captain. "You held my wife against her will! Who were the men you called?"

"No English!" he yelled, terrified.

Marta stepped forward and fired a series of questions at the man in Hungarian and then German. Turning to Donovan, she said, "He says he has no idea what woman you're talking about or what men you're talking about."

"Maybe this will remind him," Lauren stepped out of the shadows and walked to the clearly terrified captain. The man shrunk from her and began speaking to Marta.

"He says there was a reward offered, and a phone number," Marta translated. "That's all, no name. They came by boat. Oh, and he also offered to share the reward with you."

Donovan hit him, a quick powerful jab to the face that easily broke the man's nose. "Tell him no thanks."

"We've got it!" Montero called out as she came running up the stairs.

"Did you see anyone down there?" Lauren asked.

"No," Montero said. "Are we looking for someone in particular?"

"Forget them," Lauren said. "Let's get out of here."

Montero signaled Trevor to pick them up and the turbine spooled back up. The helicopter lifted off and climbed overhead. Moments later, Trevor was in position, hovering only inches above the bridge. Michael helped the women first and then offered a hand to Donovan.

Donovan paused, turned, and punched the captain one more time, this time in his midsection, dropping him to his knees. He thought that should suffice to keep him out of the picture while they departed. He was about to join Michael when he had one last thought. He held up his index finger for Michael to wait, went into the bridge, and with more strength than he knew he possessed, snapped the tug's wooden steering wheel free from its housing, walked back out into the night, and flung it overboard.

Then he climbed aboard the helicopter. Seconds later Trevor lifted off from the top of the bridge, and they all watched as the tug's searchlight sprang to life only moments before the bow of the barge slid up onto a muddy bank, turned sideways to the current, and began taking on water. As Trevor banked north toward Budapest, Donovan looked back as an entire row of cars broke loose and slid into the Danube.

"Donovan," Lauren yelled from the rear seat where she, Montero, and Marta sat huddled over Montero's laptop. She motioned for him to put on his headset. When he did, Montero handed him the computer.

Donovan looked at the screen, and in seconds understood exactly what he was seeing. There was a series of waypoints, latitudes and longitudes, no names, just numbers and letters. Just below was a picture of a man, and a name: Aleksander Kovalenko. Below that was a pencil drawing, a sketch that could only be described as a warhead.

"That's the guy, Aleksander," Lauren said. "He's the one who abducted me, and then left when he got a phone call that something had been fixed. Then he asked about the weather and a line of thunderstorms. He thought the flight could get out before the system arrived. Do you have any idea where those coordinates are?"

"Trevor," Michael asked. "Can I borrow your GPS, I need to type in some coordinates."

"Sure," Trevor said.

Donovan waited while Michael typed in the first set of numbers and the moving map display pinpointed a spot in Slovakia.

"No airport even close to this waypoint," Michael said, "Maybe it's the first fix and not the point of origin."

"Type in the destination," Donovan suggested.

Michael did, and the GPS instantly shot to a point seven hundred and seventy miles northeast. Michael cycled the range on the moving map until the destination was clearly visible.

"Bloody hell," Trevor mumbled when he glanced at the screen.

Michael keyed his microphone. "This flight plan starts in Slovakia and ends in Moscow."

"We have to stop him," Lauren said. "Moscow could very easily launch their own missiles at the United States, or anyone else they think might be responsible. It's one of the theoretical triggers for an extinction-level nuclear exchange."

"If this guy starts from Slovakia," Donovan said. "He'll be in Russian airspace fairly quickly."

"He'll be invisible," Lauren said. "If the sky is full of fighters, or he thinks they've been warned, he can turn around, land somewhere, and wait until another day."

"Or pick a different target, in a different country," Montero added. "He can do about anything he wants. We don't even know what this plane looks like."

"I think we might," Lauren said. "Montero, on your phone, run an Internet search for any aircraft named *Phoenix*."

"Is this it?" Montero held up her phone so Lauren could see.

"Yes." Lauren handed the phone to Donovan.

The forward sweep of the wings was unusual but not innovative, the construction looked to be composite, every edge was rounded, the twin vertical stabilizers were canted outboard. If a radar beam did hit this aircraft there were very few hard edges to send the signal back to the antenna. If it were coated with some sort of radar-absorbing material it would vanish from a radar screen.

"I gather the engine is buried in the fuselage," Michael asked as he inspected the photo. "How fast, how high? What kind of range are we talking about?"

"These are specs from twenty years ago." Donovan thumbed down to the technical data. "Two hundred seventy-five knots at thirty thousand feet, with a no-reserve range of twelve hundred nautical miles. Does the jet exhaust come out between the vertical stabilizers here in top of the fuselage?" The tiny photograph made it difficult for Donovan to make out the details.

"Yes," Lauren said. "Daniel was trying to reduce the noise footprint by deflecting all of the jet noise upward, away from the ground."

"We need to call Calvin," Donovan told Lauren. "Bring him up to date."

Lauren dialed and Calvin picked up immediately. "Calvin, I'm handing the phone to Donovan."

Donovan took the phone, pulled off his headset. "Calvin, we have the jump drive. There is a flight plan from Slovakia to Moscow. We also have a name, Aleksander Kovalenko. Lauren knows what kind of aircraft Daniel built, it's one of his earlier designs, the *Phoenix*. Google the thing."

"I just did. You think this is what Kovalenko has?"

"You know him?" Donovan asked.

"I know of him. He's a former Ukrainian Air Force officer. He was flagged as someone rumored to have ties with Chechen terrorists. He's Ukrainian by birth. He was a fighter pilot in the Ukrainian Air Force. He flew MiG-29s, spoke half a dozen different languages, and was a rising star until he was grounded under mysterious circumstances. The rumor is he killed someone, or was suspected of killing someone; a Russian. When Kovalenko was drummed out of the service and disappeared, there was speculation he finally unraveled over the latest Russian-Ukrainian issues. I just pulled up his file; it looks like his uproar goes way back. A large portion of Kovalenko's family was killed in Stalin's forced famine of the Ukraine. Stalin was a real bastard. When it comes to genocide, Hitler was a sissy compared to Stalin. In two years, Stalin starved seven million Ukrainians. Three million of them were children."

"I remember the history. Russia and most of Ukraine have issues that go way back," Donovan said. "So, the Moscow thing makes sense? The man doesn't like Russians, and he found a way to launch a first strike at Moscow."

"What you have is a theory, zero hard evidence. I can tell you right now, if I try to sell this to the Pentagon, no one is going to believe that one man can fly undetected into some of the most heavily defended airspace in the world. If we send NATO fighters to the border of Russia, it's only going to incite tensions. I can promise you, the current administration won't sign off on any of this. I will make a call to a contact I have at the Pentagon and see what they think, but what I need is proof."

"What about the Russians?" Donovan said. "Can we warn them?"

"They'd go bat-shit crazy," Calvin said. "We'd risk them making a preemptive launch, or scaring this guy off and then we'd have stirred up a mountain of diplomatic and military trouble and still be faced with the same threat. No, we have to have rock-solid proof, or do nothing at all."

"What if I provide you the proof?" Donovan's frustration was growing. Lauren's very real fear that the Russians might counter-launch if they thought they were under a large-scale attack was real. Washington D.C. would be at the top of their list. "Calvin, I believe my wife, and she thinks there's going to be a terrorist strike on Moscow, tonight. If you won't try to stop it . . . I will, but I need your help."

"You've got it, within the limits of my power, absolutely."

"I'm going to give you the first waypoint. There's no airport close, so we think it's a first fix. The airport Kovalenko is using could be anywhere west of there." Donovan read off the numbers and then Calvin read them back for accuracy. "Find the airport. Maybe the airplane hasn't taken off yet."

"What did he say?" Lauren asked as Donovan disconnected the call.

"Nothing good. We might be on our own." Donovan handed the phone to Lauren and then put on his headset. "Trevor, Budapest Airport. And fly fast."

CHAPTER TWENTY-FIVE

"THIS IS GOING to be fast and dirty. I'm going to come in low, without lights," Trevor said. "I'm not going to talk to the control tower, so when we touch down, it'll only be for a moment. My plan is for us to be on our way again before anyone knows we were ever there."

"We know the Gulfstream is at the airport," Michael said. "What about fuel?"

"That's the variable," Donovan said. "I have no idea how much fuel was onboard when the charter pilots landed, but all I need is enough to get to the Russian border. We know where the *Phoenix* is going to be, we're just not sure when it will get there. The Gulfstream is two hundred twenty-five miles an hour faster. I can cover some ground and I'm hoping I'll get lucky. If I can prove the threat exists, then maybe people will listen."

"Quit saying I. We're both going," Michael said. "We'll do this the right way."

Donovan looked at Lauren and found the conflict in her eyes. He pulled off his headset and leaned close to kiss her.

"I don't want you to go," Lauren said as she intertwined her fingers with his. "We just found each other again. I can't lose you."

"There's no one else." Donovan kissed the back of her hand. "It's a reconnaissance mission. If we can find this plane in time, chances are the Air Force can shoot it down before he can start World War Three."

"Simple reconnaissance?"

Donovan heard the wariness in her voice. He also remembered Kristof's warning about nothing being simple. "Yes, I know it's a long shot, but we have to try. Reach out to William. Through the State Department he can work on shielding you from the CIA. I'll find you in Vienna when it's over."

Lauren raised her chin and they kissed.

"So," Trevor asked. "I'm dropping the two of you off and everyone else goes to Austria with me?"

"Yes," Donovan said. "We'll either get airborne quickly, or we won't at all. If we don't, we'll contact you."

"Let me know. I'll have men close," Marta said. "We have safe houses in Budapest."

"Lauren, the hard drive needs to go with you," Donovan said. "But Michael and I will need the coordinates so we can plug them into the Gulfstream's GPS once we're airborne."

"I've already sent them to your phone," Montero said. "Is there anything else you'll need?"

"No, just the coordinates and a phone," Donovan said.

"If you get airborne, where will you eventually land?" Montero asked the one question that hadn't been mentioned.

"That'll all be dictated on how much fuel we have to play with," Donovan said. "There are plenty of airports out there." Donovan and Michael both knew that fuel was only one of many considerations.

"Here's how we all stay in touch," Marta handed Donovan her Blackphone. "Once you're airborne, it'll switch from land-based connections and revert to satellite. To boost the signal, take this tiny suction cup and attach it to any piece of metal connected to the airframe and your entire aircraft becomes an antenna. It's fully charged."

"Where are you going when you get to Vienna?" Donovan asked.

"Undecided," Marta replied.

"I understand," Donovan knew Marta was being cautious. If any of them were caught, she didn't want a trail leading straight to her destination.

"We're about five minutes out," Trevor announced. "I'll swing in over the General Aviation ramp, find the darkest place to touch down, and then you two are out the door."

"Sounds good," Donovan turned to Lauren and found that her headphones were around her neck and she had a cell phone to her ear. She looked up and their eyes met, hers wide with surprise before they narrowed. Donovan knew she was calculating something. He'd seen the look a thousand times. She ended the call and quickly pulled her headphones back over her ears.

"That was Calvin. They may have spotted the *Phoenix*. He sent the satellite image," Lauren opened the photo on her phone and studied it for a moment and then handed it to Donovan. The photo was grainy black and white and it took a moment for him to orient himself. There was an open door, big enough for a hangar. There was barely enough light from inside the building to cast light on something sitting outside the door. Only half of the object was illuminated, but Donovan could see one of the forward swept wings and the twin tails. It was the *Phoenix*.

"Where and when?" Donovan said as he handed the phone back to Lauren.

"Seventy-three nautical miles northwest of Budapest, near a small town named Galánta, Slovakia. It was spotted four minutes ago, but now it's gone. It could be back in the hangar, or it could have already taken off."

"Anything else?" Donovan asked.

"Yes, Calvin said that even with this image, the Pentagon says there is nothing to be done. He also issued a very serious stipulation. If we think we can stop Kovalenko, do it, but on our side of the border. Under no circumstances are we to cross into Russian airspace."

"So in other words," Michael said. "If we can't stop him where NATO can go in and clean up the pieces of the American-made aircraft, we're to let it go and the nuclear detonation will erase the evidence."

"Heads up, everybody," Trevor said. "The Budapest Airport is twelve o'clock and one mile. We're coming in from the southwest, as far away from the control tower as we can get. With all of the ground clutter, I doubt if we're showing up on their radar, and hopefully, at this hour, they'll never see us in the dark."

Both Donovan and Michael strained to find the green-and-white Gulfstream they'd chartered in D.C.

"There," Michael pointed.

Donovan found the Gulfstream, and it couldn't have been in a worse position. It was parked with the nose pointed towards three other airplanes, blocking any forward exit, which meant that they'd have to find a tug and push it out to be able to taxi. Donovan's hopes plummeted until his eyes were drawn down to the cargo ramp where he spotted a row of freighters being prepped for the night's flights. In the halo of lights surrounding the ramp sat a Boeing 727 freighter. The blue airplane with white lettering down the side, was sitting with its navigation lights on, the cargo door open, and a fuel truck was just pulling away.

"Michael," Donovan said. "What do you think about the Skybridge 727?"

"Brilliant," Michael said and slowly smiled. "Of course the freight ramp makes it an entirely different kind of operation. The

Phoenix could already be airborne and this is going to take us a little longer than if we'd been able to jump in a Gulfstream."

"It also turns us into hijackers or terrorists. The 727," Donovan asked. "Yes or no?"

"Yes, but it's been a long time," Michael said, holding up his bandaged hand. "We'll need a third person."

"I'm in," Montero said without hesitation.

"You're with us, then," Donovan nodded. "We're taking the 727."

"I alerted some of my men. They've just arrived street side," Marta said. "They'll provide some distractions to give you time to get airborne."

Donovan studied the ramp, buildings, and the row of cargo aircraft. "Trevor, do you see that hangar straight ahead? That large shadow, just this side of the cargo ramp, can you let us out there?"

"I see it," Trevor said. "No problem."

"Perfect." Donovan turned to Michael and got a resolute nod in return. When he looked at Lauren, the expression on her face and the look in her eyes told him that he was loved, to be careful, and to come back to her—it was all he needed. Donovan glanced at Montero. "You ready?"

Montero didn't hesitate. She stuffed her laptop into her backpack, threw off her seat belt, and stepped to the ground the instant the helicopter touched down. She ducked under the rotor blades and fell in behind Donovan and Michael as they ran through the shadows until they were pressed up against a brick wall in the dark as the helicopter lifted away into the night.

"The best way for us to get out to the airplane is to act like we belong," Montero said. "I say we walk out there and see what it takes to get airborne."

"Let's do it." Donovan took a quick peek around the corner

of the building and motioned for Michael and Montero to follow. With Montero between them, they headed out to the Boeing
727. The ramp wasn't overly busy. Budapest wasn't anyone's cargo
hub, so the few freighters on the ground were scattered out along
the perimeter of the apron. There were bright lights illuminating
the entire area, but as far as Donovan could tell, they didn't draw
anyone's attention.

Donovan headed toward the portable stairs that would take
them up to the forward door. As they drew closer, the noise from
the Boeing's 727 auxiliary power unit drowned out nearly everything. He didn't see anyone around the plane, and it didn't
look like the cargo had arrived yet which meant the crew of three
would most likely be in the cockpit. The 727 was designed over
fifty years ago, back when all modern jetliners flew with three
crewmen.

Montero stopped, as did Donovan. He could see she held a
Glock in one hand, a phone in the other. She'd received a text
message. "That was Marta. Her men found the Skybridge captain
and first officer outside, smoking. We don't have to worry about
them."

"Okay, there should only be one guy," Michael said. "We don't
need him to fly the thing, but I need to ask him some questions
after I disable the cockpit voice recorder. There's no use docu-
menting our string of felonies. Montero, can you blindfold him
so he can't identify us? Once we're finished chatting, we'll leave
him behind."

"Let's start out playing nice," Donovan said. "And we'll see how
it goes."

Montero nodded, holstered her Glock, and dug briefly into her
backpack until she found her roll of duct tape. She stripped off
two twelve-inch strips, overlapped them lengthwise, so she'd made

a section of tape, twelve inches long and nearly five inches wide. She knew what she was doing, and it made the tape seem lethal.

She nodded that she was ready and then turned and led the way up the stairs. Donovan, with Michael right behind him, caught up to her just as she vanished through the main fuselage door. Donovan took a quick look over Montero's shoulder into the cockpit. A solitary young man with two stripes on his shoulder boards sat at the flight engineer's panel.

Montero timed her advance perfectly. When the flight engineer leaned over to pull something from his flight bag, she crept up behind him, slapped the tape over his eyes, and put him in a full nelson to control his flailing arms until his initial panic burned itself out.

Michael went forward and ripped the area microphone from the overhead, and then snapped the wires. He went to the engineer's panel, threw a few switches, and picked up a clipboard. He scanned the paper and then turned to the engineer. "Sit still and we won't hurt you. What's your call sign?"

Montero increased her pressure on the flight engineer's shoulder sockets.

"Skybridge 770."

"Destination?" Michael asked.

"Vilnius, Lithuania."

"What's your estimated time of departure?"

"Fifteen minutes ago, but our freight has been delayed."

"Thank you," Michael said and looked at Donovan. "I'm done with him. Take him down and move the stairs away from the plane. Make sure he doesn't run screaming into the terminal."

"Don't hurt me," the young man begged.

"I'll take care of him," Montero said. "How do I get back aboard?"

"I can lower the rear airstair," Michael said. "Make it fast."

Montero pulled the engineer from the chair while Donovan maneuvered the young man's hands behind him and wrapped two loops of tape tightly around his wrists. They propelled him down the stairs. Donovan found the controls that electrically moved the stairs back from the fuselage. He motored around the nose of the 727 and left the stairs parked in the grass beyond the wing.

Montero gave the flight engineer a quick, harmless jab to the midsection that doubled him over, taking the last of the fight out of him. She pressed a swatch of duct tape over his mouth, careful to leave his nose clear. Finally, she eased him to the ground, pulled a sturdy plastic tie from her pack and secured his ankle to the steel frame of the stairs, well out of reach of the controls.

Michael had already lowered the rear airstair and as Montero ran up, Donovan made a quick check of the 727's exterior. He pulled the chocks from behind the nose tires, went back to the tail and climbed the airstair up through a narrow metal hallway and emerged into the rear of the plane. Without seats or cargo it seemed cavernous. The second he was aboard, Michael began raising the steps.

"I never knew you guys flew Boeings," Montero said, slightly winded. She looked at Donovan and then Michael, waiting for either to reply. "Oh, for Christ's sake, you don't fly Boeings, do you?"

"I am a fully rated Boeing 727 flight engineer," Michael said and shrugged. "I flew for Northwest Airlines for exactly eight months before I was furloughed. I never went back."

"While not technically a 727 pilot," Donovan added, "when I was in Africa, the guys used to let me fly all the time when I was riding jump seat."

Montero pushed past them both as she left for the cockpit,

her voice echoing in the empty fuselage. "I have about a hundred hours in a Cessna! Even with the three of us on board, we still don't make a goddamned Boeing pilot!"

"You're going to have to fly," Michael said as he held up his bandaged hand. "I'm going to put Montero in the copilot seat. I'll run the engineer's panel until we're ready for takeoff then I'll switch with her. I'll need her to help. It might be a little clumsy, but it'll work."

"We can do this, right?" Donovan asked. "Just the three of us?"

"In our sleep," Michael said as he stopped and secured the main cargo door.

Donovan slid past Montero and eased into the captain's seat. He adjusted the height, the travel, and the rudder pedals until he was happy and then secured his harness. Michael pointed for Montero to sit in the copilot's seat and then began flipping switches on the engineer's panel.

"We've got thirty-five thousand pounds of fuel, so we're good," Michael said. "Call ground control for a start clearance and let's get this thing in the air."

Donovan breathed in the familiar smells of the forty-year-old cockpit, shifted his mindset to his time in Africa, made sure his transmit button was for the correct radio, and then raised the microphone to his mouth. "Budapest, Skybridge 770 request start clearance."

"Skybridge 770, start approved," the controller replied in a normal tone.

Donovan stowed the microphone, and made room for Michael to lean in and flip switches on the overhead panel as well as the center console.

"Fuel pumps on. Starting number one," Michael said as the starter began spinning the first of the three Pratt & Whitney engines.

Under Michael's tutelage, Donovan did his part to start the other two engines while Montero kept her eyes on the ramp looking for anyone who looked like they might try to stop them.

"There's a car coming from the left," Montero said. "Yellow lights flashing."

"Good, that's the follow-me vehicle," Donovan said as he, too, spotted the car. "He'll lead us out to the runway."

"Generators are on, we're good," Michael said. "I'm shutting down the APU. Montero, I need you to swap seats with me. Donovan, call for taxi."

Donovan did as he was told, and moments later they were issued taxi instructions to runway one-three right. Michael threw on the taxi lights, Donovan released the brakes, added a touch of power, and the big jet began to move forward.

"Go easy on the throttles, we're really light," Michael said. "I'm going to do everything quick and dirty. I'm setting the flaps at fifteen degrees for takeoff. Slats are down, trim is good, spoilers are stowed. Do we have a clearance yet?"

"Not yet," Donovan said as the follow-me car flashed his lights and pulled way. The departure end of runway one-three right was dead ahead. Donovan knew better than to question anything Michael was doing. Despite a bandaged hand, he was in a zone, and everything was flowing as it should. Donovan trusted Michael with his life—and was about to do it again.

"Engine instruments look good, as do the flight instruments. Altimeters are set, three times. Takeoff data set. Get ready, I'm going to call for takeoff clearance." Michael's hands were flying around the cockpit as he spoke. Satisfied, he picked up the microphone. "Skybridge 770, ready for clearance and takeoff."

"Roger Skybridge," the controller said. "Hold your position."

"Shit! What does that mean?" Montero said, she jumped up from her seat and began looking out each window, searching to see if security was headed their way.

Michael flipped on the radar, the probe heats, and waited on the landing lights.

Donovan saw no reason for the delay. There was no other traffic. "I'm not sitting here all night. If we don't get a clearance soon, I say we go anyway."

"Wait a little longer," Michael said. "It complicates everything if we blow out of here without a clearance."

Donovan flexed his fingers in preparation to push the throttles forward.

"Skybridge 770, Budapest tower, you are cleared to Vilnius as filed. Climb to flight level two-four-zero. Squawk 4721."

Michael blew out a breath as he set the transponder code, dialed in the departure frequency, read back the clearance, and then turned to Donovan. "Let's get the hell out of here."

"Skybridge 770, you are cleared for takeoff one-three right, contact departure airborne, and have a nice night."

Donovan lined up with the centerline of the runway and pushed all three throttles forward. He felt Michael reach out with his left hand and fine tune the engines until they reached take-off power. With no cargo, the 727 lunged forward and picked up speed rapidly.

"V-one," Michael said.

Donovan knew that they weren't stopping. In the event of an engine failure, they'd take the airplane into the sky and deal with the problem there.

"Rotate," Michael called.

Donovan eased back on the controls and the nose wheel lifted free from the pavement, followed moments later by the mains. Donovan made a quick adjustment to level the wings and called for Michael to raise the landing gear.

Michael threw the lever and the wheels retracted smoothly into the fuselage and the airspeed increased. "Pull back on the throttles until I can get the flaps up." Michael said, as he set the flap lever, switched frequencies, and called departure control.

"Budapest control. Skybridge 770 with you climbing to flight level two-four-zero."

"Radar contact, cleared direct LITKU intersection, climb to flight level three-zero-zero."

"Copy, direct LITKU climbing to flight level three-zero-zero."

"Uh, Skybridge 770, Budapest. Confirm you have SIGMET Charlie Six for thunderstorms along your route."

"That's affirmative," Michael said and turned to Donovan. "Give me a minute and I'll find out what SIGMET Charlie Six is all about. Flaps and slats are up. Go as fast as you want."

Donovan nodded and pushed up the throttles. The airspeed needle climbed rapidly to the redline. Donovan felt the slight buffet from the impending overspeed and backed off the throttles enough to hold his speed just at the edge.

"Navigate to this fix," Michael said to Donovan as he engaged the flight management system. "Now, hand me your phone. I need to start entering those coordinates from the jump drive."

Donovan dug it from his pocket and handed it to Michael. Out ahead of them, he saw the first flash of lightning on the horizon, then another. The higher they climbed the more frequent the bursts. As he leveled the Boeing at thirty thousand feet, it looked like the entire northern sky was one continuous wall of lightning. Tendrils of white-hot cloud-to-cloud lightning spiderwebbed across miles of boiling clouds, punctuated by monstrous strokes of cloud-to-ground bursts.

Montero leaned in between them. "I'm sorry about my out-burst earlier. What can I do?"

"Get that phone to work," Michael said. "We need to talk to Calvin. He'll know about the SIGMET."

"What's a SIGMET?" Montero asked.

"It's pilot talk for Significant Meteorological Information, as in the line of severe weather dead ahead." Donovan said. "Oh, and just so you know—earlier, you weren't wrong. Technically, there's *not* a Boeing pilot among us."

CHAPTER TWENTY-SIX

"THAT'S SKYBRIDGE." TREVOR pointed up to the lights of a rapidly climbing aircraft. "They made it off."

"They're airborne," Lauren spoke into her phone.

"That's good," Calvin said. "How are you holding up?"

"Really, we might be a few hours from Armageddon, my daughter is at ground zero, along with most of the other people I care about. What do you think?"

"That's not what I was talking about," Calvin replied. "Though as one of the people at ground zero, I appreciate your concern. I was thinking more along the lines of how you might feel about a side trip to Slovakia? I've talked with the Pentagon, and there are military assets being tasked with getting to the hangar where we spotted the *Phoenix*, but you're our closest operative. I wouldn't ask you to go back into Slovakia if it weren't imperative we get there first."

"What are you asking?" Lauren said.

"If you were to get there soon enough and found the proof we need about an attack on Moscow, perhaps the administration could be convinced to take a different stance on stopping the *Phoenix*."

"The *Phoenix*, if it makes it to Moscow," Lauren asked, "how soon will it arrive?"

"We can only approximate the takeoff time from the single

satellite image we have," Calvin said. "We're estimating an ETA over Moscow in one hour and thirty minutes."

"How long does Donovan have until the *Phoenix* gets to the Russian border?" Lauren asked.

"Forty-eight minutes," Calvin said. "It'll be close, but from what we know about the *Phoenix*, if Donovan flies the Gulfstream flat-out, he should be able to catch up."

"He's not in a Gulfstream," Lauren said. "He and Michael are flying a Boeing 727."

"Back up. I assumed he and Michael were going to give chase in the G-V they chartered. You're telling me they hijacked an airliner?" Calvin asked. "Any idea what their exit strategy might be?"

"I'm sure he's got something in mind," Lauren said. She didn't want to contemplate the fact that there might be no need for an exit strategy. Instead, she factored in everything she'd just heard and considered the tactical implications of getting to the hangar before the Slovakian authorities. "Let's discuss the Slovakian operation. To be honest, I don't think we have the fuel."

"Talk to your group. I'll send you the coordinates. You're less than fifty miles away. In the meantime, can you help me reach Donovan? There's an AWACS aircraft orbiting over Poland, and we need to all link up to establish secure communications throughout this operation."

"He's got a satellite phone. I'll text you the number but I'm sure you'll be hearing from him shortly."

"What was that about?" Marta asked as Lauren finished the call and sent a text message.

"The DIA wants us to fly to the hangar in Slovakia where they spotted the *Phoenix*," Lauren explained. "It's only fifty miles away. The tactical benefits might be significant."

"I get that," Trevor replied. "But if we divert to Slovakia, we don't have enough fuel to fly out of Slovakia. I don't think that's such a great idea, for you, especially."

"What kind of fuel do we need?" Marta asked.

"Jet-A, it's essentially aviation-grade kerosene," Trevor said.

"Lauren, can I borrow the phone?" Marta held out her hand. "Trevor, where are we, exactly?"

"I'm following the M-1 highway to Győr." Trevor held up his map of Hungary. "We're about right here."

"Győr is here." Marta pointed. "How long of a flight is it from our current position?"

"Twelve minutes."

Marta punched a number into the phone from memory and spoke rapidly in Hungarian. Moments later she disconnected the call and handed the phone back to Lauren. "Győr Airport, there's no control tower, only one man on the night shift. Land—and we'll have our fuel."

"Trevor, how long will it take us to fly from Győr Airport to these coordinates? It's the hangar where the *Phoenix* was spotted." Lauren handed him her phone. The screen glowed with Calvin's latitude and longitude message.

"It's only forty miles," Trevor said after he entered the data. "No more than fifteen minutes."

"There's the Győr Airport," Marta said. "My man on the ground told me that there's no one around. He said to land on the grass between the transient aircraft and the airport office."

"Do you own the place or something?" Trevor asked, but Marta remained silent.

Lauren decided she knew the answer to that question. Smuggling was no doubt a part of Marta's business, so it would make sense to control a small airport. "Marta, I don't know what to expect when we get to Slovakia. How are we set on weapons?"

"I thought of that too," Marta said. "Trevor and I are both armed, Michael left his shotgun behind, so we have that. We'll collect some more weapons when we're on the ground."

"All I want to do is be quick about this," Trevor said. "I'm not shutting anything down. It's a quick turn. Be careful, the main rotor will be turning and also keep in mind there's a tail rotor back there you can't see. Grab what you need. As soon as we have fuel, we're out of here."

"I'm assuming you can you handle a gun?" Marta asked Lauren.

"Yes."

Marta raised her right pant leg, removed a small automatic, and handed the weapon to Lauren. "Hopefully you won't need it, but best to be prepared."

Lauren took the weapon, pointed it to the side, and slid back the action to check that there was a round in the chamber. There was. She cupped the gun in one hand and the phone in the other, feeling more in control than she had for days.

"Here we go," Trevor announced as he made a tight turning approach into the wind while feathering off the speed. They touched down softly, and Trevor reduced the turbine engine to idle.

Lauren and Marta made their way out into the warm night air. In the distance an engine growled to life and a set of headlights flashed as a fuel truck gathered speed across the ramp, pulling onto the grass just out of the rotor arc. Marta holstered her weapon when she saw the driver jump from the cab. She spoke to him and then turned away as he reeled out the thick hose. Trevor stepped out of the pilot's seat, stretched, and then hurried to open the fuel door. Moments later, the heavy aroma of kerosene filled the air as the truck began to pump their badly needed fuel.

"We need weapons," Marta yelled to the man fueling the helicopter.

He pointed toward the truck. Mindful of the rotor blades, Lauren followed Marta, who climbed up into the cab and handed down an automatic rifle and extra clips of ammunition. Lauren carried the additional items to the helicopter and secured them in the back row of seats. The pump pushing the fuel wound down, signaling that the helicopter's tank was full. The hose was re-wound onto the reel and after a quick thank you, the truck drove off, and they climbed back aboard the helicopter.

Lauren and Marta now rode up front with Trevor. He spooled up the engine, the rotor accelerated, stabilized, and he pulled the machine into the air and headed north toward Slovakia.

CHAPTER TWENTY-SEVEN

"CALVIN? IT'S MONTERO." She winced as lightning lit up the entire cockpit, the line of thunderstorms seemed to sit directly off the left wing.

Donovan turned to her and held out his hand for the phone. "It's Donovan. We're about to deviate from our original flight plan so we can cross each waypoint looking for this guy. What's our weather situation?"

"Give me your exact position," Calvin said, dispensing with any pleasantries.

"We're ten miles west of waypoint number three."

"The line of weather shouldn't be a factor. The worst of the thunderstorm activity is north of your route, until you approach the border of Belarus, which is where you'll have to break off pursuit, anyway."

"Okay, next issue. We're about to cause some problems with Air Traffic Control, but we can't help that right now. It would be nice to know if we draw the attention of anyone's military."

"We're patched in with an AWACS flight," Calvin announced. "This connection is secure. You're talking with the tactical director—his call sign is Merlin."

"Merlin here, I'm fully briefed on your mission, and we're in a position to extend a watchful eye for as long as it's required."

"Merlin, call us Skybridge 770," Donovan said, relieved at the sound of the calm professional voice coming from the nerve center of the unseen AWACS flight. The venerable Boeing 707 with a massive rotating antenna perched on top of the fuselage, gave it eyes and ears that covered vast segments of the sky. "We're going to throw the rulebook away. Please keep us advised if we're about to have any company."

"We copy, Skybridge 770. With the weather to your north, you've got the sky pretty much to yourself. Closest traffic is forty miles south of your position, and it's all civilian."

"Merlin, I'm going to hand you off to another member of our crew. She'll relay anything we need to know." Donovan handed the phone to Montero. "We've got an AWACS watching over us, call sign Merlin, we're Skybridge 770. I suggest you tighten your seat belt."

Michael had the microphone in his hand, waiting.

Donovan used his thumb and clicked off the autopilot. He could feel the rumble from the three powerful engines behind him. He watched the mileage to the next waypoint counting down toward zero. When they arrived, it would be time. They roared across waypoint three and Donovan banked the Boeing hard to the right, added power, and allowed the nose to climb without losing any speed.

"Slovakia Control," Michael transmitted on cue. "Skybridge 770. Mayday, I repeat, Mayday! We're descending from flight level three-zero-zero."

Donovan pulled off some power, leveled the wings, and dropped the nose. The Boeing gained speed, and Donovan used the throttles to maintain their maximum forward velocity. He knew that each deviation in altitude showed up on the controller's radar screen.

"Skybridge 770, this is Bratislava Control, you are cleared to descend to ten thousand feet, maneuver as needed. Please say the nature of your emergency and your intentions."

Michael turned to Donovan as he slid the microphone into its holder. "I'm going to let him sweat for a little bit. What altitude are you going to level off?"

"Eventually I'll make it twenty-eight thousand feet." Donovan made a hard turn to the right, followed by another steep bank to the left, and then he allowed the 727 to plummet quickly from thirty thousand feet to twenty-six thousand feet before pushing the throttles up and raising the nose in a climb that pinned them all in their seats.

Donovan leveled the Boeing at twenty-eight thousand feet and watched as Michael adjusted the weather radar. Red dominated the entire structure of the angry squall line. The gradients between the yellow and green were sharp and defined. High above him, out the left window, the anvil tops soared above forty-thousand feet. Their new course put them on the flight path from the jump drive, and parallel with the line of advancing storms. They didn't have to worry about the *Phoenix* going any further north. Only someone with a death wish would penetrate that weather.

"Skybridge 770, Bratislava Control, come in, please. Say the nature of your emergency and your intentions."

"I'm going to tell him we're having control problems," Michael said as he reached for the microphone.

"Yeah, and then add that we have smoke in the cockpit," Donovan said as he made another turn, not as abrupt as before, but it would still show up on radar and look like an airplane with problems. "Once they realize how severe our emergency is—make us dark."

"Bratislava, this is Skybridge 770, we're having control problems. We also have smoke in the cockpit. We're going to—"

Michael stowed the microphone and nodded his satisfaction with the deception. To make them dark, he quickly shut off the transponder and then switched off all the outside lights. To the controller it would look like a transponder failure, or a complete loss of electrical power. Skybridge 770 was now only a faint blip on his screen.

Donovan offered Michael the controls, and without losing a single knot of airspeed, Michael continued the erratic turns. Without the transponder, Air Traffic Control had no idea what their altitude was, so they could sit steady at twenty-eight thousand. Donovan held his hand out behind him without looking, like a surgeon requesting an instrument, and Montero slapped the phone in his palm. "Merlin, you still there?"

"Affirmative, Skybridge, nice work. Bratislava seems to have bought your deception; he's going nuts trying to raise you on the radio. I show you on course."

Donovan studied the weather ahead, both on the radar and visually. "I'm thinking we need to offset six miles to the south. This guy might fly his course, but he isn't going to fly any closer to this weather than we are right now. With all of this lightning, I'm thinking if we're sitting to the south, we might actually have a chance to catch sight of his silhouette."

"I copy, good idea. Do you want vectors or can you provide your own offset?"

"Vectors."

"Roger, turn five degrees to the right, we'll call your turn back to the left."

"Michael," Donovan said. "Five right."

Michael nodded and made the turn.

"Calvin, what's the math looking like?" Donovan asked, knowing that the DIA was still on the line.

"We've estimated his speed and time of takeoff against yours. You'll reach the border before he does—which means you'll pass him at some point. There's a window. It's not very big, but you'll have one."

"Merlin, do you show anything on your radar?"

"Negative, Skybridge. As far as our radar is concerned, he's undetectable."

"How long until it's possible that we've passed this guy?" Donovan asked, not caring which of the two brain trusts might venture a guess.

"Somewhere between eight and thirteen minutes," Calvin said.

"I understand." Donovan turned and handed the phone back to Montero. "Eight minutes until we might be in a position to spot the *Phoenix*. Everyone stay sharp."

CHAPTER TWENTY-EIGHT

"I TRUST EVERYONE is ready?" Trevor asked the two women to his right.

Lauren had the pistol tucked into her back pocket. Marta had given her the twelve-gauge shotgun. Sitting nearest the door, Marta held the assault rifle as if it were a natural part of her daily routine. They had no idea what to expect, but Trevor had suggested that during a helicopter assault, it's the helicopter itself that usually gets the enemy all riled up. His suggestion was to drop the two women on the roof since it looked flat in the satellite image, and then keep going as if he were going to land elsewhere. He promised the tactic would draw out the bad guys. If it was too hot, he'd swing around and pick them up for a calculated retreat.

"I see the hangar," Marta said as she unlatched the door.

Lauren's practiced eye took in the structure. The building perfectly matched the image Calvin had sent. Each window was completely dark, as were the surrounding buildings.

Trevor used distant lights as a reference to clear the trees and then pulled into a hover only inches above the roof. Lauren followed Marta and they jumped to the metal surface and ducked as Trevor roared overhead and swung around as if he were about to land. Marta reached the edge first, the rifle at her shoulder. When Lauren joined her, Marta gave her the thumbs-up signal and then went over the side.

Lauren waited until Marta had made her way down a drainpipe onto the lower roof of what they guessed was an attached shop area. Lauren slung the strap of the shotgun over her head and slid down the edge of the roof on her stomach until she had a firm grip on the drain. She reached the next roof and hurried to the edge and repeated the process. A hundred yards away, Trevor was hovering scant feet above the ground ready to draw fire and climb away.

Marta motioned Lauren to follow her to an exterior door. The door was locked and Marta pointed at the lock, then Lauren's gun, and stood back. Lauren took two steps back, leveled the twelve-gauge and pulled the trigger. The gun bucked in her hands and she blinked against the jet of fire that shot from the barrel. There was a round hole where the lock once was.

Marta, without hesitation, kicked the door inward, and they both rushed inside to find themselves in a dark hangar. Marta swept the interior with a flashlight. When the beam touched the twin tails of a black aircraft in the rear of the hangar, she froze and played the light on a partially constructed stealth aircraft.

"We're in the right place," Lauren whispered. "Come on, we need to check out the rest of the hangar."

There were three other rooms, two were machine shops filled with equipment, the third was a small windowless apartment that held a tiny kitchen, bathroom, and twin bed. Lauren guessed she was looking at Daniel's prison cell.

"All clear." Marta found a light switch and a single row of lights above them illuminated, casting a dim glow. "You start looking around. I'm thinking we don't have much time. I'm going to go stand guard by the door. If anyone shows up, I'll start shooting and draw them away from here toward the west. If that happens, you make your way to the roof where Trevor can find you. Then come find me."

Lauren already had her phone out and began taking pictures of the partially complete aircraft. She ran her finger along the black radar-absorbing coating and found it was slightly rough to the touch. Each imperfection would not only absorb radar impulses, but reflect the energy in a different direction, dissipating the signal. Lauren swung the strap of the shotgun free from her neck and then set the weapon aside so she could hoist herself up to get a look into the cockpit. She was shocked to find an ejection seat. She shot more pictures and then backed away to examine the tail. The engine was installed but exposed. The twin tails reached well above her head. She took a burst of photos and then went around to the back of the plane. She raised the camera and then stopped and cocked her head. Something seemed different. Perhaps it was all the open access panels, but this airplane looked different from Daniel's designs all those years ago at MIT.

Lauren ducked and turned at the bark of gunfire. It sounded close. She snatched the shotgun, raced to the wall, and flipped the switch to plunge the hangar into darkness. Crouching, she waited as her eyes adjusted. She pocketed her phone and swung her weapon into position and listened. Outside, she heard the helicopter lift off and fly away, her signal to try to make it back to the roof. Lauren was contemplating her next move when a door on the other side of the hangar opened, and the hangar lights snapped back on. Before she could hide, someone spotted her and yelled.

Lauren ran. She sprinted deeper into the work area, past the second airplane, and slid to a stop behind a large steel toolbox on wheels. She leaned against the metal and flinched as shots were fired, echoing loudly. She felt slugs impact the toolbox and went down on her stomach. When she looked around the edge, she saw a man approaching cautiously. He wasn't wearing a uniform, but his movements seemed professional and practiced. She brought her shotgun around to fire, but the man darted to the side just as Lauren pulled the trigger. From behind a crate he popped up and fired three times, the bullets ripping into the containers that sat on top of the toolbox. When they fell on Lauren, her shotgun clattered to the floor, and several cans scattered and rolled away.

Lauren's calf felt wet and sticky. A thick reddish liquid saturated her leg as it spread out in a pool on the concrete floor. For an instant she thought she'd been shot, then three feet away, she saw a can of hydraulic fluid roll to a stop, a bullet hole in its side. Lauren left the shotgun lying on the floor and reached into her pocket. She stayed low and let out a groan to mask the sound of the hammer click from the pistol Marta had provided. Lauren held her breath, as footfalls told her the man was rushing toward her. The instant he stepped around the toolbox, she fired until he dropped to the floor. The astonished expression was still etched on his face as he collapsed.

Lauren jumped up, grabbed her shotgun, and sprinted across the hangar to a metal ladder bolted to the cinder-block wall. It led to a hatch on the roof. In one smooth motion she aimed the shotgun at the light switch and blew it apart, plunging the hangar into darkness. With yellow-orange spots still dancing in her eyes, she felt the coolness of the metal ladder and started climbing. The ceiling was easily twenty feet high and the hydraulic fluid smeared on her feet made the rungs slippery. Her hand finally touched the ceiling and when she felt for the latch on the door, she also found a small padlock she hadn't noticed from below. She yanked on it twice, hoping for a fail, but it held tight.

Below her, the door swung open, and from the faint light outside, Lauren could make out two men, both carrying weapons. When they couldn't find the light switch, they called out several times for someone named Tomas. Lauren assumed it was the name of the man she'd shot, and in the darkened hangar they received no response. After several long moments, the two men closed the door and left.

Lauren stood on the ladder and considered her dwindling options. If she made too much noise, the men would return, if she went back down to the hangar floor she could no doubt find something to pry apart the lock, but then she'd have to make the climb back to the roof. She heard the sound of the helicopter getting closer and stopped to listen. Lauren made up her mind. She looped her left arm through a rung in the ladder and aimed the shotgun up into the darkness and fired.

The flash of light from the muzzle blast told her she'd missed. She jacked in another shell and the spent casing fell away. Outside, she could tell that the helicopter was coming in fast. Keeping the location of the lock fixed in her mind, Lauren used the side rail of the ladder to align her next shot. She squeezed the trigger, trying not to jerk; the gun fired and the lock fragmented and rained down on her. She climbed as fast as she could and slammed the heel of her hand into the metal hatch. It was heavy and the rusty hinges screeched as they moved. Lauren climbed up one more rung and pushed, leaned into the hatch, and pressed with her shoulder. She inched it to vertical. The helicopter now sounded as if it were almost on top of her. With one more lunge the hatch swung all the way open and crashed to the roof.

A spark erupted from the ladder and fragments stung her hand. Lauren realized that someone had shot at her from below. She tumbled out the hatch, spun around, pumped a new shell into the chamber, and using just her arms, aimed the shotgun down the ladder and fired.

Muzzle flashes from the ground caused Lauren to duck and sprint to the center of the roof. The noise from the helicopter faded as Trevor was forced to come around for another pass. Lauren searched the dark sky and couldn't spot the helicopter even though the shock waves from the rotor blades reverberated in her chest. Sound of more gunfire rose above the noise of the rotor. Lauren knew she didn't have much time. She reached for her phone and quickly found one of the pictures she'd just taken as an instant of clarity struck her, a detail from a time long ago. Daniel's dying words echoed in her memory. He told her he'd changed—different from before, but he wasn't talking about himself. Daniel had changed the *Phoenix*. She pushed several buttons and half a world away, Calvin Reynolds had an email. She called his number, and he answered before the second ring.

"Lauren, where are you?" Calvin asked.

"I'm at the hangar. Calvin, there's another *Phoenix* in the hangar, about ninety percent complete. I sent you a photograph and I found something. A flaw!" Lauren heard Trevor growing closer and she felt a downpour of rotor wash. She crouched and lowered her head to try to insulate the phone from the roaring sounds coming down around her. "Daniel changed it! The jet exhaust is close to the tail. From above and behind there's a heat signature— there has to be!"

Muzzle flashes from the ground drove Lauren to lie flat on the roof. Trevor never wavered. He came in low, and Lauren understood he wasn't stopping.

"What's happening?" Calvin shouted.

Lauren yelled into the phone, "Did you hear what I said about the infrared? Use it!"

"Lauren!" Calvin shouted into the phone as Lauren jammed it in her pocket.

Lauren brought herself up into a crouch. The left skid of the helicopter was almost within reach. As the helicopter roared overhead, she jumped and clutched the skid with both hands. She was about to pull herself up so she could swing her leg around the cold metal when she was hit from underneath, lost her grip, and fell back to the roof of the hangar, hitting hard on her left side. All the air rushed from her lungs. She gasped for breath, struggling to get to her feet. More shots were fired from behind her, and Lauren turned. In the dim light she saw a soldier standing over her, holding a pistol, aiming it up at Trevor and Marta. Lauren drove her heel in the soldier's kneecap, toppling him off balance as the bullets from his weapon flew wide.

Crouching in the open door of the helicopter, Marta let loose a burst from her machine gun and the soldier went down, collapsing face first to the roof.

Lauren tried to push herself up using her left arm and found it couldn't support her weight. Pain ripped in waves from her wrist, up her arm, into her shoulder. Another more focused throbbing seemed to radiate from her left thigh. Trevor began to ease lower to the roof, as if he were going to land so Marta could get out and help her into the chopper.

A withering burst of automatic weapons fire raked the cockpit, bullet holes puncturing the metal, forcing Marta to dive away from the open door. Lauren watched with growing disappointment as Trevor, with no other choice, climbed and peeled away in self-defense. The sound of the rotor blades quickly retreated in the night sky. Lauren needed to get up and start moving, find a way to escape.

She made it onto her knees, protecting what felt like a broken left arm.

Turning to get her bearings, she heard the footsteps behind her. Before she could react, she was kicked back to the ground and then rolled over on her back. When she saw the face with the white bandage, her hopes dissolved into the night.

Aleksander roughly frisked her, finding her weapons as well as her phone. He studied the phone and understood that there was a call in progress. He brought it to his ear. "Who is this?"

Lauren couldn't hear what was being said and had no way to know if Calvin was still there. Her last hope was that he was listening.

"Well, Calvin," Aleksander said, the triumph in his voice evident. "Understand that Lauren McKenna's death is on you."

CHAPTER TWENTY-NINE

"Merlin says Russian fighters just lifted off from Baranovichi Air Force base in Belarus," Montero said as she leaned forward from the flight engineer's panel. "ETA is twelve minutes."

Lightning exploded from below them and hundreds of tendrils climbed up into the thunderstorm before winking out, followed by more multiple bursts. Donovan never looked away, squinting from the brightness and scanning the sky for the *Phoenix*. With each new burst, he strained to spot the small jet. "Ask them how much longer we have before we reach the border?"

"Six minutes," Montero relayed.

"We're running out of time," Michael said.

"Is there any chance we passed him already?" Donovan asked, knowing the answer was yes. "When we get to the border, I want to circle and wait . . . just in case."

"What!" Montero said into the phone then leaned forward. "Merlin says we have traffic at eleven o'clock, six miles. It's the *Phoenix*, he's level at fifteen thousand feet."

"How is that even possible?" Michael looked from Montero to Donovan, then back out the forward windshield.

Donovan held his hand out for the phone, then pressed it to his ear. "Merlin, confirm you have the *Phoenix* on radar?"

"Donovan, it's Calvin, we have a faint infrared signature. Lauren found him, it's confirmed—we have the *Phoenix*. Be advised, the satellite needs to be above and behind the *Phoenix* for the IR signature to register. If *Phoenix* turns broadside, due to the tail configuration, we'll lose contact."

"Is there any NATO fighter that can reach the *Phoenix* in time?" Donovan asked.

"Not this close to the border," Merlin said.

Donovan handed the phone back to Montero then turned to Michael. "Calvin's got him. He's giving off an infrared signature."

"Where is he now?" Michael asked.

"Right in front of us. He's at fifteen thousand feet." Donovan pulled all three throttles back to idle, extended the speed brakes, then banked the Boeing 727 steeply and let the nose drop far below the horizon while keeping the airspeed pegged just below redline.

"Montero," Donovan said over his shoulder. "Tell Calvin we're going to need constant distance and altitude information to the *Phoenix*."

"He's at eleven o'clock, five miles, still at fifteen thousand feet," Montero reported. "We're one hundred and fifty knots faster."

"I want to know what kind of terrain is below us," Donovan said. "How much room do we have to play with?"

"Merlin says stay above two thousand feet, and we won't hit anything. *Phoenix* is still at eleven o'clock, four miles," Montero replied. "We're five minutes from the border."

Donovan did the math. He needed to lose fifteen thousand feet in two minutes. It was going to be close. "Michael, put the landing gear down!"

"We'll lose the doors!" Michael said as he reached for the lever and pulled it down.

The sound of the wind shrieked as the massive landing gear was forced out into the three-hundred-and-twenty knot slipstream.

Donovan knew, just as Michael did, that as fast as they were fly-ing, the gear doors had instantly ripped away, but the massive gear and struts were still locked into place. The sudden drag made it feel like the bottom had dropped out from underneath them.

"He's eleven o'clock, two and a half miles," Montero yelled above the noise.

Donovan made a turn, first to the left, then to the right, as he continued to lose altitude. They blew through some clear air tur-bulence at twenty-two thousand feet that shook the plane vio-lently. Donovan focused on the artificial horizon located in the center of his primary instrument cluster. Wings level, they flew into smooth air once again, and he and Michael desperately tried to spot the *Phoenix* out in front of them.

"Eleven o'clock and two miles." Montero said. "He's ten o'clock and a mile and a half."

A great explosion of lightning illuminated the entire thunder-storm cell off to their left. Donovan winced and moved his head to the side at the sheer magnitude of the energy released.

"I saw him!" Michael yelled. "Level off, we need to come in from above."

Donovan immediately stowed the spoilers, added power, and leveled the Boeing. "Where is he?"

"I lost him. He was ten o'clock and a mile. All I caught was a momentary sight of the aircraft's silhouette," Michael said. "It's him, I promise. Hold this heading."

As Donovan scanned the dark sky, waiting, until it was once again lit up by a rippled burst of lightning. Less than half a mile off the nose and slightly below them, Donovan spotted the *Phoenix*. He pushed the nose down until the small jet was centered in his windshield and threw the throttles forward.

"The main gear strut and tires hang down six feet. No more

than that, all it'll take is a kiss," Michael said calmly. "Whatever you do, don't clip him with our wing or we're all going down."

The dying lightning kept the *Phoenix* illuminated as Donovan held the 727 in a steep dive. All he needed to do was touch any part of the small composite *Phoenix* with the heavy-duty strut of the Boeing's main gear, and the smaller airplane would fold up and disintegrate. Donovan clenched his teeth and added more power, ignoring the unnerving sensation of intentionally closing on another airplane at one hundred and fifty knots. The *Phoenix* nearly filled the entire windshield. The last of the lightning ebbed and there was only blackness as Donovan gripped the controls and waited for impact.

An instant later, another flash of lightning told Donovan the entire story. The *Phoenix* was below him, diving and beginning a tight turn—fully intact. Donovan yanked the throttles all the way to idle and banked as hard as he dared in an effort to give chase. He could feel his arms grow heavy in the two-g turn. He twisted his neck to try and find the small black airplane, praying for another bolt of lightning.

"Calvin says they've lost him!" Montero yelled, her voice shaking.

"Come on," Donovan said to anyone who might be listening. A series of cloud-to-cloud bursts lit up the northern sky, but neither Donovan nor Michael could locate the *Phoenix*. "Damn it!"

Montero called out. "They've reacquired him! He's back on his original course, down at three thousand feet. He's twelve o'clock, two and a half miles. We're two minutes from the border."

Donovan pushed all three throttles to the stops and pointed the nose down. He knew he wouldn't get another shot. The airframe began to buffet, but he ignored the dangerous message and continued the dive. Lightning ripped overhead. In front of them, a massive cloud-to-ground stroke of lightning arced downward and lit up the entire sky. The *Phoenix* was straight ahead. Donovan didn't dare blink. He held the vibrating controls, making dozens of tiny corrections to try to hold the Boeing steady while screaming down at over three hundred knots.

"He's turning," Michael called out. "And he's headed down."

"He knows we're here, but he can only spot us when there's lightning," Donovan said as he urged the 727 to close the gap. "He doesn't know we can find him in the dark."

"Calvin says he turned south, and then they lost him, but they're plotting his arc," Montero called out. "Turn fifteen degrees left, there should be a small town out there."

Donovan banked hard. The ground was coming up fast, and he felt the dryness of his mouth as he focused on the glow from the village. In an instant, he saw the *Phoenix* create an eclipse, its silhouette revealing both its course and altitude. Donovan kept the Boeing in the turn, picturing the *Phoenix* in his mind as he turned and descended to intercept.

"AWACS says we're less than a thousand feet above the ground!" Montero cried out.

Donovan had hoped for one more burst of lightning to show him the way, but the sky remained frustratingly dark. "Michael, turn on all the landing lights!"

Twin beams of intense light erupted from the wings and expanded outward, illuminating the *Phoenix*. The Boeing was close enough that Donovan saw the pilot snap his head around as the 727 overtook the small jet.

Donovan watched in frustration as the pilot of the *Phoenix* climbed away and snapped the nimble jet to the side. Without hesitation, he pulled the throttles to idle and cranked the Boeing in a punishing turn to stay behind the *Phoenix*.

"Kill the lights!" Donovan ordered as lightning rippled from the base of the storm in front of them.

Michael once again made them black—and waited.

Pressed in his seat by the g-forces, Donovan craned his head forward to try to spot the *Phoenix* in the turn. The lightning wasn't as blinding as it discharged deep within the cloud. The subdued orange background was perfect, and seconds later, Donovan spotted the *Phoenix*.

"I've got him in sight," Michael said. "Do you?"

"Yes," Donovan kept the Boeing in the turn; the 727 was accelerating quickly. "Get ready with the lights."

The *Phoenix* had leveled its wings. Donovan, in the blacked-out 727, going a hundred knots faster, thundered toward the *Phoenix* from behind. There was no way the pilot of the other plane could see what was coming. "Lights!"

The landing lights lit up a cone of the sky in front of the Boeing, and in the middle was the small elusive black jet. Donovan held the controls tightly and didn't flinch. An instant later they all felt the impact of the *Phoenix* as it resonated through the entire 727. On the instrument panel—the right main landing gear safe light winked from green to red.

CHAPTER THIRTY

"Calvin says he's down!" Montero called out. "The *Phoenix* broke up in flight and the debris landed in Poland."

Donovan slowly eased the 727 out of the dive, thankful that the controls still felt firm in his hands. A bright flash of lightning just off his left told him the leading edge of the cold front was almost on top of them.

"Merlin says we've crossed the border into Belarus airspace," Montero yelled above the noise of the slipstream. "We need to turn back. Fighters are four minutes out."

"Can we get back in time?" Michael asked, the urgency in his voice undisguised.

Donovan had no illusions about the Russians' intentions. Without hesitation, he threw the Boeing into a steep left turn and slammed the throttles to the stops. Against every ounce of training against retracting damaged landing gear, Donovan turned to Michael and called. "Gear up!"

Michael never hesitated as he took the gear lever in his hand and pulled it upward. "Montero, tell them we need a heading for the closest border!"

Donovan felt the Boeing surge forward as the landing gear tucked into the wings. He began converting their energy into a climb.

"The fighters are now in missile range," Montero relayed. "The closest border is on a heading of three-zero-five degrees, but it takes us into the worst of the thunderstorms."

"This is going to get rough!" Donovan kept his turn until they were headed three-zero-five. The 727 was climbing and accelerating straight at the wall of weather.

"We don't have any idea if making contact with the *Phoenix* caused any structural damage," Michael said as he pulled hard on the straps of his harness. "Rough air penetration speed is two hundred and seventy knots."

"I do know one thing," Donovan said as he glanced down at the airspeed indicator, which read three hundred knots. "Russian missiles most definitely cause structural damage."

"Ignition and the anti-ice are on," Michael said, his hand on the altitude alerter. "What altitude are we climbing to?"

"Lauren told me something once and I believe her. We're going up to twenty-eight thousand feet," Donovan shouted as the first blast of heavy rain pelted the windshield and serious turbulence rocked the Boeing. Donovan grimaced as he pulled the throttles back to avoid an overspeed. A moment later they were pressed in their seats as the 727 was forced upward in a massive updraft. Donovan's control inputs did nothing as the Boeing flew upward, helpless in the violent thunderstorm. Lightning crackled in the air around them, and in a rare occurrence, the thunder could be heard above the beating of the rain and the three-hundred-knot slipstream. The altimeter spun wildly up through fifteen thousand feet.

"We'll never get above this thing!" Michael shouted as he put one hand on the glare shield to brace himself. "Lauren knows better than most that the worst turbulence is going to be at the freezing level. This is only going to get worse the higher we climb!"

"That's what I'm counting on!" Donovan replied. "They'd be crazy to follow us!"

"They don't have to," Michael replied. "Only the missiles do."

Another burst of lightning bombarded the cockpit like a strobe light, freezing everything in the moment. Donovan saw the strain as well as the determination on Michael's face, and the distress on Montero's. The next bolt of lightning struck the Boeing on the nose and millions of volts coursed harmlessly through the aluminum tube and exited the airframe somewhere behind them in a huge flash.

The staccato pounding from the turbulence rocked the 727. Behind him in the night sky, Donovan knew the massive wings were flexing wildly from the thunderstorm's punishment. The noise from the slipstream rose and fell in the maelstrom. The rain decreased, and then a different roar drowned out everything else. Donovan sat helpless as hail pounded the glass and aluminum. The radar was worthless. All it painted was solid red echoes. Lightning lit up the sky around them. Donovan saw the cracks in the glass of his windshield. He hoped it would hold.

"I've lost them," Montero shouted. "The phone went dead."

Donovan understood that the storm would interrupt the satellite signal. The connection didn't really matter, as there was nothing anyone could do to help them now. They were through twenty-six thousand feet and the hail stopped as abruptly as it began. The turbulence worsened, and Donovan could only maintain their altitude plus or minus a thousand feet. The lightning seemed to fill the air around them. Donovan couldn't remember a thunderstorm as bad as this. Every muscle in his body was wire taut as he willed the Boeing to stay together and reach the calm air on the other side.

"How bad could a few missiles have been?" Michael quipped as another round of severe turbulence tossed the 727 around the sky.

"It can't be much further to the backside of this thing," Donovan replied, "Right?"

"I hope not," Michael said. "Look, I can see lights, dead ahead."

Donovan saw them as well, and even though the thunderstorms had allowed them a glimpse out the backside of the front, it wasn't done with them yet. The next onslaught of turbulence caused Donovan to wince. It sounded like a sledgehammer was pounding the skin of the plane; the instrument panel was shaking so violently it was almost impossible to read. Two more rapid explosions of lightning lit the entire sky. Donovan's eyes swam with pinpricks of brightness, and he blinked furiously to clear them. With one more intense onslaught of turbulence, the Boeing seemed to float upward as if weightless, then plummeted with such force that the final jolt threw Donovan's chin down into his chest and he bit the side of his cheek. The metallic taste of his own blood filled his mouth as the 727 burst from the clouds and sailed into the clear night air.

Donovan took a finger and gently probed his cheek, it came away stained red.

"I told you thunderstorms could hurt you," Michael said as he spotted the blood.

"No shit," Donovan loosened his harness. "My windshield's cracked, how's yours?"

"About like yours. It's not too bad."

"Guys," Montero leaned forward. "I just reconnected with Merlin. He says they detected three missiles launched by the Russian fighters."

Michael shot Donovan a surprised look.

"As fast as they were coming, I didn't think they were kidding," Donovan said.

"Did you know?" Montero asked. "Lightning, hail, and missiles? Did Lauren tell you that would work?"

"It's all we had," Donovan said. "Lauren and I had a conversation once about thunderstorm activity, the freezing level, lightning and hail versus heat-seeking missiles. I had my doubts, but it seems she was right."

"First of all, she's a genius, a weather guru. Secondly, she's your wife. She's always right," Michael said. "Automatically, every time, it's a rule, even when she's wrong. Ask anyone. Though I'm glad she was right this time."

Donovan knew the moment had served its purpose, Michael's rant had momentarily lifted the stress, but they had problems. "Michael, are those the lights of Warsaw?"

"Probably, let me find a chart."

"Merlin, hang on," Montero said. "Calvin, say that last part again."

Montero's tone troubled Donovan enough for him to turn and look at her.

"Calvin, I'm handing the phone to Donovan. You need to explain to him what you just told me." Montero placed the phone into Donovan's outstretched palm.

"Calvin, what's going on?" Donovan said as he turned over the controls of the Boeing to Michael.

"We've lost contact with Lauren, the helicopter—everyone," Calvin said. "Can you try to reach them?"

"Shouldn't she be in Austria by now? Where was she the last time you spoke to her?"

"She was at the hangar in Slovakia where we spotted the *Phoenix*. She found a second stealth under construction, which is how she figured out it was vulnerable to infrared detection."

"You lost contact with her in Slovakia?" Donovan could barely contain his disbelief.

"She volunteered. They were only thirty miles—"

"Calvin, how soon can assets go in to rescue her?" Donovan

did his best to rein in his growing fury. "Don't bullshit me, I want reality, not estimations."

"SEAL Team Two is being scrambled as we speak. Someone in Washington finally woke up, and solutions are being explored. "

"Ask him for Lauren's coordinates," Michael said, his fingers poised above the flight management system.

Calvin rattled them off, and Donovan repeated them and watched intently as Michael began punching the buttons on the flight management system.

"At best speed, she's forty-five minutes away," Michael reported.

"What are you three thinking about doing?" Calvin asked.

"Calvin, hang on for a second," Donovan said. "Merlin, can we get to, say, Bratislava, Slovakia, without getting shot down?"

"I can keep the Polish Air Force from attacking, but when it comes to Slovakia, no, you wouldn't get very far with a straight-up border incursion. Mayday or not, you're starting to be classified as a terrorist who hijacked an airliner."

Donovan glanced over at Michael, who ran a finger across his throat to signal Donovan to put Calvin and Merlin on hold. Donovan put his palm over the phone so they could talk privately.

"The Carpathian Mountains," Michael said. "They're between us and Lauren."

Donovan hesitated for a moment as he processed what Michael was telling him, and then an understanding smile crept onto his face.

"I'm just saying," Michael said, "mountains are a great place to hide."

"At night?" Montero asked, as she connected the dots of the conversation.

"Do we have the fuel?" Donovan asked.

Michael loosened his straps and twisted in his seat until he could see the fuel quantity on the flight engineer's panel. "Going fast, down low—it'll be close."

"What do we do when we get to this hangar?" Montero asked.

"It's an airport, which means there's a runway," Donovan said. "Chances are we have the element of surprise."

"Exactly," Michael said as he cinched himself back into his seat. "Who expects help to arrive in the form of a crashing 727?"

"Crashing?" Montero leaned in between them. "Who's crashing?"

"We are," Donovan said. "More like an emergency landing, since we probably won't be able to put the gear down."

"Oh," Montero's expression never changed.

"All we need are some eyes," Donovan looked at the phone then back to Michael and Montero. "Are we all good with this? It ends with us on the ground in Slovakia."

"Polish jail, Slovakian jail." Michael shrugged. "How much difference can there really be?"

"If we get caught with Lauren, there could be a great deal of difference," Montero added. "She's wanted for murder and espionage."

"We're terrorists," Donovan said. "I'd say the general task at hand here, is to not get caught. Can we do that?"

"Is there any way you can talk to Merlin using one of the radios?" Montero asked. "That way, I can use the secure phone."

"Are you going to call Marta?" Donovan asked.

"We need to talk to her, or Kristof, tell them we're coming," Montero said. "They're our best chance of getting out of Slovakia."

"Okay, this thing is happening," Donovan said, thinking how to get everything he wanted, and then brought the phone up to his ear. "Calvin, with the infrared satellite, do you have a useful horizon for the Carpathian Mountains?"

"We're checking. What do you have in mind?" Calvin asked.

"Merlin," Donovan directed his next question at the AWACS crew. "Is there a way for us to communicate with each other via radio? We need to free up this phone."

"We can establish a VHF link on one thirty-seven point seven-five. Though it won't be secure."

"It might not need to be," Donovan said, feeling the beginnings of the rush that formed when a plan was coming together in his head. "Merlin, our plan is to fly directly to Pegasus. Can you help us thread our way through the Carpathian Mountains low enough to avoid detection by the Slovakian air force?"

"Theoretically, it might be done," Calvin said. "We'd need to calculate the optimum routes using different variables, and run some simulations based on known geographic overlays."

"Calvin, we don't have time. This needs to happen now. Merlin?" Donovan let his question float out into space.

"We've got the latest software updates that allow us to pull up existing topography and interface it with our primary radar," Merlin replied. "We can vector you through the mountains. Our capabilities combined with space-based assets should allow you to fly into Slovakia under their radar. Give me an entry point."

"Start calculating, we'll use Krakow, Poland, as our initial starting point."

"I understand," Merlin said. "Krakow. And your exit point?"

"My suggestion is Galánta, Slovakia," Calvin replied. "It's close to where we think she's being held. We'll need to be careful to avoid the Slovakian Air Force base at Badín."

"Calvin, how long is the runway where they're holding Lauren?" Donovan asked.

"It's just over five thousand feet. Is that long enough?"

"It will be tonight," said Donovan.

"If we're going to sell this," Merlin said. "I need a diversion, a big one. Right now you're a hijacked 727, and radar installations from the entire region are tracking your position, plus I think half of those sites are reporting directly to CNN. We need to focus all those watchful eyes on one point. Skybridge 770 needs to crash."

"Is there a sparsely populated area between here and Krakow?" Donovan asked.

"Affirmative," Merlin replied. "Fifty miles dead ahead, outside the small town of Kielce, sits a ten-square-mile forested area that would be perfect. The terrain in that area is roughly eight hundred feet above sea level. I'm thinking some more of those erratic turns, a final Mayday followed by a big dramatic descent afterward. I'll pass along some breaking news for CNN to wet themselves over."

"Perfect." Donovan allowed himself a small smile at the beauty of Merlin's plan.

"Use your Skybridge 770 call sign on the emergency frequency, one twenty-one point five, and then once you're down low and level, your new call sign is Dragon one-one. It's a legitimate military handle we'll borrow from a unit in England who flies F15s. They're quiet tonight, but all of the prying ears are used to hearing them airborne."

"I understand," Donovan said. "No wonder they call you Merlin."

"Tell me that again after all this works," Merlin said calmly. "Your primary VHF is one thirty-one point seven five, backup is one twenty-eight point two-five. Fly heading two-four-zero for Krakow; you're free to descend at your discretion.

Donovan read back the frequencies, and as he did, Michael dialed each one of them into the radios. "Merlin, we're switching to VHF. Calvin, whatever you do, don't lose her." Donovan hung up the phone and handed it to Montero.

"I take it there's a plan?" Montero asked as she took the phone.

"We're going to send out a final distress call as Skybridge 770 and then plummet to our deaths," Donovan explained. "Michael, once we've accomplished that little task, our new call sign is going to be Dragon one-one. Merlin will vector us as if we're a military flight while reporting that Skybridge 770 has crashed."

"I like it." Michael nodded. "When do we start?"

Donovan looked out the cracked windshield at what lay ahead of them. The plains of Poland were scattered with the lights of farms and towns. From thousands of hours of being aloft, he easily spotted the darkened area forty miles in front of them. "Michael, one o'clock, forty miles, that dark spot is lightly populated forest. Merlin says the ground is eight hundred feet above sea level. If there was ever a time and a place to give Air Traffic Control some theatre, this would be that time."

Michael picked up the microphone and double checked the frequencies.

On the horizon was the glow from Krakow, and beyond, where the lights ended, was the beginning of the eight-thousand-foot tall Carpathian Mountains. Donovan saw the flashes of lightning that marked the trailing edge of the distant squall line.

"I'm ready when you are," Michael said.

Donovan took the controls from Michael and they both shared a knowing glance. Then Donovan pulled the nose up sharply, pinning them all into their seats. As they soared upward, he banked the 727 hard to the left, and then just as quickly, made another urgent turn in the opposite direction. He eased back the throttles and allowed the nose to fall well below the horizon until they were pointed steeply downward. Then he pulled the lever to deploy the speed brakes. Panels flew open from the wings and created a massive amount of drag. The entire 727 shook and vibrated as Donovan made another abrupt turn as the altimeter unwound.

The lights on the ground seemed to tilt and fill the windshield, as Donovan pointed the wildly oscillating Boeing toward the dark forest below.

"Skybridge 770," Michael transmitted, his voice a convincing blend of professionalism and stark terror. "We've lost control, we're—going down. I repeat. Mayday, we're—"

CHAPTER THIRTY-ONE

ALEKSANDER ENDED THE call, opened the back of the case, pulled out the battery, and tossed it aside. Then he leaned down to Lauren. "How did you find this place?"

"Daniel told me," Lauren said.

"That's a lie. Daniel never knew where he was being held."

"He described it perfectly," Lauren said, though she knew she was making everything up as she went. If Aleksander knew that the *Phoenix* was being hunted through a design flaw that she was aware of, he could potentially abort the mission and the *Phoenix* could vanish.

"Dr. McKenna, you had your chance to tell me where Daniel is hiding." Aleksander slipped his hand under her right arm and pulled her to her feet. "It's time to do this the hard way."

Lauren grimaced in pain as she was propelled into the hangar. She did her best to support her broken arm. Once in the light she could see her thigh. It looked like she'd been grazed by a bullet, but, while bloody, her leg still functioned. Aleksander finally released her and pushed her heavily into a chair. He secured her right wrist to the arm of the chair with a tie-wrap and then called for one of his men. There was a quick conversation and she heard the name Tomas, the name of the man she'd killed. She steeled herself for payback.

Aleksander drew a pistol from under his jacket and jammed

the barrel up under Lauren's chin and pushed until her head was tilted upward and their eyes met. "I've just learned that you've killed another of my men."

"I killed no one," Lauren lied.

Aleksander held the pressure with his gun hand, then reached with the other and wrapped it around her left wrist, just below the broken bone, and twisted.

Lauren thrashed against the pain. He blocked her kicks, and all she could do was throw her head from side to side in an attempt to shake loose from the barrel of Alexander's pistol. A scream formed, and as it echoed through the hangar, she barely recognized it as her own. An instant later, the twisting stopped.

"Imagine hours of that." Aleksander used his gun to bring Lauren's eyes back to his. "I don't enjoy hurting people, though I have one man who relishes inflicting pain. Tomas, the man you killed, was his friend. I can always turn you over to him."

Lauren could feel the tears from her pain run down her face. She glared at Aleksander, refusing to blink or to show fear of any kind. Behind him, she saw the wings of the second *Phoenix* being removed, and the fuselage wheeled into the back of a truck. Aleksander was moving the aircraft.

Aleksander slapped her hard across the face. "You will give me your full attention when I'm speaking to you! Who were you talking with on the phone? Who is Calvin, and what does he know?"

Lauren could taste the blood in her mouth as she saw his eyes turn into hate-filled slits. "He's my handler in Vienna and he knows nothing. I was trying to send him a report when you found me."

"Where did the helicopter go?" Aleksander pushed the gun barrel harder into Lauren's flesh. "How many people were with you?"

"I don't know what the pilot's orders were in the event of a retreat," Lauren said, as she latched on to her theory that as long as she could keep feeding Aleksander tantalizing bits of intelligence, he might keep her alive. "I'm not a spy. The only reason I'm here is that Daniel requested me. We used to be friends a long time ago."

"That's the first element of truth you've spoken since we met," Aleksander said. "What is your specialty?"

"Earth Science, Meteorology." Lauren answered truthfully as a man yelled from across the hangar.

Aleksander yelled over his shoulder in return, speaking rapid Ukrainian, and then turned to face Lauren. "You and I have a history of interrupted conversations. Think long and hard about how much pain you're willing to endure for Daniel Pope. I promise we're going to have a prolonged chat very soon, one that I can assure will be very difficult for you."

Two men arrived and dragged her out of the chair into a small office, where she was forced to sit, tied to a different chair. One man opened a first aid kit, ripped open her pant leg and sloppily applied antiseptic and hurriedly wrapped the wound. They did nothing about her arm and quickly left the room. Through a dirty window, Lauren listened for sirens, beating helicopter blades, anything that would tell her that help was coming. She heard the rumble of approaching thunder, mixed with brilliant flashes of lightning that lit up the cracks around the covered window. The line of thunderstorms was almost on them and her hopes began to sink. The heavy weather would slow any rescue attempt, as well as help mask the fact that Aleksander and his men were moving. A raid, if it came, might very well find an empty hangar.

CHAPTER THIRTY-TWO

DONOVAN JUDGED THE pullout as close to the ground as possible. Michael turned on all the Boeing's lights to give any eyewitnesses on the ground something to report. At fifteen hundred feet, Donovan eased the nose of the 727 up until it was level, at the same time he stowed the speed brakes and pushed the three throttles forward until they were screaming across the ground as fast as the Boeing could go. He dropped down until the high-intensity landing lights illuminated the tops of the trees blowing past five hundred feet below them.

Michael, microphone in his good hand, killed the external lights with his thumb, making the Boeing invisible again in the night sky. Anyone watching would have seen them abruptly vanish, which was the impression he wanted to send. He switched away from the emergency frequency. Relief from the voice of the Polish air traffic controller, whose frantic calls had grown in urgency until he'd finally announced that he'd lost radar contact, was a blessing. "Merlin, this is Dragon one-one, how do you read?"

"Roger Dragon one-one, this is Merlin, I read you five by five, radar contact, turn right to a heading of two-four-five degrees. Say your altitude."

"Dragon one-one, copy two-four-five degrees, we're level at one thousand five hundred feet," Michael replied, knowing full well that Merlin knew what their altitude was down to the foot.

"I just tried Marta and Trevor and got no answer," Montero said. "Is there another number I can try?"

"Try Calvin, they might reach out to him," Donovan said. "If not, try Marta again."

"We need to save battery power on the phone, it's getting low."

Donovan focused on hand flying the Boeing at two hundred eighty knots, five hundred feet above the unseen terrain. Occasional lights on the ground gave him some perspective as to how low and fast they were flying. The Boeing was also loud. The three older-generation jet engines produced a massive amount of noise, and Donovan imagined that people for miles along their path were awakened as they roared past in the darkness.

"What's our estimated time of arrival at Lauren's position?" Montero asked.

"Roughly thirty minutes," Donovan said, glancing down at the information displayed by the Flight Management System. "Depending on how many turns it takes to make our way through the mountains."

"I don't understand. I should be able to reach Marta," Montero said as she stared at the phone in frustration. "I don't like this at all. Do we have any other exit plan out of Slovakia if we can't reach her or Trevor in time?"

"It's the middle of the night at a rural airport," Michael said. "We'll steal another airplane, or a car—we'll do whatever it takes."

"I say call Calvin," Donovan said. "He may be in contact with Marta, or he may have already devised a way to get us out of Slovakia."

"Dragon one-one, this is Merlin. Turn further right to a heading of two-one-zero degrees, climb to one thousand eight hundred feet."

Donovan did as instructed. The Boeing bounced hard as they

flew through some sharp turbulence. Below them, lights flashed past, but Donovan had no time to study the landscape other than to glance at the glow of Krakow, which was slipping behind them. Merlin was steering them away from the city, and the climb was due to the rising terrain. As the darkened 727 thundered up a valley, Donovan caught sight of a brief flash of lightning far to the south, the momentary burst silhouetting the jagged tops of the terrain dead ahead. Behind him he heard Montero talking on the phone.

"Dragon one-one, climb to be at two thousand five hundred feet in fifteen seconds, and stand by for an eighteen-degree turn to the right. New heading will be two-two-eight degrees. You are in the corridor."

As Michael confirmed the clearance, Donovan glanced at the clock and climbed. In the valley, on either side of them, unseen terrain reached well above them. He needed to do exactly what he was told. Donovan leveled at two thousand five hundred feet just as the second hand on the ancient analog clock hit the fifteen-second mark. The radar altimeter, which showed the exact distance between the belly of the Boeing and the terrain below, had been holding steady at five hundred feet, now jumped to two hundred feet as they crossed a ridge.

"Dragon one-one, turn to a new heading of two-two-eight degrees, and climb to be at three thousand two hundred feet in thirty seconds."

In the turn, Donovan inched the nose up to initiate the climb as another flash of lightning, more intense than the last, filled the southern sky. In the brief light, Donovan saw a rounded peak above them to his right, but the much closer jagged rocky spire to his left startled him by its proximity. His apprehension grew as the night once again closed in around them, leaving the now invisible terrain etched in his mind.

"Dragon one-one, descend to two thousand eight hundred, and turn left to one-eight-zero degrees."

Donovan banked hard and descended just as another staccato burst of lightning danced across the distant sky. The Boeing lurched as they flew through another pocket of turbulence. Donovan reacted quickly and held the plane steady. He'd felt the airplane try to climb and roll at the same instant, marking the turbulence as terrain induced. As the winds increased over the peaks, the rougher their route would become. Without taking his eyes from the instruments, he called back to Montero. "Ask Calvin exactly where the weather is situated. Threading our way through the mountains in thunderstorms would be suicidal."

"Calvin says the front is moving quickly," Montero replied. "Our course through the Carpathians shouldn't be impacted. He says that on our arrival, we'll encounter scattered clouds at two hundred to three hundred feet, with visibilities ranging from two to five miles in light rain. The wind will be gusty from the northwest. He said to expect standing water on the runway."

"Dragon one-one, climb now to three thousand eight hundred feet. On my mark, make a hard right turn to a heading of two-four-zero degrees."

As if to punctuate the weather briefing, the southern sky lit up, and Donovan saw the narrow, dead-end valley they were roaring through at six miles per minute. Rugged, boulder-strewn granite seemed to close in on either side of the Boeing. The radar altimeter bounced around between four to six hundred feet above the ground.

"How hard of a turn are we talking?" Michael asked.

"No less than four degrees per second," Merlin said calmly. "Start your turn now."

Donovan banked the Boeing hard to the right to thread them between the next set of mountaintops. He had ten seconds to be on the new heading and for the first time he noticed the inside of his mouth felt like cotton. Scattered lights came into view as they crossed the ridge. He held the heading as the 727 raced along the outskirts of the small town, the deafening sound of their passing would echo off the hills and no doubt confuse a startled population.

Michael turned and spoke to Montero. "What does Calvin have to say about Marta and Trevor?"

"Calvin says he can't reach them, and Merlin can't positively identify them, either. No one knows for sure where they are."

"Is there any other support on the way?" Donovan asked.

"Not that we can count on," Montero replied. "We may very well be on our own."

"Dragon one-one, descend to two thousand nine hundred feet and turn left to a heading of two-three-zero degrees."

Donovan made the course corrections, and the Boeing shuddered as turbulence rocked the airliner. He expected it to grow worse the closer they flew to the squall line. Snaking out before them was a road. At this hour he only spotted a few vehicles, either their taillights or headlights visible in the clear mountain air. It gave Donovan a brief sense of perspective in their blind headlong rush through the mountains, a momentary reprieve, and he took several slow breaths in and out to steady himself. He needed Lauren to be alive, yet he had no illusions about their chances of a successful rescue. That they held the element of surprise went without saying, but that wouldn't last long, and they had no idea what their opposition would be like. They'd be trained, that was a given. But would they be alert and ready, or asleep and slow to respond? He and Montero both had handguns; Michael was unarmed, having left the cumbersome shotgun in the helicopter when they landed at the Budapest Airport. Less than twenty rounds between the two of them. He didn't want to think about the odds of their success in finding and rescuing Lauren, let alone getting out of the country alive.

The turbulence worsened and the airspeed needle jumped past the redline and the controls began to shake in his hands. Under the new onslaught, Donovan was begrudgingly forced to pull the throttles back to slow the Boeing.

"We have a problem," Montero said. "Calvin says the emergency GPS signal from Lauren's Blackphone shows that she's on the move."

"What do you mean emergency?" Donovan asked.

"It means someone removed the main battery without punching in the correct exit code. Every thirty seconds, using the phone's backup battery, a location ping is sent via satellite."

"Is she on the ground or in the air?" Donovan asked, knowing exactly why the battery would have been removed from her phone.

"Ground," Montero said. "Satellite confirms two vehicles, a large truck, and a sedan leaving the airfield, traveling west."

"We just lost our runway." Michael spoke the words that he and Donovan both understood all too well.

"This was always going to be a crash landing," Donovan said as he glanced over at Michael. "All that matters is we walk away."

"Look at the upside," Michael added. "Our element of surprise just went way up."

"Guys," Montero said. "Calvin says that they just turned south, the road they're on takes them into the trailing edge of the weather."

"Ask Calvin if we're going to reach her before she drives back into the teeth of the storm?" Donovan asked.

"He says it's too soon to tell for sure," Montero relayed. "But at the moment, it looks like the storms are going to be a factor."

As more lightning exploded on the horizon, Donovan could see that the valley closed dead ahead. The turbulence eased, and with a new determination, Donovan pushed up the throttles and once again pegged the airspeed needle against the redline—and held it there.

CHAPTER THIRTY-THREE

RAIN FROM THE line of thunderstorms pelted the roof of the hangar, at times sounding louder, as if hail had joined the downpour. Lauren could hear the howl of the wind as it rattled the metal roof of the building. She supported her broken forearm as best she could, finding that if she didn't move, it was more numb than painful. She intently watched as the men finished loading the truck. She'd studied each item, trying to decide if any of them might be a second nuclear device. Aleksander was nowhere in sight, and she wondered what he was doing. What if Daniel's body had been recovered? The lie that Daniel was alive was the only reason she was still alive. The longer she sat and processed the realities, the darker her thoughts became. She couldn't help but wonder if Aleksander's threats about an extended conversation had been hollow words, and that instead of taking her with them, they were going to kill her and leave her to be found by the Slovakian authorities. She glanced at her watch. If Donovan and Michael had failed, then a large portion of Moscow would be destroyed in less than an hour. If they had averted the attack, had they survived? Her thoughts, as always, darted to Abigail and what would happen to her little girl. She wondered how many parents had felt what she was feeling, the helplessness of knowing that their treasured children could very well grow up without them. Abigail would be well taken care of, in the safe, loving environment of William's niece and dear family friend, Stephanie VanGelder. In sixteen years, on her daughter's twenty-first birthday, she'd be told the truth of who she really was, that her father was the late Robert Huntington. Along with the shock, questions, and frustration, would also come the reality that she'd just inherited billions. From Lauren's own experience, she knew it would be a harsh truth for their daughter to absorb. Lauren felt her eyes tear up at the thought of Abigail as a grown woman. Abigail would have vague memories, and of course pictures, but what would always remain were the unanswered questions.

Lauren offered a small prayer up to the universe, not for herself, but for Abigail, and for Donovan to still be alive, and make it home to raise their daughter. The rear door of the truck slammed shut and brought Lauren back to the present. From her right came Aleksander, a scowl on his face as he pocketed his phone and drew his knife. With a quick cut, Lauren's wrist was released from the chair. She had no defense as Aleksander pulled her to her feet and pushed her toward the door. Agonizing pain radiated from her left arm and she spotted the smear of blood from her leg wound on the seat of the chair.

"Let's go!" Aleksander shouted to everyone in the hangar as he roughly propelled Lauren forward, his hand an iron grip on her right bicep.

Lauren limped forward before he brought her to a stop and spun her aside so he could open a door that led out into the pouring rain. He pushed her toward the rear door of an older BMW and shoved her inside. He climbed in after her and forced her to scoot across the bench seat until she was situated behind the driver. Aleksander produced another tie-wrap and secured her left wrist to the armrest in the door. He pulled the seat belt across her torso, clicked it into place and pulled it tight.

The driver and another man sat in the front seat and once the truck pulled past them, they swung out and fell in behind the larger vehicle. The rain had let up slightly, and Lauren could see patches of pea-sized hail on what little grass lined the rough track that led away from the secluded hangar. Lightning lit up the sky, and with each flash, she hoped to see armed soldiers, weapons drawn, assaulting the convoy in an attempt to retrieve the second *Phoenix*, and in the process, rescue her. But with each successive burst, the two vehicles moved away from her last known position and picked up speed. With each minute, she was going deeper into the rabbit hole, and realistically, no one would ever find her in time.

CHAPTER THIRTY-FOUR

"WHATEVER HAPPENS, WE'RE going to need to do it in a hurry," Donovan said to both Michael and Montero. "Once we're exposed to Slovakian radar, the situation becomes fluid, and we'll have to react fast."

"Dragon one-one, maintain present heading and descend to one thousand nine hundred feet. You'll exit the corridor in three minutes."

"Calvin says infrared analysis confirms that Lauren is in the trail vehicle, the sedan. She's seated in the back seat behind the driver."

"Is he sure she's alive?" Donovan said with more force than he intended.

"Yes," Montero said with equal force. "Calvin says he's positive."

"Ask him about the weather and brief us on the road itself," Donovan said, clinging to Montero's words. The trailing edge of the towering squall line was just off their left wing. Almost constant lightning allowed him to see the valley beneath them and the downward sloping terrain on both sides that was going to expose them to Slovakian radar in moments. He felt like a mouse sneaking along the baseboard in a room full of cats. Speed and surprise were their only weapons.

"Calvin says at our present speed, we'll intercept the convoy in five minutes. Weather over the target is scattered clouds at four hundred feet, overcast at two thousand feet. Frequent cloud-to-cloud, as well as cloud-to-ground, lightning, with intermittent moderate rain. Wind is variable from two-four-zero to three-zero-zero degrees, at twelve knots, with maximum gusts estimated at twenty knots," Montero relayed. "He also says they can't locate or contact Marta or Trevor. The helicopter seems to have vanished. We're on our own, guys."

"Donovan, wait a minute. We need to think about our speed," Michael called out. "If we're suddenly a target on their radar going three hundred knots, it's going to set off all kinds of alarms. If we're going a hundred and fifty knots, we'll look like a small plane. That doesn't seem nearly as threatening, and it might buy us some time to find a viable exit strategy."

Donovan pulled all three throttles back to the stops and deployed the speed brakes. The Boeing slowed dramatically.

"Guys," Montero said as she leaned forward. "If people start shooting, remember where Lauren's sitting. If this goes the way I plan, we'll be driving her out of here in that car."

"Dragon one-one, you're cleared to descend to twelve hundred feet. In one minute you'll exit the corridor and be free to navigate at your discretion."

"Merlin, Dragon one-one, I copy," Michael said. "Thanks for your help this evening."

Donovan had the 727 slowing through one hundred and eighty knots when Michael advised he was lowering flaps. As both trailing and leading edge devices pushed out into the slipstream, the Boeing slowed even more. Michael continued to lower flaps, and Donovan carefully added power until their airspeed was pegged at one hundred fifty knots.

"We're ten miles from intercept," Montero said. "Calvin says the road they're on is a two-lane paved highway. There are scattered trees along the side, and due to the proximity of a power plant, there are massive cross-country transmission lines spider-webbed across the area."

Donovan clenched his jaw and felt the Boeing buffet from the gusty surface winds. At one hundred and fifty knots, it felt like they were crawling over the ground. The lightning was now horizon to horizon as well as high above them. Rain drops began hitting the fractured windshield.

"Calvin has calculated the probable route the convoy is taking. We'll arrive overhead of the convoy at a stretch of highway that runs relatively straight for a mile, but in the center of that section of road are power lines that bisect the pavement at ninety degrees. They've counted at least six individual transmission lines."

"For God's sake, don't hit the wires," Michael said as he strained to look out the window and spotted two vehicles on a distant road. "I have no clue what happens when 727s encounter power lines, but it can't be good."

"We're not going to make an overhead pass. These guys know airplanes. A low-flying 727 will tip them off, and I want complete surprise. Michael, you said it earlier, and I think you're right, we probably damaged the main gear when we took out the *Phoenix*. We're landing this thing gear up. It'll be more predictable," Donovan said as he scanned the road in the distance for any other traffic. The low, scattered clouds complicated the job. "I'm going to come around and set this thing down so as to come to a stop right in front of them. Montero, ask Calvin if he can guide us around to land into the convoy—or damn close to it."

"Let's go over this one more time just to be clear." Michael spoke, but his eyes remained forward, searching. "You've got one more notch of flaps you can call for. Once they're down, in this wind, your final approach speed is one hundred twenty knots. The gear stays up, but don't let it float. Fly this thing all the way to the ground until it touches. Hell, keep flying until it stops. Even though we'll be on our belly, you'll have reverse thrust."

"Got it," Donovan said as the Boeing was pelted by heavier rain and forward visibility dropped to a mile.

"Once we're stopped," Michael continued, "leave the engine shutdown to me. You worry about getting Montero on the ground. She's our best weapon. Each of these side windows is an emergency exit. In the small compartment above each window you'll find a knotted rope. Throw it out and use it to escape."

"I see them, two o'clock—two miles." Donovan's eyes narrowed as he spotted the two vehicles. "It's got to be her."

"Calvin says turn to a one-eight-zero degree heading. In two minutes you'll turn due west, cross over a small town, and the road heading northwest out of that town is the one we want. He says to touch down as close to the edge of town as possible. The straight section of pavement is five thousand feet in length, and don't forget the power lines halfway down."

Donovan glanced at the second hand on the clock and marked the time. He pictured Calvin's instructions, trusting the man to get it right. Behind him he heard Montero check her pistol.

"Your turn will be in fifteen seconds," Montero said, then hesitated. "Oh shit! Merlin just said that we're about to have company—MiGs—and they've gone supersonic to intercept us. They'll be here in eight minutes."

"Damn it," Donovan said. Through the rain he spotted the lights from the town and added power. "Michael, so much for slow and nonthreatening. Leave the flaps where they are for now; we're flying this approach faster than one-twenty. They can't shoot down an airplane that's already on the ground."

"Flaps are standing by," Michael said. "Fly her as fast as you want!"

Donovan added more power. He held the Boeing in a thirty-degree bank and felt like he could touch the rooftops of the houses below. The rain reduced the visibility to less than a mile, and he still didn't have the road in sight. He knew going around wasn't an option.

"Calvin says the road is eleven o'clock, we're almost on top of it."

"There it is!" Michael called out. "We're high and fast, get us down!"

"Final flaps!" Donovan called out as he searched for and spotted the road through his cracked windshield. He slammed the throttles to idle. The last section of flaps slowed the airplane dramatically. The Boeing 727 seemed to stagger in the crosswind and turbulence and began to drop heavily toward the ground as Donovan reacted and added power.

Michael hit the switches, and the landing lights pierced the darkness, revealing the wet pavement.

Donovan pulled back on the controls to try to arrest the descent rate and deplete his speed. The Boeing was still hurtling over the ground at one hundred and fifty knots when the landing lights illuminated the thick power lines that stretched across the road. Donovan's hand flew to the speed brakes and pulled the lever. The 727 shuddered as it staggered and dropped under the wires. The cables flashed overhead, and Donovan felt something impact the tail, but the Boeing continued downward, and the belly of the 727 struck the pavement hard.

The airframe screamed in protest as Donovan went to maximum reverse thrust. The controls shook in his hands. The noise was deafening and the landing lights winked out as debris shattered the glass filaments, plunging them into darkness. A vicious impact slammed them all forward and then to the side as the right wing hit something solid and the Boeing began to rotate. Donovan did everything he could to slow the rotation, and as he did, he caught sight of the headlights ahead.

The Boeing hit something solid, and the straps from his harness bit into Donovan's body, the nose swung hard to the right, and this time there was nothing he could do. He kept his hands on the controls, fighting until the end. He heard the ear-piercing screech of metal tearing and separating. Every muscle in his body went rigid as something behind him snapped, and the Boeing's nose lurched off the ground, rolling to the side, and then fell heavily to the ground. In the dark, Donovan tried to hold on. The cockpit tilted and then crashed into the rain-soaked field, coming to a stop on its side.

Dazed, Donovan found he was hanging sideways in his seat. He turned to Michael, who groaned, having cupped his broken fingers to try to protect them. It took Donovan another moment to comprehend that the dim light coming from outside the shattered windows was the unmistakable flickering light of flames.

CHAPTER THIRTY-FIVE

LAUREN CAUGHT SIGHT of strange-looking lights ahead and to the left. They were low and moving fast. At first, she had no idea what it was, a helicopter or an airplane? As the unknown craft turned toward her, the lights from a small town illuminated the underside of the object, and she knew exactly what she was seeing. Her emotions soared—a Skybridge 727—the one that Donovan and Michael took from Budapest. She sent silent thanks to Calvin for not giving up on her. He was the one person who could have pinpointed her location. As she continued to watch, her relief was short-lived, and from unbridled joy, she plummeted to the depths of her worst fear as the Boeing, clouds of water vapor billowing from flexing wings, sank heavily toward the ground. In an attempt to rescue her, Donovan, Michael, and Montero were about to crash, and she was going to witness the unthinkable.

Slow to understand what he was seeing, the truck driver ahead of them finally applied his brakes, which focused Aleksander's attention to what was happening ahead of them. When he grasped the enormity of the danger, he began yelling at the driver in Ukrainian.

The Boeing leveled its wings momentarily and then descended steeply. In the brightness of the landing lights, Lauren saw the 727 maneuver to try to fly underneath massive high-power lines. Sparks erupted from at least one severed line, and the ends whipped and snaked in the darkness. The Boeing seemed to stagger and then impacted the road on its belly. For the first time, Lauren realized the landing gear was still retracted. The immediate shower of sparks sent spots across her vision. The right wing severed a tree in an explosion of bark, dirt, aluminum, and the misting jet fuel was instantaneously ignited by the sparks. A ball of fire erupted and curled skyward, a trail of flames chasing the crippled Boeing as it continued to careen toward them.

Lauren was pushed against her seat belt as the driver slammed on the brakes and brought them to a sudden stop. He threw the car into reverse, swung his head around to try and guide the car, and punched the accelerator. Out the windshield Lauren could see the truck containing the second *Phoenix* obliterated as the left wing of the Boeing ripped through the flimsy metal.

To Lauren, it all seemed to be happening in slow motion. The truck, nothing more than a fiery chassis resting on its tires, rolled into the ditch and lurched to a stop. The main fuselage of the 727, its right wing severed, spun into a muddy field. Huge clods of dirt were thrown upward as the tail section, with the engines still attached, buckled and then separated. Both nacelles came apart while flying into the air and tumbled wildly toward the car. The roar of the engines was replaced by the crumpling of aluminum as the tail impacted the road surface, broke apart, and cartwheeled into the darkness.

Debris peppered the BMW, shattering the windshield. The driver lost control, yelling as he fought the fishtailing sedan, bringing it to a panicked stop in a geyser of water from the rain-filled ditch. Lauren had braced herself but her head bounced hard off the padded headrest. In the light from the raging fire, she could see the forward fuselage of the Boeing resting on its side in the field, a huge rip in the aluminum starting just forward of the wing root nearly severed the entire tube in half. She didn't see anyone emerging from the wreckage.

Aleksander yelled again in Ukrainian, and all three men piled out of the BMW, weapons drawn. Lauren was trapped, she could do nothing but watch as they ran toward the 727 leaving her alone. She used her thumb to push the button that unfastened her seat belt, and with her broken arm on the door's armrest, she moved her torso to gain some leverage, and then she yanked at the armrest with her good arm, trying to free herself. She finally sat back, spent—still firmly attached to the door.

When Lauren turned her attention outside, a wave of pure panic shocked her entire body. A lake of burning jet fuel, the flames licking far up into the sky, was expanding from the wrecked wing that had destroyed the truck and was flowing toward the BMW. She savagely began pulling against the armrest, trying to wrest it free from the door. The pungent odor of fuel filled the car. When she felt the first hint of the intense heat on her bare skin, she began to scream.

CHAPTER THIRTY-SIX

MONTERO WAS THE first to react. She unsnapped her harness and lowered herself from her seat.

Donovan released himself and moved toward Michael, helping him out of his seat as Montero vanished through the cockpit door.

"I'm good," Michael said as he found his feet and stood on unsteady legs, careful with his bandaged hand. "Hell of a landing. Now let's get out of here. I'll follow you."

When the sound of automatic weapons reached him, Donovan drew his own weapon. The gunfire was coming from the direction Montero had headed. Together, he and Michael opened the emergency hatch above them, and Donovan stuck his head out. Through the rain and smoke, he saw that the cockpit was still connected to the wing structure, but just barely. The right wing had been torn off and was burning, as was the truck. Through the smoke in the light of the fire, Donovan spotted two men moving toward a section of severed fuselage. Then another sound reached his ears, a woman screaming.

Donovan snapped his head in the direction the screams were coming from and found only smoke. A second later, he caught sight of the sedan in the ditch. The light from the intense blaze allowed him to make out the silhouette of someone flailing in the back seat. Donovan was about to leap from the hatch, when a burst of gunfire ripped into the metal only inches away, forcing him to duck back inside the cockpit.

"I saw her!" Donovan turned to Michael. "Lauren's trapped in the car and it's burning."

They both turned as Montero came rushing back into the cockpit.

"Can you drop to the ground without getting shot?" Michael asked. "The second you're clear of the exit, Montero will come up shooting and cover you."

"There're two guys with automatic weapons," Montero said in a rush. "They've got us cut off from back there."

"I'm going out this exit. Cover me. I have to get to Lauren." Donovan pulled himself up toward the exit.

"Donovan, wait!" Montero called out.

Instead of only taking a glimpse, Donovan went up and through the exit at full speed, rolled over, and dropped the almost ten feet to the soft soil below. Montero began firing the instant Donovan hit the ground.

Donovan took off toward the BMW as bullets slammed into the ground just behind him. He cut to his right, trying to use the smoke to mask his moves, but the muddy ground made it hard to stay balanced and pick up speed. The next volley of bullets sizzled through the air around him. He cut again and braced for the next burst, the sound of Lauren's cries for help spurring him on. Then her screams were drowned out by a new sound.

He drove himself forward as a familiar helicopter blew past only feet above his head, the rotor downwash parting the smoke and curling it downward. He glanced back as he ran and saw Trevor fly into the circle of light created by the fire, and hover directly between him and the gunmen. Automatic weapons fire rained down from the helicopter, and cut down the two exposed men. Despite the cold rain, Donovan could feel the heat intensify as he neared the car. He put his sleeve up his face and slid to a stop at the open rear door; Lauren was on the opposite side. Their eyes met and Donovan had never seen such fear on his wife's face. Her terror sprung him into action and he crawled to her, seeing instantly that she was secured to the door. He also saw the blood that had saturated the fabric on her left leg.

"My left arm is broken," she cried, fear warbling in her throat.

Donovan raised his pistol. "Close your eyes!" He pushed the barrel against the black plastic of the tie-wrap that held her, and pulled the trigger twice. The heavy .45 caliber slugs easily cracked and parted the plastic, and Lauren, now free, slumped against him.

The rising heat started to blister the skin on the back of his neck. He put one arm under Lauren's knees, and scooted her toward the door as best he could. She slid across the smooth leather until Donovan had her out of the car and in his arms. He pulled her close and began to run, carrying her away from the flames.

Trevor banked hard, away from Donovan, sliding the helicopter into a hover behind a cluster of trees. It was then that Donovan heard the roar of the MiGs coming in low from the east. Donovan swerved to take cover in the ditch. He dove and turned, hoping his body would cushion the impact for Lauren. Holding her tight, he landed on his back, and splashed into the soggy ditch. He scrambled and threw his body over hers, placing himself between Lauren and what was left of the 727.

The MiGs streaked overhead low enough that Donovan could see the underside of their wings, the missiles hanging there. The roar of the MiGs receded into the distance, and both Donovan and Lauren took in the scene. Dozens of fires burned brightly, engulfing what remained of the Boeing, as well as the BMW and truck. Having seen the destruction, the roar from the fighters receded into the stormy night and disappeared.

"Did you get to the *Phoenix* in time?" Lauren asked.

"Yes, once Calvin had an infrared position via satellite we were able to down it in eastern Poland," Donovan said, his ears alert for any sign of the MiGs coming back around. Gathering his wife up into his arms, he stood, and once again began moving away from the wreckage as quickly as he could. He ran until his arms ached and the sharp pain in his side couldn't be ignored, yet stopped only when he heard the staccato beats of a helicopter drawing closer.

Donovan felt the rotor wash pour over him as Trevor touched the skids to the ground thirty paces in front of them. Relief washed over him as the door slid open and he lifted Lauren into Michael's waiting arms. Donovan was about to climb in when a perfectly round hole formed in the metal next to his head. He swiveled in time to see the muzzle flash of another bullet being fired. The sound of the turbine engine and spinning rotor blades masked the sound of the gunshot. Donovan ducked and launched himself into the cabin just as Trevor lifted off. The helicopter swung to the left, flying straight at the shooter. Trevor turned on the helicopters landing lights which both illuminated and blinded Aleksander.

Donovan crouched in the open doorway as Aleksander staggered backwards, firing wildly. In the harsh light, Donovan saw the action on Aleksander's pistol lock open—he was out of ammunition. Trevor brought the helicopter down until the skids were just above the ground. As they neared the terrorist, Donovan pushed off the skid, slamming into Aleksander and driving him down into the ground.

As Trevor made a tight circle to come back around, Donovan swung hard, releasing the rage he'd harbored since he'd first heard that Lauren was missing. Aleksander staggered backwards from the fist to the jaw, recovered, and then charged forward. Donovan delivered three vicious body blows, knocking Aleksander to his knees. In a fit of rage, screaming at Donovan, Aleksander leapt forward and pulled his knife from his belt.

The lights from the returning helicopter caught Aleksander midstride, his knife raised, as Donovan squeezed off the first shot. The .45 caliber slug hit center mass. Aleksander's legs buckled and he went back down to his knees. With an expression of shock coupled with fury, he gripped the knife in preparation to throw it at his enemy. Donovan squeezed the trigger again, and the pistol jerked in his hands. The second slug hit Aleksander in the middle of his chest. The man who would have killed millions dropped the knife and toppled sideways, dead in the muddy field.

Donovan lowered his gun and found Montero at his side. "We need to go!" She said over the noise from the helicopter.

"Where's Daniel's jump drive?" Donovan asked, his eyes still fixed on Aleksander's corpse.

"I'll get it." Montero turned and ran back to the open door of the helicopter and then quickly returned.

"Here," Montero said as she pressed the drive into his hand.

"We have all the information copied, right?" Donovan asked.

"Yeah," Montero replied. "Do it and let's go."

Donovan knelt down and slipped the drive into an inside pocket of Aleksander's jacket and left it there. There would now be no doubt what the man had tried to do, and how he'd intended to make the unthinkable a reality. Donovan stood. He and Montero hurried to the waiting chopper and climbed inside. Michael and Marta were up front, so he and Montero sat in back. Donovan went to Lauren and wrapped her up in his arms as if he'd never let go.

CHAPTER THIRTY-SEVEN

"CAN WE GET Calvin on the phone?" Michael asked, once Trevor had leveled off over a roadway headed west. "I'd like to know if those fighters are still around looking for stuff to shoot."

"No, the only satellite phone we had finally ran out of battery." Montero said. "I'll bet Merlin is still up there, though."

"Trevor, can I borrow one of your radios for a quick broadcast?" Michael asked. "It'll just take a minute."

"Go ahead, mate," Trevor replied. "I sure as hell don't need to chat anyone up, seeing as we're trying to sneak out of Slovakia."

From memory, Michael dialed in the secondary frequency they'd been given and keyed the transmit button. "Dragon one-one, calling Merlin, you still up?"

"Affirmative, Dragon one-one, Merlin is still here."

"Copy that," Michael continued. "Do you still have me on radar?"

"Affirmative, Dragon one-one."

"I was just wondering if there was any traffic between my position and my destination?"

Through his headset, Donovan listened to Michael's carefully worded message.

"Your present heading looks good. There is some commercial traffic at your twelve o'clock and twenty miles but it's all well above you. Previous military activity seems to have disengaged."

Donovan turned to Lauren and hugged her gently. She looked up and offered him a weak smile through the pain. Donovan leaned down and lightly kissed her, their lips lingering for the briefest moment.

"Merlin, thank you again for all your help. Dragon one-one, out."

"Okay," Montero said to Marta the instant Michael was finished. "I'm really at a loss to understand where you guys came from. Please, tell us where in the hell were you?"

"We waited in the area after Lauren was taken. Three seconds earlier and we would have had her," Marta said. "We were taking heavy fire and had to exit the immediate area, but we weren't going to leave her, so Trevor circled around until he found a place for us to land, under a bridge of all places. The storms were coming, so I set off on foot to see if I could find Lauren, using the weather as cover. I was able to work my way to within a hundred meters when I saw Lauren forced into the back of the sedan. Moments later, a truck pulled out of the hangar and drove away, and the car followed. It was pouring rain, there was even some hail and it was slow going back to where Trevor waited."

"She was a sodden mess," Trevor added. "I fired up the chopper and we took off to try to follow them, but we couldn't see them. Visibility was so bloody poor, I had to set us back down. When the backside of the thunderstorms finally pushed through, the visibility improved enough and we were able to get airborne."

"The first thing we saw in the distance was a shower of sparks," Marta said. "We had no clue what we were seeing. Seconds later there was an explosion, and Trevor had us on our way as fast as he could fly. You can't imagine our shock when we saw the crashed Boeing we'd last seen in Budapest, as well as the destroyed truck. It was obvious what needed to be done when we spotted the muzzle flashes from the men with the automatic weapons. You know the rest."

"I can't thank everyone enough," Lauren said. "I'm sorry you had to save me again."

"How did you manage to figure out that the *Phoenix* had an infrared vulnerability?" Michael asked Lauren. "It was genius."

"When I saw the second aircraft in the hangar, it was slightly different from the image we pulled off the Internet. It took me a little bit, but I realized that Daniel had compromised his original design and built in a weakness."

"Incredible," Montero said, almost with a sigh. "Where are we headed now? What's the plan?"

"First, we need to get the hell out of here, and into Austrian airspace," Trevor said.

"Do you have something in mind?" Michael asked. "Trying to bolt across the border will probably draw unwanted attention."

"Fortune favors the bold," Trevor said as he switched on all of the helicopter's lights so as to appear as a law-abiding flight. "Marta and I discussed this earlier. We're flying straight into the heart of Bratislava as a medevac flight. We navigate to the university hospital and act like we're going to land. Once we're at rooftop level, we dash for the border. It's less than five miles."

"What about radio communication? You're going to have to talk to someone, right? " Michael asked. "How do you sell all this to Air Traffic Control?"

"I'll speak to them using English, mixed with my natural Eastern European accent," Marta replied. "Trevor will tell me what to say."

"Once we're across the border," Trevor added. "We'll get Lauren medical attention straight away."

"Amen to that," Lauren said, her eyes growing heavy.

Donovan looked at the glow of lights on the horizon. Bratislava was coming up fast. He liked Trevor's plan; the pilot had already pulled off some of the most skilled flying he'd ever seen. He pictured the geography, and guessed that they were only twenty or twenty-five miles from the border.

In the darkened cabin, the bright red light suddenly lit up Trevor's instrument panel like a neon billboard.

"Trevor," Michael asked. "What's happening?"

"Nothing good." Trevor's eyes danced over his instruments. "It says we're losing engine oil. The gauges confirm the light. The engine is overheating—fast."

"What's the plan?" Michael asked.

"The book says we should land immediately and be ready for an autorotation if the engine seizes," Trevor replied.

"We're not doing that, are we?" Marta asked.

"No," Trevor said as he tightened his harness. "We're twenty miles from the border. That's ten minutes, max. I say we press on and pray that the engine keeps running for another ten minutes."

"Trevor, should we still fly directly over the city?" Donovan asked. "Or would it be safer to skirt the city, and then if we had to autorotate to a landing we'd be in the open country as opposed to the city?"

"Straight over the city is the shortest distance to the border, it's still the best play," Trevor replied. "I can set this thing down on a rooftop or in a parking lot if I have to, and we have a better chance hiding in an urban environment."

"What's our weapon and ammunition situation?" Montero asked.

"I have about twenty rounds for the machine gun and two full clips for my Glock," Marta replied.

"I only have six rounds left," Donovan said.

"Okay, hiding is a far better option than fighting," Montero said. "I agree with Trevor, an urban setting works to our advantage. Marta, do you have any contacts in Bratislava?"

"No. There's a strict division of business between us and the

Slovakians," Marta explained. "There was a bloody turf war started years ago, and much ill will still exists. In fact, I'd rather be captured by the authorities than the Slovak mafia."

"Good to know," Montero said. "Is there any chance your associates in Austria could cross the border and pull us out?"

"Perhaps, but it would take time."

"I hate to break up your strategic meeting," Trevor said. "But it's time to talk to Air Traffic Control or we'll have a whole new set of problems."

"I'm ready." Marta turned her attention to Trevor.

"I'll control the push-to-talk switch," Trevor said. "I'll tell you what to say, then I'll use the word *go*. This means that the microphone is hot, and that you need to repeat exactly what I've just said. I'll stop transmitting the moment you're finished, and we'll wait and see what you need to say next. Is that clear?"

"Yes," Marta said as she nodded and blew out a quick breath.

Donovan watched with anticipation. Pilot speak was an art, and controllers expected not only familiar phrases, but a certain cadence as well. This could go badly in a hurry.

"Here goes," Trevor said. "Bratislava tower, this is Med-Air helicopter zero-two. How do you read? Go!"

Donovan marveled as Marta repeated perfectly what Trevor had said word for word.

"Med-Air zero-two, this is Bratislava tower, go with your message."

"We're ten miles east, request transition through your airspace at one thousand five hundred feet," Trevor said to Marta. "Go."

Once again Marta convincingly repeated what she'd been told to say.

"Med-Air zero-two," the seemingly bored controller replied. "Say your destination?"

"University hospital helipad. Go." Trevor said.

Donovan marveled at how relaxed Marta sounded. Then he realized she was in charge of a huge crime syndicate, and was no doubt well practiced in saying what was needed to get people to do her bidding.

"Roger Med-Air zero-two, cleared to transition, report leaving one thousand five hundred."

"We're beginning our descent at this time, Med-Air zero two," Trevor said as he nodded his approval. "Go."

Marta gave herself a little fist-pump as she made the final transmission that allowed them to continue.

Covering ground as fast as he could, Trevor was flying only a thousand feet above the city. Donovan was helpless to do anything except hold Lauren and hope that the engine kept turning. Below them were narrow, tree-lined streets, and houses with sloped roofs. There seemed to be few places to land a helicopter, regardless of how well Trevor could fly. Downtown was situated slightly to the left. Straight ahead was a cluster of buildings that looked to be a university. Just beyond, in the distance, lay the Danube and the border to Austria.

"Okay, folks," Trevor said. "This thing could go to shit at any moment. If we go down, hold onto something solid and brace yourself for impact. Do not panic and do not try to get out of the helicopter before I give the word. There's a rotor brake, let me stop the blades from spinning before we make a run for it—does everyone understand?"

Donovan eyed the instrument panel and spotted the oil temperature gauge. The needle was in the red. Next to it was the oil pressure gauge—and it showed zero. As if he were having the same worrisome thoughts, Michael turned toward Donovan with an expression of concern. They'd all hear the engine when it quit, and would know they were going down. Trevor would autorotate, which allowed the airflow in the descent to keep the blades turning. Only a few feet above the ground, Trevor would convert the energy of the still-spinning blades to arrest their free-fall into a smooth touchdown.

"We're obliged to act like we're landing just ahead at the hospital," Trevor continued. "I'll be slowing momentarily, and then we'll make a quick left turn and we're going to go like bloody hell for the river. According to the navigation display, once I make the turn, we need to stay in the air another two minutes to cross the border. Once we're in Austria, I'll be setting this thing down while we still have an engine."

Everyone in the cabin remained silent as Trevor began slowing the helicopter under the pretense of landing. At two hundred feet above the ground, Trevor killed the lights, banked to the left and accelerated.

Ahead, winding like a black snake through a maze of lights, was the Danube. Donovan could see their position on the moving map display on Trevor's panel. Their course put them toward the nearest point where the land on the other side of the river was Austria.

"We're almost there," Trevor said, it sounded as if he was talking to the engine.

Montero tried to settle lower in her seat and pulled on her harness. Donovan reached over and tightened the straps securing Lauren. Her eyes were open and she gave him a weak smile and closed them again. They'd all gone without sleep, but Lauren had been running for days on end. They'd come this far, and he vowed to do everything in his power to protect her from harm.

The ambient light from the buildings and streetlights on the ground abruptly dimmed and Donovan looked up from Lauren to the terrain. They'd flashed over a road, below them were trees, then a row of what looked like apartment buildings, and beyond that appeared to be the dark water of the Danube.

Donovan felt the subtle shift in the vibration of the airframe. The vibration quickly accelerated and was joined by the sound of screeching, tortured metal which reached a crescendo and ended in a muffled boom that sent glowing hot debris tumbling away from the helicopter. The loss of the engine noise was immediate and total. The only the sound came from the spinning rotor blades.

Trevor dumped the collective and the bottom of the helicopter felt like it collapsed out from underneath them as they dropped toward the ground. He maneuvered the chopper into a descending U-turn in an effort to turn back toward the highway.

"Everyone hang on," Trevor called out. "This could get a bit messy."

Donovan held Lauren as tightly as he dared. She turned in her seat and buried her face in his chest. Below them were nothing but trees, but, straight ahead, Donovan caught the sight of lights. Trevor was using street lamps from the thoroughfare to illuminate his touchdown zone.

A different roar reached Donovan's ears. He had no idea what was generating the sound, only that it was growing louder. A quick search up and down the roadway showed no incoming traffic. Michael, too, was searching for the source.

Trevor pulled on the collective and the spinning blades bit into the air, arresting their drop and slowing the helicopter only seconds before the skids lightly kissed the asphalt. "Everyone stay put!" Trevor ripped off his headset as he reached overhead and pulled on the rotor brake handle. Ten seconds later, the spinning blades creaked to a stop.

"We've got company," Michael said as he popped open the door and the sound of another helicopter roared above them in the night sky. "It's a Russian-made Mil-35. The Slovakian Air Force flies them."

Donovan released his harness and then reached across to un-buckle Lauren. Up front, Marta, Trevor, and Michael had already jumped to the ground. Donovan gathered Lauren in his arms and with Montero behind him, stepped out of the chopper. He looked up at the machine; it was military gray and dwarfed their now use-less EC-130. The Mil-35 hovered menacingly, bristling with guns, and fully loaded rocket launchers hung from twin weapons pylons. Trevor had set them down on an overpass. There were only two ways to run, and as the gunship lowered its landing gear in prepa-ration for touchdown, their escape route dwindled to one.

Donovan turned and spotted a police car, blue-and-red lights lit up as it rushed toward them. From behind, the helicopter flattened its descent, roared only feet over their heads, and the entire nose of the gunship seemed to erupt with smoke and flames. Tracers arced out from the large-bore cannon and shredded the pavement in front of the police vehicle, throwing huge chunks of asphalt up into the air. The driver braked hard, but couldn't avoid the deep potholes created by the cannon shells. The front end of the car dropped hard. Donovan saw sparks as the undercarriage hit and then bounced the vehicle into the air. It slid sideways and came to a halt. Donovan saw the officer climb out through a window and take cover behind what remained of his car. He was well out of small arms range.

Above him the Mil-35 had swung around and was descending again. Donovan put his head down and turned to shelter Lauren, using his back to shield her from the brunt of the massive rotor wash. Once the helicopter was down, the pilot eased off on the pitch of the blades and the hurricane force winds abated.

Donovan watched as a fuselage door opened. It was Kristof, cane in hand, motioning for them to hurry.

"Oh, dear God," Marta cried out as she spotted her father and began to run toward the helicopter.

"It's Kristof," Donovan told Lauren as he hurried toward the helicopter. Trevor climbed in first and then turned to take Lauren from Donovan's arms and lift her aboard. Michael followed Montero, and the second they were inside, Kristof slammed the door closed, and the big helicopter went to full power and lifted free from the bridge.

Marta yelled above the noise. "We need to destroy the helicopter."

Kristof nodded, spoke into a microphone, and the pilot immediately swung around smoothly until the entire fuselage vibrated as the chain gun sent a barrage of cannon shells into the EC-130. As they swept south, Donovan caught a glimpse of what was left of his multi-million dollar Eurocopter. It was burning fiercely, the rotor blades resting on the ground as if the machine had been swatted like an insect and set on fire. Donovan joined Lauren, where a man had an open first aid kit and was tending to her broken arm.

"I brought my doctor," Kristof said. "I hoped no one would need him but me."

Donovan turned and looked into his friend's eyes. The earlier anger had vanished, filled by a sense of relief, as well as a measure of pain. Donovan didn't know what to say. He put out his hand so they could shake, but instead he got a hug from his oldest friend.

"I'm glad I made it in time," Kristof said low enough so only Donovan could hear.

Donovan returned the hug. "Thank you. I'm sorry I deserted you."

"In many ways you were always with me," Kristof said. "I've been thinking about our shared past all day, and when I became worried, I reached out to William. He's the one who kept me apprised of . . . events. He's still on the line. You were in serious trouble, it seems, so I decided I'd use some of my inventory to help you complete your mission. Most of all, I had to make sure you brought Marta home to me."

"You and William?" Donovan said as he took the Blackphone Kristof offered. Donovan's mind reeled from the implications of his two oldest friends pooling assets to help him. For a man who'd operated on his own for so long, Donovan's feelings almost over-whelmed him. He put the phone to his ear. "William?"

"Kristof said he'd found you," William said. "I gather everyone is safe?"

"Lauren has some injuries, but a doctor is working on her now. I think she'll be fine."

"I'm glad. Now listen carefully. There isn't much time. Kristof is flying you to a remote area in Austria where you'll be met by members of SEAL Team Two. You'll be transferred to a CV-22 and flown to the Air Force base in Aviano, Italy. There's a State Department Boeing 737 standing by for you. The jet is courtesy of a grateful President, his way of saying thank you."

Donovan kept listening; he liked what he was hearing, but he knew William always saved the best for last.

"Due to Lauren's retrieval of Daniel's files, Mr. Quentin Kirkpatrick of the CIA has been relieved of his duties. He was arrested last night and transferred to a federal detention facility for his actions regarding Daniel Pope. I don't think we'll hear from him anytime soon."

"What about Daniel's daughter?" Donovan asked.

"Daniel Pope's daughter is recovering nicely, and she was

informed personally by the Secretary of State regarding the news about her father, and the fact that he died a hero. Oh, and before I forget, the President also assures me that you and your team are being granted full immunity from any and all crimes committed in the interests of averting this disaster. As far as anyone knows, none of you were in Europe during the time in question. In fact, you've all been in Canada. Get some rest. There will, of course, be some debriefings. Calvin and I will do what we can to minimize those necessary evils, and I will, of course, meet you upon arrival."

"Thank you, William, for everything. We'll see you soon." Donovan disconnected the call and handed it to Kristof as he felt the helicopter start its descent.

"We're here," Kristof said as a sad expression settled on his face. He patted Donovan on the back as the wheels of the helicopter touched the ground.

"I don't want to leave like this," Donovan said. "Me in a mad rush to get out of Eastern Europe."

"Then don't," Kristof said. "Come back and visit. Just don't wait too long."

Donovan stepped off the helicopter. Not far away sat a CV-22 Osprey, both engines idling, ready for a quick lift-off. He turned as Michael handed Lauren down and Donovan once again had her in his arms. In a rush, everyone said their goodbyes.

Marta took time to give Donovan a fierce hug and then a quick peck on the cheek. "We'll see you both soon. We have a deal, remember?"

Marta pulled back and then gave Lauren a gentle hug. "Travel safe."

"Trevor," Donovan said, "you're the best. Thank you."

"It's what you hired me to do. I'm happy to help. You did some good work out there yourself."

Marta and Trevor climbed back aboard the helicopter with Kristof. Donovan carried Lauren toward the CV-22, and they were met by two soldiers, one who introduced himself as Lieutenant Commander Mathews. He turned and escorted them up the ramp into the Osprey where Donovan gently laid Lauren down on a stretcher. A medic immediately buckled her in and then put a headset over her ears.

"Dr. McKenna, I'm going to give you something for the pain," the medic said as he efficiently started an IV line and inspected the temporary cast on her arm.

Donovan sat next to her as the meds kicked in and the pain etched on her face began to subside. He held her hand as the CV-22 lifted off and rapidly climbed away. When Donovan looked around, he saw that besides Mathews, there were four other SEALs aboard, as well as one other person, who, while wearing full combat armor, was far older than Mathews and his team. Donovan felt the unique sensation of their upward flight transitioning into forward flight, the engine pylons swiveling and transforming the hybrid aircraft from helicopter to fast-moving airplane.

Across from Donovan sat Michael and Montero. Donovan slid his headphones into place to cancel out the noise, and found the channel quiet. Montero closed her eyes, followed quickly by Michael. Donovan, too, could feel the ebb of adrenaline being replaced by profound exhaustion. The need for sleep was almost overwhelming.

"It happens all the time," Mathews said. "I've seen battle-weary soldiers fall asleep in minutes. I think it's a combination of being free to let down their guard, coupled with the vibration of the CV-22, that knocks them out."

The medic positioned the inflatable cast and turned his attention to Lauren's leg. Using scissors, he cut away her bloody pant leg, removed the soggy dressing, and began to examine the wound. He, in turn, dug in his bag and laid out an antibiotic, gauze, and tape. As Donovan watched, it occurred to him that he and his wife would now have similar scars on their thighs.

In the aisle, the older man was coming his way. He signaled for the SEALs to disconnect their communication systems. As he came to where Michael and Montero slept, he pulled the plugs on their headsets so they wouldn't wake to what was being said. He stood and looked down at Donovan, plugged his headset in, and asked the medic to disconnect. The medic immediately complied, giving Donovan the impression that this was a common occurrence. He and the stranger were now the only two who were connected.

"Mr. Nash, my name is Kensington. I'm here to answer some of your questions."

"You're CIA." Donovan had no doubt at all who Kensington worked for, and the man made no attempt to deny the accusation. "Just so you know, I'm not very happy with you people right now."

"I'm sorry about what happened to your wife," Kensington said. "It was a monumental breakdown at Langley, and we're taking every step possible to ensure that nothing like this ever happens again."

"Go on," Donovan said.

"Was the second *Phoenix* completely destroyed?"

"Are you asking me if the Slovakian authorities will be able to tell it's a stealth aircraft?"

"That's correct."

"They'll know. If I were you, I'd gear up with a plausible story. Or, perhaps think about telling the truth. You didn't create Aleksander Kovalenko. He's Ukrainian, and his desire was to kill Russians. America wasn't involved, only in that we stopped the attack and killed him."

"He's dead?" Kensington asked as if he needed to hear the news twice. "Where's his body? How did he die?"

"Near the crashed Boeing 727," Donovan said. "He was killed by gunfire, and it's possible that he has the jump drive that Daniel Pope created."

Kensington's eyelids fluttered briefly, as if in shock, while he processed what he'd just heard.

"I never saw what was on it myself, but I hear it had flight plans, pictures of Kovalenko, a file on Daniel Pope, as well as the tactics that Quentin Kirkpatrick used to coerce him to go undercover."

"You did this on purpose, didn't you?" Kensington asked. "You made sure we couldn't cover up what took place tonight. I'm going to have you arrested for treason."

"Let's get a few things straight. The Boeing waiting for us is courtesy of the President, who's going to get a full briefing of all the events, including this conversation we're having right now." Donovan stood, going chest to chest with Kensington, and looked down at the man who was a good four inches shorter. "If you ever mess with my family, you don't get deniability. You'll get a shit-storm."

"You don't get to talk to me like that!" Kensington snarled.

"In your upcoming debriefing at Langley, you know, the one where you're going to try to save your job, you tell your superiors that the CIA can expect my cooperation, as long as the agency buries the file on my wife that Kirkpatrick used to blackmail her, and leave me, my wife, my family, and my friends alone—forever. Now, is there any part of that you need me to repeat?"

"You can go to hell, Mr. Nash! We'll use whatever we deem necessary—"

Turbulence rocked the Osprey, and Donovan used the opportunity to end the conversation. He swung a forearm and hit

Kensington square in the nose and felt cartilage splinter. Blood poured down Kensington's face, covering his mouth and chin.

Kensington reacted quickly and brought his fist up to strike back when his legs were cut out from underneath him. He went down hard, slamming his head on the steel floor and lay there stunned, gasping for breath.

Mathews sprang to his feet and winked at Donovan as he grabbed Kensington by the arm and helped him sit up. "Sir, you need to strap in, the turbulence can be dangerous."

Kensington yanked off his headset, turned, and allowed Mathews to help him to his feet and lead him away.

"Nicely done," Montero's voice filled Donovan's headset.

Across the aisle, Donovan found that her eyes were open and her headset plugged in. She'd been listening the entire time. When needed, she'd taken Kensington's legs out from under him. Donovan smiled. She'd had his back, and at that moment he knew that she always would.

"Can I interest you in a full-time job?" Donovan said and watched as the words had their desired effect. Montero, despite her fatigue, smiled.

"Maybe," she replied. "What's my title going to be?"

"Chief of Security for Eco-Watch."

Montero shook her head. "I like Director of Security better, and nowhere does the name Veronica appear—anywhere."

"Done. How much do I have to pay you?"

"I trust you to be fair," Montero said as she shrugged. "When do I start?"

"You already have," Donovan said. "From the moment we began this mission."

"If I work for you, will you promise to do what I tell you to do?"

"We both know I can't really make that promise."

"I know, you'll always be a pain in the ass, but we have a deal, anyway," Montero reached across the aisle and the two of them shook hands.

Donovan nodded his approval and saw that Lauren looked to be sleeping peacefully. He leaned back and closed his eyes. He focused on the noise of the slipstream, which was the sound of going home, and within a minute, he ,too, drifted off to sleep.

EPILOGUE

"YOU BOUGHT YOUR five-year-old daughter an entire equestrian center?" Lauren said, using her good hand to poke her husband in the arm.

Donovan shot William an accusatory look and then refocused on his wife. They were sitting in the vacant bleachers at the stable. As promised, they'd made it back for Abigail's riding lesson. Abigail had been thrilled to see them both, though initially upset about Lauren's injuries. She'd finally decided that her mother's cast was cool, and Lauren let her draw pictures on the smooth plaster. Abigail had finished her lesson and was in the stable attending to Halley's post-ride grooming.

"I assumed you'd already mentioned it to your wife," William said with a subtle smile on his face.

"It was going to be a surprise," Donovan said, but the second the words were out of his mouth he heard how hopeless his defense sounded. With everything that had happened, he'd forgotten to mention the eight million dollars William had spent acquiring not only Abigail's horse, but the land, and finally the center itself.

"It's partially my fault," William said with a shrug. "Donovan asked me to look into acquiring the property the center leased. You know, since he'd already bought the horse to keep Abigail happy."

"This was after I found out they were selling Halley, because developers were in the process of buying the land, and the center was going to shut down, permanently," Donovan added. "With everything going on, I forgot I'd asked William to look into the situation."

"When I studied the deal, it made sense to buy everything," William said. "Don't worry, Abigail never has to know."

Lauren rolled her eyes. "If she does, you two get to explain it to her."

"It'll be fine," Donovan said. "If she grows out of her horse phase, we'll sell the place and put the money toward her next passion."

"How much money are we talking about?" Lauren asked.

"Eight million and change," Donovan admitted. "We'll use the profit from the equestrian center to start her a savings account, so that when she's old enough to learn to fly, we can buy her a plane."

"God save us all," Lauren mumbled. "Anything else I should know?"

"The insurance check for the helicopter came through," Donovan said. "Though I split it up and used part of the money as a show of appreciation for Trevor, as well as an anonymous cash gift to Daniel's daughter. Oh, and I also gave Montero a signing bonus so she could move out of the country house into her own place. I also bought her a car."

"You've been a busy man. There's our little girl now." Lauren stood to hug her daughter.

Donovan helped as she used her single crutch to keep pace with the other three as they headed toward the parking lot.

"See everyone later. I need to run," William said as he headed toward his Jaguar. "Abigail, I'm so proud of your riding. I'll see you next week."

Abigail gave him a hug and then waved goodbye.

"You know, it's a beautiful day, I love being with my family, and I thought we might go out to the farm," Lauren suggested.

Donovan smiled. Though it hadn't been a farm for decades, for generations it was his mother's family's home, the only place from his days of being Robert Huntington that Donovan had retained.

Abigail squealed with unbridled joy. The farm was one of her favorite places. "Is Aunt Veronica going to be there?"

"I believe so," Lauren said. "I told her we might drop by for lunch."

Donovan lifted his daughter up into her seat and fastened her belt. Then he took Lauren's crutch and helped her into the passenger's seat. He slid behind the wheel and moments later, they were cruising west on Route 50.

"Daddy, can I get a pony?" Abigail said as she looked up from her tablet. "We could keep it at the farm, and I could move out there so it wouldn't get lonely."

"You'd stay at the farm all by yourself?" Lauren asked.

"No, you'd want to move with me," Abigail explained as if it were obvious.

"I don't know," Donovan said. "Maybe someday we can talk about a pony."

"I'm getting a pony!" Abigail yelled, nearly overcome with joy.

"Donovan!" Lauren said shaking her head in disbelief. "You're spoiling her. What are you going to do when she's a teenager?"

"Visit her regularly at the convent," Donovan said, as he made the turn on Oatlands Road and sped toward the farm before he said anything else he'd regret.

He wheeled into the driveway and stopped at the control panel to the gate, slid his keycard and punched in the code. The security at the property was complex and effective. He pulled through and continued up the driveway, swung around to the rear of the massive stone house, and parked outside the garage next to a brand-new black BMW 5 Series. Across the grounds he could see Montero jump up from a chair on the patio and come toward them.

"You bought Montero a new BMW?" Lauren asked as she smiled and shook her head in mock disbelief.

"Good afternoon," Donovan called out as he helped his daughter out of the car. The second Abigail's feet touched the ground she bolted for Montero. The two were close.

Donovan then helped Lauren to the ground, making sure her crutch was in place. When he turned, he was shocked to discover they had company.

Kristof stood, his cane in his right hand, Marta supporting his left side. Donovan felt tears push to the surface as he quickly covered the distance to where they waited. He hugged Marta, and then turned toward Kristof, and found the face of his youth, the smile that had launched a thousand adventures, and they hugged.

"Come," Lauren said. "Let's move to the shade of the patio."

Donovan pulled away and found that Kristof's eyes were as damp as his own, but they were clear and vibrant. He wanted to speak but couldn't find his voice and he turned toward Lauren to see his wife hugging Marta.

"The little girl with Montero is our daughter, Abigail," Lauren said as she moved from Marta to Kristof. "I'm so glad all of this worked out."

"Lauren. Thank you for everything. I'm so happy to be here," Kristof said and then opened his arms and got a hug and a kiss. He then turned to Donovan. "Bobbie, this place is magnificent; exactly the same as I remembered. It's like going back in time."

"That's the whole point," Donovan managed to say. "Exactly how is it that you're here?"

"Lauren may have mentioned that your chartered Gulfstream was still in Budapest," Marta said. "The doctors cleared him for the trip, and here we are. We just arrived a few hours ago. Montero picked us up and brought us here."

"Please, let's go sit. You must be tired from your trip," Donovan said as he put his arm around his wife. Marta helped her father, and slowly, they made their way to the patio. As they settled around the table, Montero joined them, while at the same time keeping an eye on Abigail, who'd headed for the tire swing.

"I'll bring out some sandwiches in a minute," Montero said, then looked at Donovan and winked. "So, Abigail tells me you're buying her a pony?"

"I guess I am," Donovan held his hands up in surrender.

"Though, technically, you already have," Lauren replied and began telling the story.

Donovan put his hand on Kristof's shoulder. "Thank you for everything you and Marta did for us in Europe. I owe you so much, and now this. Somehow, you being here feels like old times, like we've never been apart."

"Maybe we haven't," Kristof said.

"I agree." Donovan smiled. "Remember in England, the day we decided we'd race?"

Kristof's eyes grew wide as if surprised by the memory. "There's no way that Mustang you flew was faster than my Lamborghini."

"I think we proved that I was faster from zero to one hundred and fifty," Donovan replied and smiled at the thought of them both out on that long ago runway.

"I had you from zero to one hundred," Kristof said, laughing. "The bet was best two out of three."

"The local constabulary put an end to our nonsense," Donovan said, transported back in time with Kristof, to a story told many times. "He told you your car couldn't be out there, even though it was an old RAF base turned private airfield."

"Then you buzzed him," Kristof was nearly in tears and he wiped at his eyes. "He heard you coming, but couldn't figure out where you were. You flew over so low he practically soiled his uniform. We both nearly went to jail. That chap almost burst a blood vessel trying to find any laws we'd broken."

"Do you remember the time we were in Monaco, and we were invited to that party aboard some prince's yacht?"

"Oh, dear God, he hated me for ending up with some Italian model he'd just met." Kristof immediately began laughing.

"We woke up with a massive hangover, out to sea, headed to Barcelona." Donovan said as he reached under the table and squeezed Lauren's hand to say thanks. Until this moment, he had no one to share his youth with who had actually been there. She squeezed in return, and her eyes told him she was happy.

"Well, what did the two of you do then?" Marta asked.

"Yes, I'd like to hear this story as well," Lauren added. "But first, I think this occasion deserves a celebratory drink. I say we should open some champagne."

"Perfect. But before we start drinking," Kristof said as he turned to Donovan. "Bobbie, what's in the garage?"

A smile came over Donovan's face. "There are a few cars in there, but one in particular might interest you. It's a Ferrari, one that you don't see every day."

"Ferraris are everywhere, except . . ." Kristof's eyes grew wide at the sudden possibility. "No."

Donovan nodded. "A 1963 250 GTO."

"Dear God! How long were you going to wait to tell me about this?" Kristof planted his cane in an effort to rise. "Excuse me, ladies, but drinks are going to have to wait a little longer."

Donovan helped Kristof to his feet, and it felt as if the years of animosity were shedding by the decade. He and Kristof, their mutual love of automobiles rekindled after all these years. At least for the time being, he could forget that his friend was sick. All that mattered was this moment, and he affectionately put his arm around Kristof's shoulder. When he glanced back at Marta and Lauren, he saw they were smiling and talking. Lauren waved as he and Kristof, at the moment more like overjoyed boys than men, headed for the garage.

CPSIA information can be obtained
at www.ICGtesting.com
Printed in the USA
BVHW08s1239110818
524180BV00004B/15/P